A Trifling Cold

A Pride and Prejudice Variation

Lory Lilian

Contents

Title Page

Copyright

Chapter 1   1

Chapter 2   16

Chapter 3   33

Chapter 4   48

Chapter 5   61

Chapter 6   77

Chapter 7   93

Chapter 8   107

Chapter 9   124

Chapter 10   138

Chapter 11   152

Chapter 12   168

Chapter 13   179

Chapter 14   192

Chapter 15   207

Chapter 16   220

Chapter 17   232

Chapter 18   244

Chapter 19   263

Epilogue   274

The End   277

Chapter 1

*I*t is a truth universally acknowledged that a young man in possession of a good fortune must attend balls from time to time, even if he loathes them. Especially when such events are a good opportunity for a close friend to be properly received in the community in which he has recently leased an estate.

Attending such a ball was one of the greatest favours Darcy had ever done for his friend Bingley, particularly considering that he had skillfully managed to avoid a similar, but much more grandiose, event at St. James' Palace recently. In the carriage that took them down the country lane towards the Meryton assembly, Darcy glanced at Miss Caroline Bingley and Mr and Mrs Hurst, wondering how he had allowed himself to be dragged to such a tedious event; it would have been much more pleasant to spend this cold, autumn evening reading a book or writing to Georgiana. Miss Bingley's insinuating smiles irritated him, and he turned his attention to outside the window. It was a dark night and he could not see much, but it was better nevertheless.

"Darcy, you look so ill-humoured that people will be frightened from the moment they see you. That is not the way to make a good first impression," Bingley said with a large smile of anticipation on his face.

"Bingley, I accepted the invitation for your sake. The first or second or third impression of the people in Meryton is not my concern in the slightest."

"If this is your opinion, you may as well return home."

"Charles, do not be rude. Mr Darcy has done you a favour

by coming. And you should appreciate his honesty. He is not a man to conceal his feelings, you know that," Miss Bingley said.

"I do appreciate his honesty, Caroline. Except when his expression of it is unfairly harsh."

"It is quite a stupid way of spending the evening; we cannot deny that," Mr Hurst intervened. "Why not stay at home with a good dinner and some fine wine? We barely know anyone here and we surely do not intend to dance."

"Speak for yourself," Mr Bingley responded. "I intend to make as many acquaintances as possible and dance as often as I can."

"None of us doubted that, Bingley. However, I must say Mr Hurst expressed my own opinion quite accurately," Darcy added.

"But Mr Darcy, I hope you do intend to dance at least one or two sets," Miss Bingley enquired meaningfully.

"Indeed, it is an absolute must. Besides, neither Caroline nor I will dance with anyone else," Mrs Hurst insisted.

"What my sisters mean is that as long as you are kind and polite to them, they do not care how you behave towards others," Bingley said with a laugh.

"Charles, you are horrible," Caroline cried.

"Indeed you are," Mrs Hurst added.

Mr Darcy remained silent upon the subject until the carriage stopped in front of the assembly. Music, voices, and laughter could be heard from within, spilling out into the village street. Bingley exited the carriage first, then turned to hand down his sisters, who looked around with displeasure.

Mr Darcy was reluctant to leave the carriage but he finally climbed down, glancing along the road for just a moment before returning his attention to studying the building critically and finally following his friend inside. As he did so he considered whether it was too late to simply return to Netherfield. And yet, he stepped forward through the door, and stopped, staring at the gathering of people who watched them with unconcealed curiosity.

∞∞∞

The Bennet family attended the Meryton assembly eagerly, as balls were among the favourite distractions for all the sisters excepting Mary, who repeatedly declared she would have preferred to stay at home with their father and spend the evening reading or practising the pianoforte. Her complaints, however, were ignored by her mother and sisters, whose full attention was concentrated on the door where Mr Bingley was expected to enter.

Mr Bennet had been among the first to visit Mr Bingley when he arrived at Netherfield. Mr Bingley had quickly returned the call, but only spoke to the master of the house in the library. Mrs Bennet had sent him an invitation to dinner soon afterwards, but Mr Bingley was unable to accept the honour, as he had been obligated to return to town on an urgent matter.

The girls were disappointed and Mrs Bennet quite disconcerted. She feared that he might always be flying about from one place to another, and never settle at Netherfield as he ought to in order to bind himself to one of her daughters.

Lady Lucas quieted her fears a little, with the news that Mr Bingley had only travelled to London to invite his family and friends to join him at his new home. The number and identity of the people in that party were widely speculated upon but remained mostly unknown. Therefore, the ball was the first opportunity to receive answers to their numerous questions and to learn more about Mr Bingley's character.

The gentleman finally arrived, accompanied by a party of four: his two sisters, the husband of the eldest, and another young man. Sir William–the only one who could claim a close acquaintance with Mr Bingley–immediately hurried to welcome him and was introduced to the others in the group. His wife–Lady Lucas–also made their acquaintance, and others soon followed.

Mrs Bennet was becoming desperate. Without Mr Bennet, nobody was in any hurry to introduce her and her daughters to the object of their interest.

However, rumours reached them in the blink of an eye, then spread through the room, as quick as the music itself. Mr Bingley was good-looking, gentlemanlike and amiable. His sisters were elegant women, with an air of decided fashion, but also of obvious self–sufficiency, which met with some criticism around the room. His brother-in-law, Mr Hurst, looked like any other gentleman in his thirties.

But his friend Mr Darcy soon drew everyone's attention by his fine, tall person, handsome features, noble mien, and the report, which was in general circulation within five minutes after his entrance, of his having ten thousand a year. The gentlemen pronounced him to be a fine figure of a man, the ladies observed his severe yet handsome features, his dark eyes and impressive posture and declared he was much more handsome than Mr Bingley.

Mrs Bennet stared at him with special attention and asked her daughters to look carefully so they could identify a truly desirable gentleman when they next saw one. More than that, not even Mrs Bennet dared to imagine. No matter how beautiful her first daughter was, how clever the second one, and how lively the youngest, she knew perfectly well that they were too far removed socially to ever catch Mr Darcy's interest. None of them were good enough for a gentleman with ten thousand a year, Mrs Bennet had to admit to herself with no little sorrow.

Not long after, her disappointment diminished as she–as well as all the others in the room–observed that nobody was good enough to catch Mr Darcy's interest.

He appeared to be proud, above his company, and above being pleased. He danced one set with Mrs Hurst and another one with Miss Bingley, then stood alone in a corner, showing that he was not desirous of company, although gentlemen were scarce and more than one lady was in need of a partner. He declined being introduced to other people, and only spoke occasionally to one of his own party. His character was decided. He was the proudest, most disagreeable man in the world, and everybody wondered why he had come to ruin everyone else's mood. Not even the news that he owned a large estate in Derbyshire was enough to compensate for his forbidding, disagreeable countenance, and he lost in any comparison with his friend.

Mrs Bennet ignored Mr Darcy completely. She had more important things to do, being still exasperated by the impossibility of addressing Mr Bingley directly.

Finally, when Lydia and Kitty were dancing and Mary sat on a chair near the wall, Sir William moved towards them, together with Mr Bingley. With a superior air that showed his self-importance, he presented the eldest Misses Bennet as being "some of the most charming and admired young ladies in the entire county."

Mr Bingley bowed, smiled to Mrs Bennet, then said, "I am grateful to Sir William for performing the introductions, as I had long wished to make your acquaintance. Mr Bennet was one of the kindest gentlemen in the neighbourhood and I enjoyed meeting him, as much as I regretted not being able to accept your dinner invitation, madam."

"Oh, how kind of you to say so, Mr Bingley. We were eager to meet you too, were we not, girls?" she asked her daughters, who blushed with embarrassment. "Please feel free to come to dinner whenever you wish; the invitation stands."

"Thank you, Mrs Bennet, you are too generous. And if she is not otherwise engaged, may I ask Miss Bennet for the favour of the next set?"

"No...I mean yes...I am not engaged, sir. Yes, thank you..." Jane's face was crimson, while her eyes brightened with pleasure. Her nervousness seemed to delight Mr Bingley, who smiled and thanked her.

"It is sad that your friend does not show the same willingness for dancing," Mrs Bennet declared sharply.

Mr Bingley appeared uneasy. "Yes, well, he rarely dances.

He does not enjoy parties. Is Mr Bennet in good health? I hoped I would see him tonight."

"Yes, he is. He just preferred to stay at home. Apparently, he is very much like your friend in that respect," the lady concluded, to her daughters' deep embarrassment and the gentleman's bewilderment.

The music started and Mr Bingley led the eldest Miss Bennet onto the floor.

Elizabeth on the other hand had been obliged, by the scarcity of gentlemen, to sit down for the second time that evening. She spent that half hour watching her sister and her dance partner, who had very quickly become her admirer.

When the music stopped, Miss Bennet returned to her family and was met with her mother's delighted exclamations. Elizabeth joined them and an animated discussion started. They were careful not to be overheard by Mr Bingley, who was talking to his haughty friend in the corner of the hall, partially hidden behind a column. The gentlemen though were obviously unaware of the proximity of the ladies, who could hear them clearly enough, despite their low voices. Mr Bingley was telling Mr Darcy about his pleasure in dancing with the most charming lady in the room and pressed his friend to join him.

"Darcy, I hate to see you standing about by yourself in this stupid manner. You had much better dance."

"I certainly shall not. You know how I detest it, unless I am particularly acquainted with my partner. At such an assembly as this it would be insupportable. Your sisters are engaged, and there is not another woman in the room whom it would not be a punishment to me to stand up with."

At those words, Elizabeth smiled with amusement, while Jane blushed with embarrassment and Mrs Bennet with anger.

"You are fastidious beyond reason, Darcy. I find this to be a lovely evening with the delightful company of some truly beautiful young ladies."

"You danced with the only handsome girl in the room," Mr Darcy replied severely. Miss Bennet blushed even more and Mrs

Bennet's anger diminished slightly.

"She is the most beautiful creature I ever beheld! But her sister, Miss Elizabeth, is also very pretty, and I dare say very agreeable. Do let me introduce her to you and you will have the chance to dance after all."

"Absolutely not. I noticed her earlier. She is tolerable, but not handsome enough to tempt me; I am in no humour to give consequence to young ladies who are slighted by other men. Let us not continue this conversation, we are only wasting our time."

Astonishment removed Elizabeth's smile, as she wondered if the rudeness she had heard was real. Jane's face turned pale with mortification while Mrs Bennet's eyes and mouth remained open as fury overwhelmed her. Elizabeth quickly took her mother's arm and gently pushed her a little farther away; she wished to avoid letting the gentlemen know they had been heard. The amiable Mr Bingley did not deserve to bear such shame on behalf of his unworthy friend.

"This is...I cannot believe it! What a horrible man," Mrs Bennet spoke against her handkerchief, while her daughters begged her to calm down.

"Mama, let us not give this gentleman more importance than he deserves," Elizabeth struggled to speak in jest. "His admiration has no value and I would rather dance with a chair than with him."

"And so you should, Lizzy! What appalling manners! Is the assembly so insupportable to him? He must know he is insupportable to us, too! It would be a punishment to him to dance? This is just...it is just..."

"Mama, please calm yourself," Elizabeth insisted. "Come, take a seat and Jane will stay with you while I bring you something to drink."

She quickly walked towards the table with the refreshments, stealing a glance in Mr Darcy's direction. He was now standing against the wall and their eyes met briefly. She frowned and hoped he could see how much she despised him;

his countenance, however, remained stern and his cold gaze betrayed no feelings.

Elizabeth offered her mother a cup of tea, and Mrs Bennet regained her composure enough to go and talk to Mrs Phillips and Lady Lucas. The music started again and both Elizabeth and Jane were asked to dance, so for the following set they were engaged agreeably enough to forget about Mr Darcy.

The evening progressed slowly. Later on, Mr Bingley introduced Jane to his sisters, then asked her for the favour of a second set. His preference was soon openly displayed and it was clear to everyone in attendance that Miss Bennet's well-known beauty had charmed the new master of Netherfield.

Mrs Bennet's anger was hardly diminished by the two cups of tea and several glasses of punch offered by her friends, along with their encouragement. Having her second daughter slighted in such a manner sharpened her opinion about the arrogant man into particular resentment.

It must have been midnight when Darcy realised he had had enough of the noise, the heat, the lack of air, the curious looks, and the rumours. He wished to leave, but they had all arrived in the same carriage, and he was certain the others in his party wished to remain longer. Especially Bingley, who appeared completely bewitched by the eldest Miss Bennet. Darcy was not surprised. He had seen his younger friend enchanted many times before. Often, Bingley was quickly impressed by the beauty of a lady and yet equally easily he became bored with her. It would likely happen in this case as well.

He knew perfectly well that it was his own fatigue and the torment of the last months that had left him spent and incapable of any enjoyment. Everything he had loathed before had become even harder to bear lately.

And that evening, that ball, was the worst so far.

Everything vexed him. The people, the music, the small windows that allowed no air, the floor that trembled under his feet. One of the most distressing things was the second Miss Bennet's repeated glances towards him, her challenging expression, her eyes narrowing with curiosity, her smile twisting as if there was something on her mind that she preferred not to divulge.

Not that he would have been interested in the slightest in her–or anyone else's–thoughts. He was just intrigued by the daring of a country girl who had not even danced all the sets. One whose appearance made him ignore her and left him unwilling to make her acquaintance when requested. Her interest and curiosity in a strange gentleman was quite improper. But of course, such a lack of decorum was not surprising in that small town lost in the countryside.

When the music started again, Darcy found a proper moment to slip outside through the back door. He felt even less comfortable and more restless than usual. Something bothered him exceedingly, and he was annoyed at not knowing what. The fresh, cold air surrounded him, and the slight relief brought him some peace. He wished he did not have to go back into the middle of the crowd. Perhaps he could take the carriage, return to Netherfield, and send it back for the others. Yes, that might be the proper way of solving this insupportable situation.

He took a few steps into the muddy, slippery yard. The night was dark, but the torches offered enough light to see. Dogs were barking, the music carried out through the windows, and the voices of the people outside the assembly increased the din. He could not decide where was worse, outside or inside the ballroom. Having decided to tell Bingley about his plan, he turned abruptly to the door, colliding with someone in his haste. A cry startled him, and he almost slipped. He finally recovered, and with astonishment he noticed a lady of middle age, staring at him with apparent fury.

"Forgive me, madam; I did not notice you. I apologise, are you hurt?"

"I am not hurt, sir! But that is only because I am strong on my feet. You should be more careful, even if you do not consider us worthy of your attention and care."

The reply astounded him, and for a moment he believed his ears were misleading him. He struggled to speak politely enough.

"Ma'am, I am afraid we are not even acquainted, therefore..."

The woman–obviously one of the guests from the ball–stood in front of the door, brushing her gown vigorously.

"I am Mrs Bennet; we were almost introduced earlier by Sir William before you turned and left with such a lack of grace. My eldest daughter Jane is the most beautiful young woman here, surely you noticed her since she danced twice with your friend."

As recognition began to dawn on him, the behaviour of the woman in front of him increased his astonishment.

"Mrs Bennet..." he reluctantly said, looking for a way of escaping her distressing company.

"I am also the mother of Miss Elizabeth Bennet, the one you called barely tolerable and with whom you refused to dance. I would be curious to hear your reason for behaving in such an ungentlemanlike manner, but it is of little importance."

"Excuse me?" His shock was now complete, and he stared at the woman in disbelief.

"No excuses are necessary; only a brief answer would suffice."

"Madam, this conversation is absurd. I had better leave now, before the situation becomes even more ridiculous."

"Of course you will leave, since you are unable to answer a mere question." The lady's anger increased and Darcy felt at the edge of his self-control.

"Do you expect a gentleman to answer such improper questions, addressed so bluntly, by someone he does not even know?" His voice was sharp and disdainful.

"I expect a gentleman to behave in such a manner that these questions are not necessary, sir. Or at least not to offend a young lady who did him no harm."

He stared at the woman in front of him, startled by her accusation. She continued with no restraint while Darcy slowly lost his temper.

"I must leave you now, since I am completely oblivious to your meaning, madam."

"Do not take me for a fool, sir! You told Mr Bingley my daughter was not tolerable enough to tempt you. How could you say that out loud, so other people would hear you? She might not be as beautiful as Jane, nor as joyful as my youngest, Lydia, but everyone considers Lizzy a beauty. And she is a great dancer–fortunately she gets that from me! Not to mention she is the cleverest girl in the area, everybody agrees on that. She reads almost as much as a man; I tell you that. Of course, she is a little wild, walking in the fields all day long. God knows that until a few years ago she was climbing trees–but you could not possibly know that, so I would imagine you spoke so badly of her because you are quite impolite!"

He listened in shock, unable to understand the tumult of information thrown at him.

"Mrs Bennet, I am afraid this conversation has ended! Good evening!"

"Oh well, it gives me no pleasure to talk to you either. And I assure you that my daughter will never ever dance with you at all! Good evening!"

Darcy briskly reentered the hall, then stood stunned and still, blinking a few times, wondering what had just happened.

Never in his life had he had such a conversation, and he hoped he never would again. Why was Mrs Bennet outside? Probably taking some fresh air too. But how could she speak to him in such a manner? She had listened to his private conversation with his friend and then threw it in his face? That was unthinkable. Had the young lady–the one he had refused to dance with–heard him too?

Suddenly, the eyes of the Miss Bennet he had called tolerable appeared in his mind, but he realised he barely remembered her figure. He recollected little else but how tedious the atmosphere was, how relieved he felt after complying with his duty of dancing one set with Miss Bingley and one with Mrs Hurst, and how eager he was for the evening to end.

And then, he had met that Mrs Bennet–and there was still more to endure, the night was not yet over.

∞∞∞

For the rest of the ball, Darcy struggled to regain his usual composure. The conversation with Mrs Bennet troubled him deeply and his anger combined with contempt. What education could that lady give to her daughters? What was her situation in life? If he remembered correctly, Mr Bennet was a country gentleman, with a small estate close to Netherfield. What kind of gentleman had a wife with such poor manners?

He chose a chair in the corner of the room, looking from Mrs Bennet to her daughters. They were all good-looking; two of them appeared noisy and reckless, one too silent, the eldest one quite beautiful but smiled too much. Miss Elizabeth Bennet caught and held his attention most of the time; the more he looked at her, the more intrigued he became. Her eyes–even from a significant distance–seemed lively and enquiring. Her features were handsome and her figure pleasant. She danced and she appeared to possess the skills her mother claimed. Did she truly enjoy reading? Were her mother's words about her intelligence worthy of belief? Walking through the fields and climbing trees? Surely that could not be true. Or could it?

After some earnest scrutiny and a couple of drinks, Darcy still had not recovered from the altercation with Mrs Bennet, nor had he reached a conclusion about Miss Elizabeth Bennet. But one thing he reluctantly admitted to himself before the ball ended: she was more than tolerable and he regretted missing the chance to dance with her.

Once the evening had ended and they climbed into

the carriage to take them back to Netherfield, Darcy's usual calmness returned. Opinions about the event were exchanged and Miss Bingley and Mrs Hurst did not hesitate to express their criticism about everything that had happened.

"Mr Darcy, what do you think about the Bennet family? My brother is quite charmed by them; especially by the eldest daughter," Miss Bingley asked scornfully.

"Miss Bennet is one of the most beautiful women I have met," Darcy replied with honesty, looking outside. Mr Bingley quickly expressed his joy for his friend's favourable opinion, but Miss Bingley continued.

"Jane Bennet might be a lovely person, but her sisters are ill-behaved. And their mother! Dear Lord! Be happy that you escaped her attention, Mr Darcy. She spent the entire evening trying to gain my brother's interest in her daughters. I am sure she already imagines him as her future son-in-law. Horrible indeed!"

"Mrs Bennet is obviously searching for proper suitors to marry her five daughters. She must have understood very quickly that I am the last man in the world to entertain such a desire, so she put her efforts where she could hope for some success. I cannot but be grateful; I spent a few minutes talking to her tonight, and I have had enough for a lifetime."

Bingley threw his friend an offended and disapproving glance while his sisters laughed and continued to express their disapproval of the Bennet women. Fortunately, the carriage arrived at Netherfield soon enough, and Darcy retired to his chamber in haste. His interest in company and conversation had long ended.

∞∞∞∞

At Longbourn, Mrs Bennet took her time to relate to her husband every detail of the ball, describing the lace, the gowns, the music, the food and drink, Mr Bingley's amiability and Mr

Darcy's horrible haughtiness. She informed her husband how many sets Mr Bingley danced with Jane and how Mr Darcy refused to dance with Lizzy.

Mr Bennet accepted the torturous story stoically for half an hour, glanced at Elizabeth to see if she was upset by the offence and–pleased to see her smiling and amused–he declared he felt as tired as if he had danced every set himself. Then he disappeared into the silence of his bedchamber.

When Jane and Elizabeth were finally alone in their own chamber, the former gathered her courage to express to her sister her opinion about Mr Bingley.

"He is just what a young man ought to be: sensible, good-humoured, lively! I never saw such happy manners, so much ease, with such perfect good-breeding!"

"He is also handsome," said Elizabeth, "which a young man ought likewise to be, if he possibly can. He certainly is very agreeable, and I give you leave to like him."

"Thank you, dear Lizzy!" Jane smiled. "But I am sorry you did not have an equally pleasant time. I was so sad to hear Mr Darcy's offensive remark! I did not expect that from him. He seemed a gentleman of good character and excellent education. And Mr Bingley speaks so highly of him."

"I see no reason to praise his character, since he gave us no reason to do so. You never see a fault in anybody, Jane. All the world is good and agreeable in your eyes."

"I would wish not to be hasty in censuring anyone, but I always speak my mind."

"I know you do; you have so much common sense and still you are so honestly blind to the follies and nonsense of others! Speaking of Mr Darcy, his refusal did not offend me, as I took it as proof that a good education is sometimes not enough to keep arrogance under good regulation. I am quite grateful actually; just imagine what a torture it would have been to spend half an hour dancing with such a disagreeable man. I am happy he did not find me tolerable enough to make me endure such an ordeal!"

"Dear Lizzy, you are incorrigible." Jane laughed and embraced her. Eventually, the sisters lay in the comfort of their bed, abandoning themselves to a well-deserved sleep, thinking each of one gentleman: one with tenderness, the other with hurt pride.

Chapter 2

For several days, the assembly and Mr Bingley were the most important subjects of conversation. Charlotte Lucas–a dear friend of Elizabeth–as well as her mother Lady Lucas, agreed that Mr Bingley's admiration and preference for Jane could not be doubted. Mrs Bennet was beside herself with joy and admitted that both Lady Lucas and Charlotte were wise women, although neither could be described as handsome.

Elizabeth's ill feelings about the ball soon disappeared. She was pleased to know her eldest sister had gained the admiration of a worthy gentleman, and that helped her quickly forget a less worthy gentleman's arrogant offence.

Of Mr Darcy, the general opinion did not improve with time. He appeared in Meryton only once with his friend and even then he barely took the trouble of speaking more than a few words to anyone. His fortune was much talked about, his handsomeness was recognised, and his high education presumed from the little people knew of him. But his arrogance and his apparent unwillingness to improve his acquaintance with anyone made everyone dislike him.

Sir William Lucas was the only one who took Mr Darcy's side.

"I had the honour of meeting many members of the ton when I was presented at St. James', and I observed that pride and aloofness are not rare traits among them. And why would they not be, if they were blessed with everything one can hope for? Mr Darcy seems to have it all, truly."

Mrs Bennet completely disagreed with him.

"One can be wealthy and important, yet amiable and friendly enough. He is not. In fact, I could say he is the last man in the world I could call either. I am glad I had the chance to speak to him and give him a piece of my mind. He is truly the least agreeable man I have ever known."

"Mama, I assure you I do not care about his offence. You should not trouble yourself so much and we would do well to forget it."

"Well, I do care. I took it as a personal insult and forgetting it is impossible. He has much to do to redeem himself in my eyes."

"I doubt that will happen, or that he would have any interest in redeeming himself to you," Elizabeth concluded, hoping Mrs Bennet might put the whole incident aside soon enough.

The more her neighbours and her mother loathed Mr Darcy, the more Elizabeth found amusement in the situation. Her opinion of Mr Darcy was too low to give his words much consequence and his refusal to dance with her she considered fortunate. It was dreadful to even imagine being trapped with such a haughty man for half an hour. She had seen him dancing with his friend's sisters and, while his dancing skills were quite proficient, he appeared to be as silent and unpleasant with his intimate acquaintances as he was with those he had just met.

Happily, she did not see him much in the days following the assembly. However, one morning when she was enjoying her usual, solitary walk towards Oakham Mount she was stunned to find the very same Mr Darcy, sitting on the grass, lost in his thoughts, staring out across the valley. He had taken off his coat and hat, so his appearance was far from formal. Elizabeth observed him and recognised him only when she was too close to leave unnoticed. Furthermore, his horse and his dog, also both dark and of impressive stature, reacted to her presence, causing him to turn and face her.

He quickly jumped to his feet, brushed his hands over his trousers, and bowed to her.

Surprise kept Elizabeth silent and still, while he seemed embarrassed and uncertain of how to proceed. Only then did she remember that they had not been properly introduced, so he was a stranger to her. A stranger who had offended her without even knowing her, and who had been accordingly scolded by her mother. She felt a smile spreading across her face.

Opposite her, Darcy looked disconcerted by her amusement and equally embarrassed by their solitary encounter.

"Miss Bennet, if I recall correctly?" he said, bowing again. "Good morning, ma'am. I am Fitzwilliam Darcy."

"Indeed. Good morning, Mr Darcy. One can hardly doubt your identity, sir," she replied.

"I apologise for my appearance, Miss Bennet. I did not expect company at this early hour and in this secluded place."

"You must not worry, I am most certainly no company for you. I am as surprised as you are to meet someone here. I have been regularly walking these paths for several years and this is the first time I have happened upon someone. I shall leave you now."

"Please do not leave because of me, ma'am."

"Rest assured that I would not leave because of you. But I know these grounds well enough and I can find another path so we both can enjoy our solitude."

"You may enjoy this place–I must return to Netherfield anyway. It was a pleasure to meet you, Miss Bennet."

"Likewise, sir. I hope you found your morning ride tolerable enough," she said, unable to refrain from taking some small revenge.

He stared at her, recognising the comment and his face changed colour.

Then he bowed and turned to mount in some haste.

"Mr Darcy!" Elizabeth called to him. He looked at her, puzzled, waiting for her to continue. His apparent uneasiness amused her and gave her a strange feeling of satisfaction.

"Mr Darcy, you should be careful if you plan to ride

towards Netherfield–the ground is very unsteady for horses."

He did not expect that, and his answer sounded colder than he would have wished. "I thank you for your care, but I assure you it is not needed. I am an excellent rider."

Elizabeth rolled her eyes and shook her head.

"Of course you are, sir. My main concern was for the horse's safety. Have a pleasant day."

She started to walk in the opposite direction and quickened her pace, completely oblivious to Darcy's astonished and intrigued gaze. For a while it was quiet so she could not say if he had followed her advice about not riding down the hill. Mostly likely not–he surely did not care for her suggestion, or for the well-being of his horse.

If Elizabeth had any remaining doubts they were all gone. Mr Darcy was as unpleasant as he was ridiculously proud and haughty. If she never saw him again, it might still be too soon. However, being Mr Bingley's friend, it was difficult to imagine such a happy turn of events. The pleasant company of Mr Bingley would probably come accompanied by Mr Darcy's unpleasant presence. Or perhaps he had some business to attend and would leave Hertfordshire soon, to everyone's relief.

Little could she imagine the strong impression their short exchange had made upon the gentleman. Her lively, daring spirit sparkled even in that brief conversation and he found himself regretting that he had not stayed longer. If he had had more time to recover from the surprise, he would have certainly apologised for offending her at the ball–something that she had obviously heard and held against him. Understandably so, as he had been truly rude.

Darcy barely remembered Elizabeth's features from the ball, and he had to guess her identity. In those few minutes he had only enough time to observe her cheeks coloured by exercise, the sharp brightness that lit her eyes, the challenging lift of her right eyebrow, and the mischievous smile that twisted her pink lips. She looked quite displeased to see him and even more so after their brief conversation, but she certainly enjoyed scolding him for the past offensive remark and for his present foolish and arrogant statement regarding his riding abilities.

How could he have said he was an excellent rider? That was truly childish and had to be corrected as soon as possible.

Three things bothered Fitzwilliam Darcy as he took the reins of his stallion and walked carefully down the path towards Netherfield, followed by his horse and his dog: that Miss Bennet was brave enough to walk alone such a distance from her house; that she was either unaware or completely indifferent to his situation in life and disliked him utterly; and that she had already occupied his thoughts and piqued his curiosity more than any other young lady ever had.

He recollected her mother's words about *"Lizzy"* being very clever and about her tendency to run across the fields and climb trees–and he found himself smiling as he entered the main gate of the manor.

Even later that evening, the meeting was still vivid in his mind and he went to bed wondering why he refused to dance with her.

He still had not studied her features thoroughly, but he could see they were far from perfect. She was certainly not a classic beauty by society's standards–but it was surely a sort of beauty that was not easy to forget. Definitely more than tolerable.

∞∞∞

Elizabeth did not mention the brief encounter with Mr Darcy to anyone except Jane. She wished to avoid other discussions and arguments that could make Mr Bingley uncomfortable and jeopardise her sister's new relationship.

The master of Netherfield called on the master of Longbourn twice, but he only spent time in the library, without the pleasure of the ladies' company. But they had the advantage of seeing him from the window and admiring once again his excellent posture and apparent riding skills.

Mr Bennet's opinion about their neighbour was entirely positive too, so Mr Bingley was a subject allowed and encouraged at any time of day, among the family or with their friends from Meryton.

Of all the sisters, Jane was the most restrained and only opened her heart to Elizabeth.

"Dear Lizzy, he is indeed everything I have ever desired to find in a man. Am I wrong to admire him although we barely know each other?"

"You are not wrong at all, dearest. I give you permission to like him–you have liked others less worthy and less handsome."

"Lizzy, do not tease me!"

"I do not! I truly like Mr Bingley and I think he would be a good match for you–unless you discover some unpleasant traits that might ruin your admiration."

"I am sure everything else I might discover would be to his merit, Lizzy. Do you think he might like me?"

"He might like you? Dear Jane, whoever sees you both even for an instant, could not doubt his admiration. Just wait for him to be more in your company and to become aware of your sweet and generous heart. I still wonder how someone can have equal beauty and kindness and still be as modest as you are."

"Lizzy darling, you spoil me with your praises. I hope Mr Bingley will see at least a small part of what you see in me."

"If he does not, he must be blind. And I am sure that is not the case," Elizabeth concluded, embracing her sister.

"I hope he will not be frightened by our mother's insistence," Jane whispered. "Sometimes, all her talk of Mr Bingley seems a little too much."

"That is true, but I hope he is strong enough to bear it all, for your sake." What Elizabeth did not tell Jane was her concern about Mr Darcy, of whom she found herself thinking more than she wished to. Would he oppose Mr Bingley's connection with Jane or would he encourage it? Mr Darcy's opinion about their family could not be too high since he had never joined Mr

Bingley to call on Mr Bennet, which was not very surprising considering his argument with their mother. He seemed uninterested in attempting to know them better before judging and dismissing them as being unworthy. If only he would not influence his friend against his inclination for Jane.

Elizabeth decided it was useless to share her concerns with anyone else. For the time being, everything was just speculation and assumption. She did not know any more of Mr Darcy than he knew of them and she admitted to herself that she was tempted to judge him too, based on the little information she had gathered about him.

They all needed more time and more proof before establishing a sound conclusion. And for the benefit of Jane, she was willing to grant it.

∞∞∞

Several more days passed until a piece of news stirred up daily life at Longbourn. It came in the form of a letter, received by Mr Bennet and shared with his family in wry amusement.

"You will be as happy as I am to find that my cousin Mr Collins, the one who will inherit Longbourn at my death, has decided to pay us a visit. He seems willing to become better and more closely acquainted with you all and to restore peace between our families."

"My dear Mr Bennet, please do not even speak of that horrible man," Mrs Bennet cried.

"Well, my dear, I know we cannot forgive him for the impertinence of being my heir, but we cannot reject his attempt at friendliness either," Mr Bennet answered. "It appears he is a clergyman in Kent, and has the honour of benefiting from the generosity of a noble patroness, Lady Catherine de Bourgh."

"Could he be a sensible, reasonable man, Papa?" Elizabeth enquired.

Mr Bennet smiled. "I doubt it, my dear. In fact, if the

letter is any indication of his true self, I would rather say he must be completely the opposite. I am counting on a few days of amusement and follies."

"Well, I shall not spend a single moment with that man if I can avoid it," Mrs Bennet declared. "He might do whatever he wants once you are gone, Mr Bennet, but until then, I shall do what I please in my own home."

"That is as fair as can be expected, my dear. But let us not plan to hate him before we actually meet him. I last saw my cousin when he was only a young boy, so I am determined to give him an opportunity to prove himself, even against my intuition."

"Very well. But I will ignore the matter completely for now; I will have enough time to worry about him once he arrives. Jane my dear, go and change your gown, Mr Bingley will be here soon."

The master of Netherfield called at Longbourn that day and several more times over the coming days. Mr Darcy never joined him, but his sisters did—once. The ladies remained only half an hour, refused to eat anything, spoke only to 'their dear Jane', and invited her alone to spend a day with them 'sometime very soon, when their mutual schedules allowed'.

Elizabeth found their presence more offensive and unpleasant than Mr Darcy's absence and openly declared her relief when they left.

"Lizzy, you are too harsh on Louisa and Caroline," Jane scolded her gently. "They are caring sisters and quite pleasant companions. I agree their manners are not as friendly as Mr Bingley's, but it is because they are accustomed to a different society from ours."

"They are very elegant indeed," Mrs Bennet said, silently hoping the named ladies would not join their brother on future visits.

"They might be elegant, but to me, they look more like Mr Darcy's sisters; they surely resemble him in manners," Elizabeth laughed.

"True," Mrs Bennet admitted. "But Lizzy, you should refrain from being too blunt in your opinions about them. We do not want to upset Mr Bingley in any way. I hope he will come to dinner soon. What do you say, Jane?"

"Mama, I cannot guess Mr Bingley's intentions," Jane answered, blushing slightly.

"Of course not, my dear. And you do not have to. Just smile nicely and be as beautiful as you are, and I am sure Mr Bingley's intentions will soon become clear."

"Mama!" Jane cried. "Please do not make such statements in the presence of strangers! It would be deeply embarrassing to start rumours that have no foundation! Mr Bingley is only a mere acquaintance to me, as I am to him."

"Yes, yes, of course," Mrs Bennet replied, barely listening to her daughter while she thought of a plan to bring Mr Bingley back as soon as possible.

"Mama, will we speak only of Mr Bingley forever?" Lydia intervened. "You do not even seem to care that the regiment have arrived in town! There are many officers at least as handsome and pleasant as Mr Bingley."

"Indeed, Mama," Kitty continued, "Lieutenant Denny and Mr Sanderson; we met them yesterday, when we visited Maria Lucas."

"Yes, you told me. But what can I do about the officers? Besides, I doubt any of them have an income of five thousand a year. Of course, half that sum would suffice, if I knew any of them intended to marry. They should be camped in Meryton for at least six months, so we have plenty of time to know more about them. Now, I wonder when we should invite Mr Bingley to dinner and if it would be rude to send the invitation for him only."

Despite Mrs Bennet's efforts, due to some unfortunate

circumstances, Mr Bingley did not dine at Longbourn in the following days. He seemed caught up with other engagements and they barely saw him for almost a week.

Elizabeth easily noticed Jane's distress every time the gentleman's name was mentioned and her frequent glances outside, as well as her sudden preference for strolls in the garden, where the main road was easily observable.

It was obvious that Jane's affection for Mr Bingley was slowly growing, whether he was present or absent. However, to everyone else except Elizabeth, the eldest Miss Bennet looked unchanged in manners, serenity and calmness. Therefore, Mrs Bennet continued to make plans to bring the gentleman to Longbourn, while Mr Bennet mocked her about the subject whenever the opportunity arose.

Everything was handled by Jane with graceful silence and tentative smiles that suggested more indifference than inclination. This was what Charlotte Lucas told Elizabeth during one of their meetings.

"If Mr Bingley's admiration for Jane is clear, her opinion about him is not easy to guess even for us, and I am afraid it must be even more difficult to read for the gentleman himself. Jane's behaviour is elegant and praiseworthy, but it conceals her affection and might diminish his as a consequence. In nine cases out of ten, a woman had better show more affection than she feels. Mr Bingley undoubtedly likes your sister, but he may never do more than like her if she does not help him on."

"Charlotte, what more help does he need? She is doing everything that her nature will allow. He must be a simpleton not to perceive her regard for him."

"You should keep in mind that he does not know Jane's disposition as you do, Lizzy. Besides, they have only met a few times and have never been alone or spent a long time together. They have barely had time to converse, so if you want my advice, I would say Jane should make the most of every half hour in which she can command his attention."

"I believe Jane is showing as much of her feelings as she

feels she should. As yet, she cannot even be certain of the degree of her own regard, nor of its reasonableness. She has known him only a fortnight. She danced four dances with him at Meryton and has met him a few other times. This is not enough to make her understand his character."

"I wish Jane success with all my heart," said Charlotte. "If she were married to him tomorrow, I should think she has as good a chance of happiness as if she were to be studying his character for a twelvemonth. Happiness in marriage is a matter of chance; it is better to know as little as possible of the defects of the person with whom you are to pass your life."

"You make me laugh, Charlotte; but you know you would never act in this way yourself."

"Of course I would, Lizzy, and I will do it as soon as I have the chance."

"Charlotte, if I were to follow your reasoning, I might very well try to marry Mr Darcy and hope for a reasonable chance for happiness," Elizabeth laughed.

"You might laugh, but one could not dream of a better husband than Mr Darcy. He is rich, well educated and has an excellent situation in life. My father said Mr Darcy's estate in Derbyshire is among the most beautiful in the country. And he is very handsome, indeed one of the most handsome men I have seen. I believe all these things somehow give him the right to be proud and aloof. Any woman would be happy to know him better, would you not agree?"

"Not quite," Elizabeth laughed. "Despite his perfection in appearance, situation, education, and estate I shall gladly give up my chance to a better acquaintance. The little I know about him so far is more than enough for me. And I could readily accept his pride if he had not wounded mine."

"I understand that you cannot forget his rudeness, but hopefully you will see more of him and he will improve his manners towards you. After all, his friend may be in the company of your family rather often."

"True; but I trust Mr Darcy and I will find the means to

avoid each other, to the advantage of both."

∞ ∞ ∞

Contrary to Elizabeth's hopes, Mr Darcy did not leave the county. She met him again in Meryton, while he was with Mr Bingley and she was with her sisters. Mr Bingley's amiability seemed contagious, as his friend's manners appeared slightly softened. Mr Darcy greeted them, his glance lingering a moment longer upon Elizabeth. He then remained silent while his friend carried the conversation. However, his posture and countenance were not as severe and disdainful as they had been during the assembly, and Elizabeth amused herself by wondering in silence if he ever behaved better than that.

Furthermore, they spent an evening at Lucas Lodge, at a party hosted by Sir William. It was another chance for Mr Darcy to make everyone uncomfortable, especially herself, as his stare seemed to never leave her.

While Jane was engaged in conversation with Mr Bingley, Elizabeth enjoyed the company of her good friend, Charlotte Lucas.

"I wonder what Mr Darcy means by listening to my conversation with Colonel Forster."

"That is a question which only Mr Darcy can answer," Charlotte replied. "But I did notice he seemed to watch you with special attention."

"I should let him know that I see what he is about before I start growing afraid of him. He has a very critical eye, and his severity gives me shivers."

"I dare you to do that," Charlotte jested. "How can you possibly mention such a matter to him?"

"Well, just like that," Elizabeth said, as Mr Darcy again approached them silently.

"Mr Darcy, do you think I expressed myself well enough when I was teasing Colonel Forster to give us a ball at Meryton?"

Both Darcy and Charlotte were surprised by her query. The former responded lightly, "With great energy; but it is a subject which always makes a lady energetic."

"You are severe on us. However, you must admit that some gentlemen are energetic about balls too."

"I would readily admit it."

"But not you, I presume."

"No, indeed."

"I find dancing a charming amusement for young people," Mrs Bennet declared, as she approached with Sir William and Lady Lucas.

"I agree," Sir William added with self-confidence. "There is nothing like dancing after all. I consider it as one of the first refinements of polished societies. Would you not agree, Mr Darcy?"

"Only partially, sir; it also has the advantage of being in vogue amongst the less polished societies of the world. Every savage can dance."

His words were on the edge of politeness, but his severe tone stepped over it.

Mrs Bennet narrowed her eyes in reproach.

"Well, every savage can eat too, and still we do not avoid eating for this reason. Quite the contrary. I assume you have a good chef, Mr Darcy. Am I wrong?"

Startled, Darcy could form no reply, although Mrs Bennet stared at him, demanding one.

Elizabeth felt equally embarrassed and amused, while Sir William watched with apparent panic, fearful that the gentleman might get upset.

At that very moment, Mary started to play the pianoforte and several couples–Mr Bingley and Jane amongst them–began to dance.

"Mr Bingley performs delightfully. If only all the gentlemen would follow his example," Mrs Bennet continued reproachfully.

"Mr Darcy is adept in the art, too. I saw him dancing at

the Meryton Assembly and received no inconsiderable pleasure from the sight," Sir William declared.

"I know he danced once or twice, but it was so quick that I had no time to notice," Mrs Bennet replied, as though Darcy were absent. Sir William turned to him, to soften the rebuke.

"I presume you dance often at St. James's, Mr Darcy?"

"Never, sir."

"Do you not think it would be a proper compliment to the place?"

"It is a compliment which I never pay to any place if I can avoid it."

"Well, we are relieved to know that at least it is not only our company that displeases you and you give the same treatment to every place you visit," Mrs Bennet concluded, much to the others' astonishment.

Elizabeth searched for a reason to take her mother away from Mr Darcy, when she was startled by the gentleman's incredible request.

"Miss Bennet, would you do me the honour of dancing with me?"

She stared at him in disbelief. "Dance with you? Here? Now? You just declared your dislike for such activities."

He forced a smile.

"I hope this will be an experience to change my opinion."

She laughed. "I doubt that very much. I am afraid it would only worsen your discontent and I would rather not take the risk. But I thank you for the invitation, sir."

"Come, Miss Bennet," Sir William interjected. "You excel so much in the dance that it is cruel to deny me the happiness of seeing you; and though Mr Darcy dislikes the amusement in general, he is ready to oblige us for one half-hour."

"Mr Darcy is all politeness," said Elizabeth, smiling. "And yet, I have to persist in my refusal. Please excuse me, I am going to find Charlotte."

Elizabeth looked at Mr Darcy archly, then turned away.

Mrs Bennet shuddered. "I told you she would never dance

with you, did I not? On the other hand, with such an attitude, she will not get married anytime soon. I must speak to her," she declared, leaving abruptly.

Darcy and Sir William looked at each other, both wondering what had just happened. Sir William found a new subject of conversation about houses in town, but Darcy's interest had long abandoned him, following Elizabeth across the room.

The second Miss Bennet was certainly the most intriguing woman he had ever met and he regretted that she refused to dance with him. But her resistance did not offend him; he thought of her with increasing curiosity while considering when he might be able to see her again.

∞∞∞

On two other mornings, Elizabeth was stunned to encounter Mr Darcy in more private circumstances, on the road towards Oakham Mount. This puzzled her exceedingly. Since from the very first time she had mentioned to him that it was her favourite path and that she used to walk there quite often, she imagined he would avoid that place diligently.

Little did she know that avoiding her was the last thing Darcy intended. His interest in her increased with each new meeting, while he discovered more to be admired in her and became slowly enchanted by her uncommonly pleasing figure and the beautiful expression of her dark eyes.

Though he had detected with a critical eye more than one failure of perfect symmetry in her form, he was forced to acknowledge she was more charming than any other woman he had met. And, in spite of his assertion that her manners were not those of the fashionable world, he was caught by their easy playfulness.

He began to wish to know more of her, so he searched for any opportunity to be in her company, to speak to her, or to listen to her conversing with others.

Elizabeth was perfectly unaware of all this. To her, he was only the man who had not thought her handsome enough to dance with and made himself agreeable nowhere. Especially on solitary encounters, when he was disturbing her peaceful walks.

"Mr Darcy, how are you finding our county? You seem partial to riding these grounds, but you should not neglect other areas. There are many beauties to be discovered," she told him at their third chance meeting.

"I am sure there are, and I am determined not to neglect them. But for now I am rather enchanted by the view from this hill," he answered, and as proper as his words were, his voice stirred Elizabeth. She felt silly for her reaction and was torn between leaving and continuing the unpleasant conversation.

"I noticed a small cottage in the wood, by the pond," Darcy said. "It looks old and in a rather poor condition. Does anyone live there?"

"Oh, the Talbot cottage. My grandfather's cousin used to stay there for several months every year from spring to winter. He was very fond of nature and solitude," Elizabeth explained.

"I see. I imagine it is empty now."

Elizabeth could not understand his interest in prolonging a discussion which could give no pleasure to either of them.

"Yes. We use it rarely when my cousins and my uncle wish to go fishing."

"I see," he repeated. "I imagine there are not many fish in the bog," he attempted to joke and she was surprised.

"No, not many. But the company and pleasant time with family is more important."

"I cannot argue with that. Thank you for the kind explanation. It is lovely to have someone willing to share the little secrets of a new area."

She felt disconcerted by his friendly voice again.

"I am glad to be of use. Mr Bingley does not join you on your morning rides?"

"Bingley is not as fond of waking early as I am. What about

your sisters? Do you always walk so far from the house alone?"

"Not always, but quite often."

"It might be dangerous for a young lady to venture such a significant distance by herself," he said in earnest.

She laughed. "You are very considerate, sir, but there is no reason for such concern. I know these grounds as well as my own room; I am perfectly safe, especially with the regiment that resides in Meryton."

"You are a brave lady," he smiled. "I am sure you do not need the militia to protect you."

She startled at such a joke, and especially at his playful tone. A shiver troubled her while she stared at the dimples brought to his cheeks by his twisted smile. His amiability was so unusual that she became slightly uneasy in his presence.

"Indeed I do not. However, it is almost breakfast time, I must return home."

"May I accompany you back to Longbourn?" he asked, and she was surprised again.

"That would be unwise, sir. If someone sees us wandering alone through the woods, this might be considered a highly improper and compromising situation. We might be forced to marry to stop the gossip and I am certain neither of us wants that. Have a lovely day, Mr Darcy."

She turned and almost ran without looking back. If she had, she would have seen Darcy watching her for a long while. She reached the Longbourn gate while he was still meditating on the very great pleasure which a pair of fine eyes in the face of a pretty woman can bestow.

Chapter 3

*D*arcy's stay in Hertfordshire had become almost a torture by the beginning of November, because of his strange and tormenting reaction to Miss Elizabeth Bennet.

He could easily deceive others with his brooding and distant behaviour, as well as with his long silences. But to himself, he had to admit that he felt more attracted to her than he had been to any other woman before, despite the briefness of their acquaintance. Why could he not free himself of her image? What was happening to him?

He dreamed of her at night, losing rest. During the day he struggled to keep his distance, while yearning to be near her. He avoided her favourite paths, but more than once he rode around in the proximity of Longbourn, hoping for a glimpse of her and rejoicing in the small pleasure of being somewhere close to her.

He first thought that her mother's impropriety and outrageous manners would be enough to keep him safe. He had met Mrs Bennet and the rest of the family a couple of times, and he had even called briefly with Bingley one day. Each time, he struggled to be polite and calm and to carry on reasonable conversations for the benefit of everyone involved. He knew he would not stay long in the county and it was of no use to prolong a conflict with a woman so beneath his station; even more so since she was Elizabeth's mother.

Mrs Bennet also made some apparent efforts to improve her manners and to show more decorum, but with little success. For Meryton, even for Hertfordshire, she could be considered acceptable, but he would not allow himself to be seen in her company by his family and friends.

Mrs Bennet's faulty behaviour, together with the awareness of his duty, were strong reasons against his increasing interest in Elizabeth Bennet and they forbade him to think of her in any other way than a charming young woman that would soon be no more than a distant memory. Any connection between them should and would be unthinkable; and that realisation protected him against his own weakness for a while.

But as the days and nights passed, he realised the danger of the Bennet family, both for himself and for Bingley. His friend appeared more and more charmed by Miss Jane Bennet, whose perfect beauty would surely challenge the resistance of any strong man. The rumours—as well as his own observation—indicated to Darcy that his friend was closer and closer to making a decision that might affect his life, and very likely in a painful way. Despite her impeccable manners and serene countenance, Miss Jane Bennet did not show much affection for Bingley. She seemed to enjoy his company, but no more than that of any other amiable gentleman with a good income. Her mother, however, betrayed her resolution to secure a worthy husband for her daughter—and for her entire family. If such an event eventually occurred, Bingley would be a victim, trapped in an unequal marriage, forced to spend his life loving a woman who would grant him respect and consideration at best, but no more.

Bingley's sisters also noticed their brother's inclination and, for the first time, Darcy found himself sharing the same opinion as the two women. That realisation disturbed him and he tried to keep his judgment rational, observing his friend closely and guarding him by any means necessary.

"It appears that the Bennets have a guest. A Mr Collins, their cousin, is visiting," Bingley told his family at breakfast one morning.

"Well, the house must be full now," Caroline said. "They surely do not need more visitors."

"Very likely."

"And who is this man?" Louisa asked.

"The relative who will inherit Longbourn at Mr Bennet's death," Bingley explained.

Louisa rolled her eyes. "That is precisely what the Bennets need. Together with their lack of connections, poor situation in life and presumably meagre dowries, the notion that they will be thrown out of the house in the near future must be disturbing. I imagine the parents would do anything to secure a husband for their daughters. If only they were able to find someone to fall for their charms. In such a situation, a man cannot be too careful."

"Charles, you should be more thoughtful in your interactions with the Bennets," Caroline declared. "We were only talking to Mr Darcy the other day about your obvious partiality to Jane Bennet. This might arouse unrealistic expectations and rumours that would only harm the Bennets."

"I am astonished that you and Darcy talked about me and my partiality behind my back," Bingley replied with unusual severity. "And I am amazed at how preoccupied you are by what might harm the Bennets."

"Charles, be reasonable. We know you are very young and easily charmed. We have seen you in love so many times that we are not even surprised. But this is not London; this is a small town, with several country families to whom any special attention might be seen as a marriage proposal."

"Caroline, I have only met Miss Bennet six times so far and I intend to continue to do so. I enjoy her company and I find her the most beautiful woman I have ever met, with a sweet disposition and a generous character. Any man would be fortunate to gain her affection."

"Come now, Charles. How can you presume her generosity? You barely know her. She is serene indeed and smiles too much, as even Mr Darcy said. But she does that with everyone while you behave in a special way in her company. Everybody can see that. People might imagine more than exists."

"What more do you mean, Caroline? Does it not occur to

you that I might show exactly what I want to? Do not take me for a fool, or an ignorant child, because I am not as wise or as clever as Darcy. Who, by the way, was rejected by Miss Elizabeth Bennet when he invited her to dance at Lucas Lodge. If the Bennet ladies were so desperate to find a husband, she would never consider refusing any request from Darcy. Is this not true?"

Bingley's anger increased with every word and his rebuke towards his companion continued. The mention of Elizabeth's refusal startled Darcy and shocked Bingley's sisters. Caroline stared at Darcy in disbelief and answered disdainfully.

"Well, even the Bennet women would understand that there is not the slightest chance of Mr Darcy being interested in any of them. I cannot imagine what ridiculous reason Eliza Bennet had to refuse Mr Darcy, just as I cannot comprehend why he would ever ask her to dance with him, even more so at such an insupportable gathering."

Darcy listened in silence, musing to himself upon the subject, when he noticed four pairs of eyes watching him. The feeling of being scolded displeased him and sharpened his reply.

"If you are waiting for an explanation regarding my invitation to Miss Bennet, I have none other than the usual admiration that induces any man to ask a lady to dance. The reason for her refusal remains a mystery to me too, but I cannot see why anyone would have any interest in such an insignificant matter."

His words were light, but the tone was severe, attempting to end the conversation. However, Miss Bingley insisted.

"Well, this is the first time I have heard you speaking of admiration in anything related to the Bennets. A few days ago you were as decidedly against Miss Bennet's beauty as you were against her mother's wit. You surely remember."

"I do remember, Miss Bingley. But sometimes, people change their opinions once they know more on a certain subject."

"Apparently you are right; this is absolutely astonishing to me," Miss Bingley said contemptuously.

Darcy ceased any further discussion, disconcerted that he had allowed himself to be pulled into the debate. Caroline Bingley's manner and her embarrassing attempt to gain his attention were difficult to bear on a regular basis; but when discussing Elizabeth Bennet, it was even worse.

He suddenly realised that, as much as he considered that Bingley needed his protection against an unreasonable inclination, he was in much more danger. If Bingley had met Miss Jane Bennet six times so far, he certainly had met Elizabeth more, and that might arouse some rumours and false expectations in many, including Caroline Bingley. Perhaps even Elizabeth–which would be a painful situation. Or her mother–and that would be much worse.

"Very well, Charles, for your sake we will try to find out more about Jane Bennet. After all, she is a sweet girl and could be a pleasant friend. We will ask her to tea tomorrow. You will be out meeting the officers anyway, and that will give us the opportunity to see her in more private circumstances," Louisa offered.

"True. That will give us enough proof of her true character," Caroline added. "I shall write to her immediately."

"How lovely of you. You may invite her but keep in mind that I will judge the matter by myself. I believe it is time for me to behave as a man of three and twenty should."

Bingley retired from the table soon enough, obviously upset and preoccupied. Darcy had seen Bingley in love many times, but never so angry and impolite to his sisters. Of Jane Bennet's indifference towards Bingley, his opinion remained strong. But any insistence on the matter might push Bingley even closer to her, if only to contradict his family and friend.

He followed Bingley and caught him in the main hall.

"Do you need company?"

Bingley glared at him. "I am going for a ride. You may join me if you wish."

"Only if you are desirous of my presence."

Bingley shuddered.

"As you like. I used to like talking to you, but I would rather you not treat me as a silly young boy. Especially in matters where you do not seem to excel. I have never seen you in love, nor have I noticed any inclination towards a young lady, although many of them appear to be partial to you. Perhaps you are not such a good judge of people's feelings."

"Bingley, the mere fact that one has an inclination towards a person, does not imply that a person must respond and reciprocate it. I am not as easily attracted to people as you are–ladies or men."

"I understand that; I am not a simpleton. Please do not lecture me; come with me if you want; I will see you at the stables."

Half an hour later they were galloping across Netherfield's grounds. The weather was cold and cloudy; a soft but chill wind was blowing, brushing their faces.

Bingley took a path through the wood that Darcy immediately recognised as the one leading to Oakham Mount; in a heartbeat, Elizabeth's image filled his mind and he even glanced around for her. She was not there, but he could sense her presence even in her absence. The notion sent chills down his spine, while his stallion raced along. What was happening to him? He did not recognise his own feelings and feared he could not control them. That was disturbing, shattering his comfort. He had always been in control of his feelings, behaviours and even his thoughts. His reason was always stronger than his wishes, even when he was a child. He knew what was expected from him and never stepped over the line.

Suddenly, in the wilds of Hertfordshire, a revelation startled him. The only thing that had always been missing from his life was feelings; that inclination that made Bingley smile so much and act silly at times. That sense that gripped one's stomach and disturbed one's sleep and tranquillity.

He had read about it, heard it talked of by his eldest cousins, even by his parents. But he had never experienced it and was certain he never would. But then, why did he delay doing the only thing that was still expected of him–entering into a marriage appropriate for his family name and situation, with a lady worthy of the position of Mrs Darcy? There were many ladies he could have chosen, including his cousin Anne. Why had he silently opposed taking that step for so long? What was he expecting? What was he missing and what did he wish to have? And could all those secret desires come together and overwhelm him now, in the person of a country girl, who by anyone's judgment was so far below any other woman he knew?

She was the most enchanting person that he had ever met. And he had only spoken to her a handful of times, he had barely had time to judge her, to be certain of her character. And he did not even need that; he was simply charmed. Defeated. It was a trap set by his self-imposed reserve, hidden weakness and concealed wishes, and he had already fallen into it. .

He needed to depart from the object of his torment more than Bingley needed to do so. To Bingley, Miss Bennet's shortcomings were less powerful than her strengths. To him, Miss Elizabeth's wit, beauty, and liveliness meant little compared to her family's lack of manners, situation and connections. Bingley might choose to even marry Miss Jane Bennet. It would be his decision, his mistake, his misfortune. Darcy was forbidden by his duty and his responsibilities to even think of marrying Miss Elizabeth Bennet. He had no choice but to remove himself as far from her as possible.

"Darcy, do you believe Miss Bennet has no affection for me?" Bingley unexpectedly drew him out of his musing.

"Bingley, I have no intention to pain you but my affection and consideration for you demand I speak openly and honestly. I have not observed any particular inclination from Miss Bennet towards any man of our acquaintance, and I have seen no sign that she holds you in special regard."

"You did not hear her speaking to me, nor did you feel how she held my hand," Bingley responded sadly.

Darcy was not indifferent to his friend's distress.

"True. Which is why you must understand this is only my perception and my opinion. I cannot claim to be in possession of the absolute truth. However, the lack of decorum in some of the Bennets' behaviour can hardly be argued."

"I shall not contradict the obvious, Darcy. But she is flawless."

"I agree. And perhaps you should base your evaluation on your own judgement. This way you will have nobody else to blame, regardless of what decision you might take."

"You are right. But I have rarely been right when I have argued with you. This is why I value your opinion. However, I am sure you are wrong about Miss Bennet."

"If I gather more information to prove me wrong, I will readily admit it."

"Very well. You will see I am right if you meet them more often. Mr Bennet is a very peculiar gentleman. He seems well-read and well-educated. And very much inclined to tease people and to make sport at their expense—which makes him dangerous at times."

Darcy laughed at his friend's deep sigh.

"I have barely spoken to Mr Bennet at all, but your description sounds intriguing. I should make an effort to become better acquainted with the gentleman—and his eldest daughter."

"Well, you seem to favour Miss Elizabeth. Am I wrong in my observation?" Bingley asked daringly.

Darcy struggled to sound light. "You are not. And based on your description, I might say Miss Elizabeth resembles her father in some aspects. So I might favour him too."

"Luckily she does not resemble him in appearance," Bingley responded and Darcy concealed his laughter. "But I am quite sure you will appreciate Mr Bennet's company. He has a small library, yet neat and rich in books from what I noticed."

They rode along until Longbourn appeared in their sights. Bingley glanced at Darcy undecidedly, then at Longbourn, then at his friend again.

"We may call on the Bennets if you wish," Darcy heard himself telling Bingley, who happily approved.

"Of course I wish; and I hope you will enjoy yourself too," Bingley replied, spurring on his horse.

Darcy followed his eager friend, torn between his reasoning and the impulse of his heart. Under the sound of the horses' hooves and the blowing wind, he realised that any resolution he took regarding Miss Elizabeth Bennet lasted no longer than a breath.

∞∞∞

Longbourn was already animated when the two gentlemen arrived and asked for Mr Bennet. Bingley's arrival caused Jane to blush, while Darcy's presence distressed Elizabeth without her understanding why.

His dark gaze stirred her and his usual aloof countenance made her uncomfortable. During their short greeting, he seemed to stare at her and she instantly wondered what was wrong with her appearance. Even if it was nothing, he would surely find something with which to reproach her.

And then, as before, a small smile appeared, crushed between his lips and a dimple brightened his face. She felt her cheeks and neck burning and grew angry with herself for her silliness. Never before had she felt so clumsy and so uneasy in a man's presence; she knew she must dislike him, but the feeling was so strong and so strange that it troubled her every time they met.

"We apologise for intruding. We were taking a ride and Darcy suggested we briefly call and greet you. We will not stay long," Bingley said.

"Mr Darcy suggested?" Mrs Bennet cried. "He is all politeness, I must admit. Please do come in, Mr Bennet will be happy to see you. He is in the library; I will send for him."

"I hope we will not disturb him." Darcy said, glancing at

Elizabeth. She blushed again and averted her eyes, then replied, "Not at all, I am sure."

Her annoyance with herself grew along with her strange uneasiness in Darcy's presence.

"Indeed, he will welcome your visit," Mrs Bennet interjected. "He is speaking to his cousin who arrived a few days ago. Mr Collins, a clergyman in Hunsford. But I am sure Mr Bennet has had enough of talking to him."

"Hunsford? That is very close to Darcy's aunt's estate, Rosings, is it not, Darcy? He must know Lady Catherine," Bingley replied, attempting to advance the conversation while taking a seat in the drawing room.

At this, Mrs Bennet became increasingly animated. "Lady Catherine is your aunt? Dear Lord, he spoke of her the entire evening and morning. He seems truly in awe of the woman. I am sure she is an extraordinary lady. We already know everything about her and her daughter."

"I am sorry to hear that," Darcy responded and Elizabeth looked at him in surprise. He noticed and added, "I am sorry Mr Collins monopolised the conversation with only one subject. I have not had the pleasure of meeting him."

"I am sure you will soon, but do not anticipate any enjoyment from the meeting," Mrs Bennet mumbled, loud enough for her daughters to blush in embarrassment and for Darcy to show another smile.

"Mr Bingley, Jane has just received an invitation to tea from Miss Bingley," Mrs Bennet said moments later.

"Yes, my sister informed me she planned to invite Miss Bennet," Bingley replied, his eyes meeting Jane's distressed expression. "I hope you will have a pleasant time."

"I am sure I will," Jane replied.

The sound of footsteps and voices approaching drove their attention to the open door.

"Mr Collins, are you sure your business allows you such a long absence?" Mr Bennet was asking his guest.

"My dear Mr Bennet, I assure you that I am very honoured

by your reception and I have no reason to be hasty with my return. Lady Catherine specifically mentioned that I should stay as long as needed to accomplish my purpose," Mr Collins spoke breathlessly from the effort of walking.

Laying eyes on the guests, he stopped, while Mr Bennet moved forward, showing more pleasure than on any previous visit.

"Mr Bingley, Mr Darcy! How fortunate that you called," their host said with an unexpected burst of joy.

Greetings were exchanged, then Darcy glanced at Elizabeth once again and noticed her face frowning in some sort of panic. He looked around and spotted Mr Collins approaching him, bent over, with an expression of awe. He took a step back, wondering what was going on.

"Mr Darcy? Mr Darcy of Pemberley? The nephew of Lady Catherine de Bourgh?" Mr Collins enquired with increasing wonder.

Darcy took another step back. "How may I help you, sir?" he asked.

"This is indeed almost the most extraordinary day of my life, except one," Mr Collins continued. "I have the great honour of being under the patronage of Lady Catherine de Bourgh and I am happy to inform you that her ladyship was in perfect health when I left Rosings."

Darcy looked at the man with repugnance. "I am glad to hear that," he said bluntly.

"Mr Darcy, Mr Bingley, allow me to introduce you to our cousin, Mr Collins," Mr Bennet interjected.

"I am so honoured to meet you! I was given the living of the parish of Hunsford and Lady Catherine did me the great favour of taking me under her wing..."

"That was very fortunate, I imagine," Darcy attempted to stop his effusions, but Collins was not to be deterred from the object of his adoration.

"Words are not enough to express my gratitude for her ladyship and my delight in meeting her nephew! I know how much her ladyship praises you, Mr Darcy...She always said ..."

"Mr Collins!" Darcy interrupted him with a thundering voice, eager to close the conversation. "It would be impolite of us to speak a moment longer of my relatives, of myself or of any other subject that is of no interest to the rest of our companions."

"I humbly beg to differ, sir. I am sure my fair cousins are willing to hear as much as possible of Lady Catherine..."

"Mr Collins!" Darcy interrupted him again. "Trust me, nobody is willing to hear so much about a complete stranger. Besides, I understand that you have already shared quite a lot of information about my aunt. I doubt anybody was left wanting on this subject."

Mr Collins appeared lost. His face showed his disturbance and his struggle between praising his patroness further and contradicting her nephew.

Darcy's harsh yet amusing intervention surprised Elizabeth. Once again, she had discovered a glimpse of the character of the aloof gentleman that she had not suspected before. Each of their meetings allowed her to sketch parts of his character but she had been unable to link them together yet. The notion that he refused a conversation about his titled aunt, to the benefit of the Bennets' sanity was diverting, intriguing and contrary to what she expected of him.

Mr Collins was ready for another try, but Elizabeth spoke quicker.

"The stories about Lady Catherine were lovely," she said, attempting to call a truce. "However, perhaps a more neutral subject could be found. What if we speak of books. Or theatre?"

"Oh, this is so boring!" Lydia interrupted. "I want to go to Meryton!"

"Lydia, please!" an embarrassed Jane discreetly scolded the youngest Miss Bennet, who responded with a shrug and a dismissive wave of the hand.

"I want to go to Meryton too," Kitty supported her

younger sister. "The regiment is in town and there is always something fun to do or someone amusing to talk to!"

"And yet, you will both stay at home and bear our boring company," Mr Bennet declared, raising even more opposition. The argument between the youngest Miss Bennets and their father became awkward for the others, who kept glancing at each other. Lydia's lack of respect and Mr Bennet's apparent indifference and mockery spoke much of the young girl's manners and of Mr Bennet's parenting skills. The host, however, seemed untroubled.

"Mr Darcy, Mr Bingley, would you like a drink?" he invited his guests while ignoring his young daughters. "And Mr Collins too," Mr Bennet eventually added.

"A drink would be lovely," Bingley mumbled. Darcy only nodded in acceptance.

"Excellent. Let us retire to the library and allow the ladies some time to themselves," Mr Bennet continued. "We have had enough arguments for one morning. Please follow me."

"I agree," Collins spoke again. "Lady Catherine always says that a glass of brandy is acceptable for a man. She kindly offers me one each time I have the pleasure of visiting her."

He continued to jabber and Darcy sighed in exasperation while his annoyance increased. He briefly caught Elizabeth's laughing eyes and he unwillingly smiled at her. He thought he noticed a trace of a blush on her cheeks and a strange heat ran through his body. Did she blush because of his smile? Was she as affected by his presence as he was by hers? Had he betrayed his preference for her?

He had no time to think further, busy following Mr Bennet to the library while trying to ignore Mr Collins' repeated mentions of Lady Catherine's name. He wondered about the coincidence of Elizabeth's cousin living in the proximity of his aunt. It was just another tie to keep him attached to her.

Would he ever be capable of distancing himself from her completely? Would he be able to cut the bond that he felt strengthening between them with every meeting, every glance, every smile?

And if he were to depart from here, would he be allowed to forget her? Would he have the power to do so, when he so readily agreed to visit her, despite his own resolution to stay away from her? Sitting in the small library with her father, enjoying his drink and absently responding to some questions from his companions, he could think of nothing else but Elizabeth's crimson cheeks and her sparkling eyes.

∞∞∞

"We stayed almost two hours," Bingley said on the road from Longbourn to Netherfield.

"Yes," Darcy admitted briefly.

"Did you enjoy your time? Mr Collins was a true annoyance for you, I can tell."

"Mr Collins is a very peculiar sort of man. I hope to spend little time in his company in the future. But yes, I did enjoy the visit. You must have noticed that I did not intend to leave."

"Indeed. You seem to approve of Mr Bennet. Am I wrong?"

"You are not wrong. His manners are not always what propriety might require, but he has a special sense of humour and excellent knowledge of the world. And his collection of books is small but rich."

"He seemed happy with our visit."

"Yes," Darcy smiled. "It provided him with an escape from Mr Collins' sole company. It must be a daunting task for Mr Bennet to bear a man with so little sense and no humour."

They rode on in silence at a steady pace for some time, then Bingley spoke again. "Darcy, do you still believe Miss Bennet is indifferent to me?"

Darcy breathed deeply, choosing his words carefully. "Bingley, I spent only a few minutes with the ladies today. I barely observed Miss Bennet and she hardly spoke more than a few words. How could I have changed my opinion? But truly, I feel you are not being honest either, not with me, with her or with yourself."

Bingley stopped the horse and turned to his friend in complete puzzlement.

"What on Earth could you possibly mean?"

"You were angry earlier today at me and your sisters for expressing our unfavourable viewpoint regarding you and Miss Bennet. And now, you keep asking what I think, as if you are uncertain of your feelings and are trying to put the burden of your decision on my shoulders."

Disbelief twisted Bingley's features and his eyes opened widely in dismay.

"I am not doing any such thing!"

"Then what are you doing, Bingley? I have already told you what I believe and that upset you. I cannot conceal my opinion to please you, nor adjust it to your liking. It is you who must assess the situation properly and choose what is best."

Bingley stared at him, lost and dumbfounded, attempted to reply, then suddenly spurred on his stallion and started to gallop, leaving his companion behind.

Darcy watched him depart, hesitated a moment, then directed his horse down another road. He needed more time to himself, alone with his own thoughts–and surely so did Bingley.

Chapter 4

*T*he next morning, a heavy autumn storm overturned the peace and the plans at Longbourn. Thunder, rain and wind ruined everyone's hopes, making it impossible for the eldest Miss Bennet to honour Miss Bingley's invitation to tea. Jane was disappointed, but her sadness was nothing compared with Mrs Bennet's distress.

"This is a most unfortunate turn of events; such ill weather precisely when Jane was about to spend the day at Netherfield must surely be a curse. I wonder who harbours such ill will towards us!"

"Mama, it is almost winter; bad weather is expected. Do not be so upset, I am sure other opportunities will arise soon," Elizabeth attempted to calm her.

"Indeed, I agree with my fair cousin Elizabeth," Mr Collins interjected. "The weather was cold and wet even when I left Rosings and, although it was only fifty miles, the condition of the road was not as good as I had hoped for."

"Well, one should not travel a long distance in the winter unless absolutely necessary," Mrs Bennet replied. "But Jane would have ridden only three miles, not fifty. Perhaps you should go anyway. You may take the carriage, and there will not be much damage to your appearance."

"Mama, I will certainly not do that!" Jane answered decidedly. "I am sure Caroline will understand and will not take offence. Nobody should travel even one mile in this storm."

"Well, I am retiring to my library. I expect not to be disturbed unless something of great urgency occurs," Mr Bennet addressed his family.

"If you do not mind, I would rather stay with my cousins this morning. I would like to know them better before returning to Kent," Mr Collins declared.

The girls' despair matched their father's relief; Mr Bennet hurried to his library while his daughters remained trapped in the drawing room, with a man preaching about the importance of a good education for ladies.

"I confess, my dear Mrs Bennet, that the purpose of my visit was beyond my wish of becoming reacquainted with my cousin and seeing the estate that will one day belong to me."

Mrs Bennet's face darkened and her eyes narrowed in anger.

"My noble patroness, Lady Catherine de Bourgh, insisted I should find a proper wife. She insisted that a man of my age and position must be an example for his congregation and that I am old enough to consider marriage an urgency. So I came to Longbourn with the determination to comply with my patroness's request–which has also been my greatest desire for some time now. Meeting my charming cousins, I grow more hopeful every day that my purpose will soon be accomplished," Mr Collins concluded with a large grin.

Mrs Bennet's expression lightened and a smile twisted her lips. She spoke animatedly, moving closer to Mr Collins.

"Well, this is sound reasoning from a wise gentleman. Lady Catherine had every right to trust you with her preferment. And I assure you that one cannot possibly find more charming young girls prepared to become worthy wives than my daughters. Even Mr Bingley admitted that, and he had no restraint in showing his admiration for Jane. But then again, Jane is admired everywhere she goes, so we expect Mr Bingley to declare himself any day now."

"Mama!" Jane cried, tearful from embarrassment. "We only met Mr Bingley a few weeks ago. We cannot guess his feelings, nor presume his intentions!"

"Of course we can–they are obvious to anyone," Mrs

Bennet continued unaffected.

"Well, I confess I am a little bit disappointed, as my eldest cousin was the first who drew my interest," Mr Collins admitted.

"I understand that, but I am afraid you are a little late regarding Jane. However, I am sure you will find much to interest you in my other daughters too."

The youngest girls glanced at each other with apprehension. Jane blushed and looked at Elizabeth, who was torn between misery and laughter. A moment later, the second Miss Bennet became the recipient of the gentleman's attention.

"My dear cousin Elizabeth, I have heard that you enjoy reading. This is an admirable quality in a woman, even if her beauty is not flawless. Even Mr Darcy said yesterday that he very much approves of women who expand their knowledge by extensive reading."

The statement shocked Elizabeth and she stared at the man wordlessly. She could not decide if she was more offended by the remark about her beauty being wanting or more surprised about Mr Darcy's comment–if it was accurate. Of course, it would be foolish for her to imagine that he had made such an allusion with her specifically in mind. He must have stated his opinion in general. But the revelation that they had talked about her enjoyment of reading in the library the previous day, was still strong and puzzling.

Even more surprising for Elizabeth was that she cared about Mr Darcy's opinion. She could not stop thinking of him lately, and that notion was disturbing. She did not remember harbouring such ill feelings about a man ever before. Each time she saw him, her heart beat in a strange, restless way. Perhaps it was because she expected him to say something to offend her or to throw her one of his judgmental gazes.

She knew she was far from perfection and could accept the critique from Mr Collins. Mr Darcy said far less but conveyed far more. A single look from him was more unbearable and hurtful than his comment about her being 'tolerable'. And his strange way of smiling at her from time to time was even more tormenting, as she could not guess his meaning.

Unexpectedly, her father's opinion of him had improved after their short encounter the previous day. But then again, her father's opinion about any man would be very high after spending so many days with Mr Collins.

"My dear Miss Elizabeth, would you be so generous as to tell me what other preferences you have? I would be happy to find out as much as I can about you," Mr Collins continued.

"There is not much to say, I assure you," she responded coldly. "In fact, I would beg you to excuse me, I do not feel well. I might have caught a cold and I would rather rest a little bit," Elizabeth declared, hurrying out of the room. Her mother called to her but she decided to face the consequences rather than return. She rushed to her chamber and collapsed on the bed.

Her worst nightmare had just begun. Mr Collins had apparently decided to choose her as the means of satisfying Lady Catherine's demand to find a wife, and she had few chances to deter him from his purpose. It was sure to provoke a major fight with her mother–there was no doubt about it. But it was a battle she would happily wage.

Thank God he was so easily convinced to give up on Jane. With a quiver, Elizabeth wondered if, without Mr Bingley's presence at Netherfield, Jane would have the strength to reject Mr Collins. She knew her sister's sense of duty would have induced her to do anything to secure her family's future. If there were no other prospects, Jane would have probably accepted Mr Collins to secure her family's future.

Elizabeth shivered and pulled the covers around her. She heard the door and then Jane's sweet voice.

"Dearest, are you truly unwell?"

"I am. I am sick and nauseous and I do not expect to get better anytime soon."

Jane sat on the bed.

"Come now, Lizzy. Do not be so harsh on poor Mr Collins. He will suffer a great disappointment if he proposes and you refuse him, but he is no worse than other men."

"True. I fear my nausea comes from Mama's readiness to marry us to anyone who may come along. I am horrified that she might make similar statements in the presence of Mr Bingley or Mr Darcy."

"Lizzy darling, now you are being harsh and unfair on our mother too," Jane said gently. "Mama loves us and wants nothing but what is best for us. You cannot doubt that. She only wishes to secure our future and to ensure us a happy life."

"I know I am being unfair. And I know Mama loves us and she wants what she thinks is the best for us. But her best is the worst for me. I would rather sleep in the woods and work as a servant than marry Mr Collins. Nobody could convince or force me otherwise."

"And nobody will. If Mr Collins has any admiration for you and a little sense, he will quickly see that there is no encouragement on your part."

"I am sure he has no true admiration, nor any sort of sense. But I will do everything in my power to show him that any pursuit would fail. Let us hope he will quickly change his mind and will search for a life partner elsewhere. Longbourn is not a good place for such a quest."

"Oh Lizzy, if I could help you to calm and relax a little bit... You are so flushed and distressed, and for no reason, I am sure."

"I am just happy that Mama told Mr Collins that you are almost engaged. Otherwise, he would have declared his preference for you. That would have distressed me even more!"

"Lizzy, darling..."

"On second thoughts, you may help me: charm Mr Bingley and make him propose to you as soon as possible. That way, Mama will be too happy about your engagement to be bothered by my refusal and will no longer fear we will be thrown onto the street by Mr Collins. One daughter so successfully married will allow the rest of us a little liberty to choose."

Jane blushed. "Lizzy, we are imagining more than is there. I have seen no indication that Mr Bingley will propose to me soon—or at all. And we have nothing but suspicions about Mr

Collins's intentions too."

"I like your tendency to see only the good side of each situation," Elizabeth embraced her sister lovingly. "I cannot wait for you to marry so I can live with you. I will raise your handsome children and teach them to play the pianoforte very poorly and climb trees very skillfully," she mocked her elder sister. Jane laughed with obvious uneasiness.

"Lizzy, let us be reasonable and not make plans about my marriage just yet. I was wondering...Do you not think that Mr Darcy behaves rather strangely? Yesterday he seemed more amiable than before. But still, I sometimes feel he measures me with his severe gaze. I feel shy and uncomfortable under his scrutiny...I wonder what he tells Mr Bingley about me and our family..."

"I cannot guess what is in Mr Darcy's mind, but I assume nothing good. Surely he does not consider us worthy of his interest, but he cannot possibly find anything wanting in you. You are the most beautiful and sweetest person that ever lived. And you are a gentleman's daughter, while Mr Bingley's roots are not as healthy or as strong...Mr Darcy surely can judge these circumstances properly. He will recognise his friend's luck in gaining the genuine affection of the most perfect woman."

Tears mixed with Jane's laughter. "Dear Lizzy, forgive me for not trusting your biased and loving appreciation. I cannot hope Mr Darcy's opinion will be anything similar. I know Mr Bingley trusts him and always counts on his advice. He has mentioned it to me several times."

"I think we give Mr Darcy too much credit. Let us wonder more of Mr Bingley's opinion. His heart and admiration are surely stronger than Mr Darcy's advice."

∞∞∞

After the visit to Longbourn and their brief discussion on the ride back, the tension between the two friends remained and increased. And the bad weather keeping everyone inside was not helpful at easing the distressing ambience. Yet, Darcy did not regret his censure of Bingley, although it pained him to see his friend struggling with distress and uncertainty. It was necessary to make his younger friend aware of his indecision and lack of self-confidence. Many times Bingley had changed his mind at his sisters' insistence, putting others' opinions ahead of his own.

Even in the situation regarding Miss Bennet, he was angry when his sisters disapproved of the connection, but was not certain, or not brave enough to decide by himself and to act accordingly. He demanded to be left alone and have his decisions respected, but he actually had not decided on anything. Constantly trying to validate his feelings with Darcy's observations proved that his doubts were stronger than his wishes. And, since he himself seemed to be falling for the second Miss Bennet's charms, Darcy was unwilling to push his friend in either direction. He could not assume the responsibility of separating Bingley from Miss Jane Bennet, nor could he in good conscience lie about his observation of Miss Bennet's indifference. The only fair and honest thing to do was to encourage Bingley to decide for himself and live with his choice.

In any case, he had to cut the bond between them, as he intended to leave Hertfordshire soon. As long as Bingley remained at Netherfield, they would probably not meet again except on brief occasions.

"What nasty weather! How unfortunate for it to rain today of all days. I am afraid that will prevent Jane from having tea with us," Caroline said.

Bingley only glanced at her.

"Probably...Surely no reasonable woman would consider calling in such weather. Unless her mother forces her to come anyway," Louisa commented scornfully.

"I see no reason for mockery. Miss Bennet is a wise young lady. I am sure she will find a better time for a visit," Bingley answered, obviously displeased with the discussion.

"We will see. What do you think, Mr Darcy? Should we try a wager?" Caroline asked in jest, exchanging amused looks with her sister.

"You are joking, I am sure. It would hardly be proper to put a wager on Miss Bennet," Darcy replied coldly. "Besides, on the few occasions when I have seen her, she gave me no reason to presume she would do anything either indecorous or reckless."

He was irritated by the sisters' rudeness. Their disapproval of a presumed connection between Bingley and the eldest Miss Bennet did not justify their lack of decorum and the continuous offences against the Bennets. And judged fairly, the Bingleys were below the Bennets in regard to their origin. Miss Bennet was a gentleman's daughter and that compensated for her lack of dowry and connections.

"Miss Bennet's manners and behaviour are beyond reproach. We cannot possibly put a wager on her actions before we carefully weigh up our own. And it is breakfast time; we should eat," Bingley ended the debate.

"We were not arguing about that, Charles. Dear Jane is such a sweet person! I am only worried that, with no dowry, a mother who does not know what decorum means, an uncle who is in trade and an aunt married to an attorney, she has no chance of making even a reasonably good marriage."

"If we are concerned about decorum, this should not be a subject for us to debate. I would rather eat in peace," Bingley insisted one more time, his ire increasing noticeably.

"I confess I am quite hungry," Darcy said with cold politeness. He was not as hungry as he was bothered. Besides his wish to support Bingley, the conversation annoyed him too.

For a while, only the sound of rain and wind disturbed the heavy silence.

But it did not last long before the sisters lost their patience.

"Charles, will you be as silent at breakfast as you were at dinner?" Caroline asked.

Lost in his thoughts, Bingley looked at her absently.

"You seem out of spirits," Louisa observed.

"Mr Darcy, you spend most of the time with our brother. WIll you not tell us what has happened to ruin his disposition?" Caroline continued.

"The only one who might answer regarding his disposition is your brother himself," Darcy replied, looking at his plate.

"Such secrecy seems even stranger," Caroline concluded. "You did not even tell us where you spent your afternoon. It must be related to Charles's unusual silence."

"I am going to host a ball," Bingley suddenly declared, utterly unrelated to the conversation. Four pairs of eyes stared at him in disbelief.

"Host a ball? What for? Where on earth did this come from?" Louisa asked reprovingly.

"Charles, this is not something to trifle with. A ball is a daunting and expensive task that requires much planning and preparation. Having one here in Hertfordshire is not worth the effort," Caroline declared scornfully.

Bingley threw his sister a sharp glare.

"I have the desire as well as the means to plan and to prepare everything needed. The ball will take place on November 26th. After it is done, I shall decide if it was worth the effort or not."

Bingley's decisiveness increased his sisters' astonishment, and his answer only aroused more questions and arguments.

Darcy watched his friend in silence, wondering about the reason for such an impromptu decision. Nothing regarding a ball had ever been mentioned between them.

"This conversation is useless. I am going to inform the staff, then I will start the preparations. How hard can it be? Food, music and some decorations. I do not even have to determine the guest list, since I will invite all my acquaintances."

Bingley rose from the table and walked towards the door. His sisters followed, in a failed attempt to temper him.

They glanced at Darcy, begging for support, but he chose to pay attention to his food. He had no opinion on the matter and would surely not try to change Bingley's mind. Yet, he too was intrigued about the sudden decision regarding the ball. Had he been influenced by their argument from the previous day? The ball must be related to Miss Bennet, but what did Bingley intend to accomplish?

While wondering about his younger friend, Darcy was well aware the best thing for him would be to return to London as soon as possible. Instead, he suddenly considered that the ball might be his last chance to dance with Elizabeth Bennet.

For the rest of the day the rain did not cease and, as expected, Miss Jane Bennet did not appear. The subject was only briefly mentioned, then dropped at Bingley's request.

They were all trapped inside the house, but the tension was so heavy at Netherfield that the party separated to avoid other arguments.

The sisters spent their time in the music room, while Bingley and Darcy retired to the library.

One struggled to read, the other only paced the room, changing one book after another. Darcy smiled to himself; Bingley was not fond of reading even when he was calm. In moments of distress, books were the last thing to comfort him.

"So? What is your opinion about the ball?" Bingley eventually burst out.

Darcy looked at him sternly.

"The same as usual, about any ball."

"So do you not approve of it?"

"Bingley, it is not for me to approve anything. It is your decision and does not need anyone's blessing. For me, any ball is a waste of time and energy. But this is my flaw. I am sure most of the people in the village will be happy with it."

"I hope so. There are almost three more weeks until then. I have plenty of time to prepare everything." Again, he looked towards Darcy for confirmation.

"Bingley, I am by no means proficient in organising balls.

But I would assume there is plenty of time. It is not an Almack's ball, after all. But may I ask, why did you decide to have this ball? Is it a celebration of anything?"

Bingley glanced at him. "No... no celebration. I just thought it would be a nice opportunity for entertainment, and dancing, and conversation."

"I see...I admit it was quite a surprise."

"I know. To be honest, I thought carefully about what you said yesterday, Darcy. I might be lacking the courage to make my own decisions. I wish to change that, and I must gather more proof. Therefore, I need to spend more time with Miss Bennet... To be sure a ball grants one no privacy, but it does provide many opportunities to see one's preference. Would you not agree?"

"I do agree. Bingley. I hope you will be pleased with the outcome and will make the right decision for your future happiness."

"I am surprised to hear that. Caroline told me you intended to convince me against a relationship with Miss Bennet. Is it true?"

The answer came with no hesitation.

"It is true. I already admitted as much to you. I thought it would be in your best interest. But your anger made me reconsider. If you ask my opinion, I will readily give it. If not, I shall keep it to myself."

"Darcy, I am always interested in your opinion and your advice. I was upset because I thought you were being unfair. You do not have enough information to make a sound judgement."

"I have no means to contradict you. Therefore, I will say no more on the subject. Just let me know if I can help you in any way."

"Your support is greatly appreciated. I know how much you disapprove of the Bennet family, and it means a lot to me that you put your own feelings beneath my wishes."

"Bingley, I fear I have misled you and others with my unfriendly manners into believing my feelings to be stronger than they actually are. I do not either like or dislike the Bennet family more than any other new acquaintance. And I am sure they dislike me just as much as any other person who has met me recently. I know I am not pleasant company."

"You did fool me by plotting with my sister against Miss Bennet, and by offending Miss Elizabeth when you first met her," Bingley laughed.

"I am glad to see your disposition improving, Bingley. I did not plot against Miss Bennet, I only expressed my genuine opinion; I have always been honest with you, and I shall not explain or apologise about this matter again."

"I know you would not deceive me with dishonest observations, Darcy. And no, there is no need for any more apologies. I also noticed your meeting with Miss Elizabeth went reasonably well."

"It did; things have changed since that rude and unfair remark at the assembly. But it was not even directed at her. I was tired and irritated, and you were quite bothersome, insisting that I dance. I would have refused to dance with any woman. I only asked your sisters to fulfil my duty to you as my host."

"Yes, I know that. And Miss Elizabeth was just an innocent victim of your poor mood," Bingley smiled. "Very ungentlemanlike of you, Darcy."

"I admit it. As I said, I cannot compete with you in amiability and I have no wish to do so. But Miss Elizabeth and I have met enough times now to become accustomed to each other. I confess I have come to admire her charm and wit. She is surely one of the most intriguing women I have met."

"She is; and very beautiful too. But she looks too strong for my taste. I mean too self-confident. And she sounds very clever, she speaks so decidedly about anything. I do admire her, but I feel somehow intimidated by her. Even when she smiles, I am not sure if she is simply amused, or whether I have said something stupid and she is mocking me. I do admire her, but I could never fall in love with someone like her. I would not have the courage to spend my life with someone like that. Unlike Jane, whose smiles are... soft and heartwarming."

It was Darcy's turn to smile–half to his friend, half to himself. Everything Bingley said about Elizabeth was true. However, it was not intimidating, but enchanting. Delightful. Alluring. Dangerous for his heart and for his sanity.

A painful thought darkened his mind although he was reluctant to accept it. He was not being completely honest with his friend. He did confess his opposition to Miss Bennet. But what he did not say and what made him feel shame and guilt was his desire to avoid any connection that might bring Elizabeth near to him in the future.

"I hope she has forgiven you for offending her that night," Bingley said. "I intend to call on the Bennets rather often, and I hope you will join me."

Darcy's smile widened.

"I also hope she has forgiven me. But I cannot be certain. As you know, I asked her to dance again and she refused me. But I trust she will not oppose me calling on her father with you. I enjoyed Mr Bennet's company very much."

"Good. Good. I am glad we talked, Darcy."

"So am I. But Bingley... I might not stay long at Netherfield. I will have to return to town soon."

Bingley startled. "Return to town? When? Not before the ball, I hope!"

"No, not before the ball. But I must be with Georgiana for Christmas."

"That I understand. Is she well, I hope?"

"She is; we keep a regular correspondence. Mrs Annesley is a reliable companion. I am very satisfied with her. But I do miss my sister."

"I imagine you do. I will be sorry to see you leave, but I feel privileged that I have had your help and your company during the last couple of months."

"Likewise, Bingley. Now–you should make a list of everything you think you need for the ball and find the right people to assign the tasks to. I am afraid you cannot count much on me for that."

Chapter 5

*T*he following day brought cold yet sunny weather and excellent news arrived at Longbourn, delivered by Mr Bingley himself straight after breakfast.

Much to the ladies' surprise, he announced the upcoming ball and was immediately surrounded by happy faces, cries of joy, and countless questions.

The gentleman did not stay long but the mere fact that he brought the news in person showed his consideration and affection for the family, as Mrs Bennet readily declared afterwards.

"I am sure he is giving this ball for Jane. It cannot be any other way. And perhaps there will be an announcement, too, at the ball. Or before! Oh, what a lovely turn of events. Not that I did not expect it!"

"A ball can be very pleasant if planned carefully," Mr Collins declared. "I would just prefer to have it sooner."

"But what difference would it make to you, sir?" Mr Bennet asked.

"My dear cousin, I am worried that it might be too long for me to be absent from my duties in my parish."

"It depends on how long Lady Catherine approved of your leave," the host replied.

"We only discussed a fortnight," Mr Collins answered with obvious concern.

"Then It would surely be too long and perhaps unwise to prolong it for a ball," Elizabeth replied hastily. "Of course, it is for you to decide between the dance and your duties as a clergyman."

"I am not certain what would be the best decision. But I will give it thorough consideration, my dear cousin Elizabeth. I might write to her ladyship and ask if my presence is needed at Hunsford."

"I was wondering...would it be sensible to suggest to Lady Catherine that your presence is not needed for such a long while? What if she responds that you are not needed—would such a notion not be worrisome?" Elizabeth continued, despite her mother's scolding glances.

Mr Collins paled. "That is...Indeed... I did not think of it."

"Could you not return to your duties in Kent in the next few days and then come back for the ball, if you desire? And perhaps you could then accomplish your other unfinished business?" Mrs Bennet interjected.

Mr Collins was lost between so many suggestions and options, looking from one to another. He did not miss the sharp glares exchanged between mother and daughter, but decided to ignore them. He had more important things to ponder for the time being.

"My dear Mrs Bennet, that is very sound advice. This is what I will do. I am going to pack my belongings and return to Hunsford tomorrow. And there I will examine the situation with Lady Catherine and see what she counsels me to do."

"A truly sagacious decision, if I may say so," Mr Bennet concluded. "I will send John to help with your luggage. Now you must excuse me. If anyone urgently needs me and cannot delay, I will be in my library, reading."

∞∞∞

As soon as Mr Collins left the drawing room, Mrs Bennet demanded a private talk with Elizabeth, asking the other girls to leave.

"Mama, I am sure there is nothing we have to discuss that

my sisters cannot hear."

"Lizzy, I will not be ignored or disobeyed," Mrs Bennet said. "You will listen to me, even if I have to force you in this! Girls, leave us now!"

Elizabeth reluctantly accepted, well aware that a refusal was out of the question. She sat on the sofa, clasping her hands together, and waiting for her mother's upcoming reproaches.

"Mama, I am afraid I do not understand why you are upset."

"You do understand perfectly well, young lady. I am talking of your rude manners towards Mr Collins. Instead of praising his intention to choose a wife from among his cousins, you hold his good will against him. Instead of encouraging him, you pushed him away before he even had time to declare himself."

"I am not rude to anyone. But I shall never encourage any man's fictitious inclination towards me, as long as I know I will never be able to accept it, even less to reciprocate it. Mr Collins has no real partiality to me or to any woman. He only searches for an easy way to comply with Lady Catherine's demands."

"And why would you care about his reasons, Lizzy? Mr Collins might not be the most desirable man, but he is a perfectly eligible one and I am sure he would be a good husband to any reasonable woman."

"Mama, I do not intend to even discuss Mr Collins' qualities as a husband. The mere notion of him declaring himself is ridiculous. To me, he is of no interest except as a distant relative."

"So you are decided not to have him?"

"Mama, I am decided not to have any man that I cannot respect. And any conversation on this subject cannot be sound or serious. I hope such arguments will cease as soon as Mr Collins leaves."

"Would you rather wait to be thrown out on the street when your father dies, than be polite to Mr Collins?"

"I trust we have no reason to worry about that for a long

time. But yes, any alternative would be better than an unhappy marriage."

"Lizzy, I will never speak to you again if you do not behave more politely to Mr Collins when he returns! You must try at least to know him better. Will you promise me that? I am your mother, you owe me as much!"

"Very well, Mama. I promise I will be impeccably polite to Mr Collins when he returns. May I be excused now?"

"Yes, you may! You should be more grateful for my efforts to ensure your future and a happy family! I want nothing but the best for you all!"

"I know that, Mama. I do appreciate your care and I do know you are doing everything in our best interest; I am sorry if I do not show my gratitude often enough."

"You have always been wild, Lizzy. You are clever and pretty, but not the type that men usually look for. And you have almost no dowry. Please keep in mind you might not get a better marriage proposal–or any other marriage proposal at all."

"I am well aware of that, Mama," Elizabeth smiled.

"I know you are, and still you are stubborn and self-sufficient. Keep in mind that Charlotte Lucas is seven and twenty and already a spinster, although her father was introduced at St James'! Times passes and you will be twenty-seven in no time!"

"My greatest hope is that Jane will marry as well as she deserves and she will keep me to be governess to her beautiful and bright children."

Mrs Bennet rolled her eyes. "You are so vexing and so indifferent to my poor nerves! You find as much pleasure in tormenting me as your father does. Just wait and see what happens if I die at the same time as your father. What will then happen to you all?"

"I am sorry, Mama. I truly do not intend to torment you. And I am confident both you and Papa will lead healthy and happy lives for many years to come. I will leave you now so you may rest."

She hurried out before her mother had time to reply and hastened her pace even more, when she heard Mr Collins calling her name. If she was fortunate enough, Mr Collins would depart without her having to talk to him again.

∞ ∞ ∞

Two more days passed and the fever of ball preparations enveloped the ladies of Longbourn. Luckily, the chaos of it diminished the importance of Mr Collins' departure back to Kent, and the prospect of his return was rarely even mentioned. Mrs Bennet was too busy imagining the happy outcome of the dance and, compared to the notion of having Mr Bingley as her son-in-law, Mr Collins was not worthy of consideration.

The entirety of Meryton—or at least those families closely acquainted with Mrs Bennet—agreed that the ball must be dedicated to Jane. The Bennets were the envy of the village, but it was universally admitted that the eldest Miss Bennet—by beauty and kindness—deserved the good fortune of a happy marriage.

Jane was the most restrained of all her sisters; she attempted to temper her mother's expectations and the rumours that had been spread around, yet she met with little success. Elizabeth, her confidante and support, understood and shared Jane's concern but neither of them had much success countering the general speculations, started by none other than Mrs Bennet.

"Lizzy, I fear we are reading too much into Mr Bingley's generous gesture and are seeing something that does not exist. It pains me to imagine how disappointed Mama will be if her hopes are shattered, but I will die of shame if such reports reach Mr Bingley's ears and they are not true."

"I understand your worry, dearest. However, not even you can doubt Mr Bingley's admiration for you."

"I am not a fool, Lizzy. I have long recognised his admiration, but I am uncertain if he intends to turn it into more than a friendship. We are rarely alone for more than a few minutes and we barely discuss anything at all, without others being part of the conversation. If he wished for more, would he not have found a way to show me that?"

"Perhaps. But my darling, have you indicated to him your feelings and your wishes? Maybe he needs more encouragement."

"What do you mean, Lizzy? Could anyone doubt my preference for him? I was worried that I might have been unwisely obvious in showing what I feel."

Elizabeth smiled and embraced her lovingly.

"Unwisely obvious? My darling, on this you are completely wrong. You could safely consider showing much more; men are rarely perceptive and, while some of them presume more than they should, others do not dare to see the truth if it is not laid out in front of them."

"But Lizzy, I cannot throw myself at Mr Bingley's feet! I cannot push him to propose to me! Surely he must understand his heart and his wishes first, and then he will act accordingly."

Elizabeth embraced her again. "You are right again, dearest. How can I ever argue with you, when you are reasonable and just most of the time?"

"Lizzy, do not trifle with me. I know that sometimes I look silly to you, but I am doing my best; not everyone possesses your strength and your self-confidence. I just hope Mr Bingley can see more even if I show less."

"Well, his decision to host a ball is praiseworthy, and I suppose he made it without much encouragement from his sisters or from his friend. Let us trust his sound judgment."

"Do you think they disapprove of the ball? Mr Darcy and Caroline and Louisa...Could this be the reason why we have not seen or heard from any of them in the last few days?" Jane asked.

"Have you missed them? I most certainly have not, especially the ladies. To me, they are even more unpleasant than Mr Darcy and that is quite a feat. He is proud and haughty and has a tendency to judge and to criticise people. But he seems well-educated and even has moments when he is amiable enough. But they are conceited, and mean and rude all the time, and consider themselves to be above everyone else–which they certainly are not. Neither by wealth or situation in life or birth. Their most important accomplishment is being Mr Bingley's sisters."

"Lizzy darling, you are a little too harsh."

"I might be, but I am also very much right. Your kindness cannot excuse their disrespect. And if a certain event takes place, I am afraid you will have to fight for your position as the mistress of the house. But on that, we can worry later."

"What of Mr Darcy? Do you think he will continue his close relationship with Mr Bingley if he enters into a family he does not approve of? I know how much Mr Bingley values his friendship."

Elizabeth hesitated to respond. Strangely, to even herself, she found herself thinking of Darcy more often than she would wish to. She was disturbed by her own reactions to him, and that troubled her more than the man himself. She knew he had offended her, she knew she disliked him, she knew she should be relieved that he had not called again. Yet, she was preoccupied with wanting to know the reason for his absence after only a brief visit when he impressed her father and he even appeared to feel comfortable. Had she–or someone else in the family–been overtly rude to him? Had he noticed something that offended him? Was it her apparent impolite manners towards him that displeased him? She wondered, if the weather allowed, would he continue to ride towards Oakham Mount and might they meet again, or had he also dropped those habits entirely, to avoid encountering her?

But, most of all, she wondered why on earth she cared about him enough to be so curious about him.

She looked at Jane and responded honestly. "I do not know, Jane. It is hard to even guess what is in Mr Darcy's mind, let alone to express a sound opinion. If he is worthy of Mr Bingley's appreciation, he should be supportive and fair. If he is not, Mr

Bingley is just too kind and too generous to grant his respect and consideration to a man who does not deserve it."

∞∞∞

"Mr Collins has returned to Kent," Bingley declared during dinner.

Darcy looked at him briefly. "The Bennet family must be relieved."

"I believe so. I did not dare ask. But Mr Bennet expressed his pleasure in having the library to himself."

"I can well imagine that," Darcy replied.

"Charles, are you aware that you call at Longbourn daily? Surely you must know it is hardly proper," Miss Bingley interrupted them.

"Caroline, I am very much aware of my actions. I assure you I am doing nothing improper."

"Perhaps not improper, but unwise. Do you not question the motives which have stopped Mr Darcy from joining you?"

"I never question Darcy's reasons. But his presence or absence does not affect my own enjoyment."

"For Heaven's sake, are you not tired of spending hour after hour with the Bennets?" Louisa interjected severely.

"Not at all. I am having an excellent time, I assure you."

Darcy finally raised his eyes from his plate. "Although my acquaintance with the Bennets is brief, I also enjoy their company. Mr Bennet is a worthy gentleman, well read, with wide knowledge and remarkable wit. I understand why Bingley feels comfortable calling at Longbourn."

Bingley threw him a surprised and thankful glance.

"He might be; but his wife?" Caroline raised her voice. "Do not deny that you cannot stand listening to her nonsense and witnessing her ill manners. Admit it—you are appalled! Her behaviour is outrageous and her constant quest for husbands for her daughters is the talk of the village. You must be terrified that she will target you, too."

Her demanding tone irritated Darcy. If he needed a reason to leave Netherfield sooner, Caroline's attitude would surely be ample justification.

He cleared his throat and held his temper.

"Miss Bingley, I beg you to allow me the liberty of deciding what appals and what terrifies me. For now, you are quite far from the truth and, as rude as it might sound, I do not appreciate anyone's attempt to presume my reasons or my intentions. I dare say I am allowed to choose how to spend my days, just as Bingley is the master of his own time. We should not blame him for not sharing my own preferences."

The conversation threatened to continue but Darcy had no patience left for it. He excused himself and retired to the library, pretending he had letters to complete.

Once alone, he tried to gather himself, staring outside. It was raining again.

Despite the harsh argument, he knew Caroline Bingley was close enough to the truth. Except he was not appalled and terrified by Mrs Bennet, but by his own strong and unexpected sentiments. He fought against those and, two weeks prior to the ball, Darcy felt reasonably content with himself. His self-control and discipline kept him in check and suppressed the shallow desires stirred by Miss Elizabeth Bennet's charms. He knew Bingley called on the Bennets daily, but he chose the solitude of the Netherfield library instead. Instead of bearing the frustration of her presence, knowing he could not take the next step, he preferred to torture himself in her absence. It was the most severe exercise of self-restraint. He succeeded in keeping himself away from her, against the aching longing to enjoy her presence.

The weather became his ally; the cold and the rain chilled his temptation to ride towards Oakham Mount or Longbourn, pining for her, hoping to catch a glimpse of her. His mind was in a constant war against his heart, his reason against his wishes. But he knew he could conquer it.

Still, more often than he would wish to, his thoughts turned back to her. His days, hours, minutes were empty and lonely without thinking of her. And, while he knew it was still a weakness, he allowed himself the luxury of allowing her to fill his thoughts, as long as neither she nor anybody else was aware of it.

Never had that happened to him before. Never had he been troubled by a woman, not even those who had been intimately acquainted with him. Never did he long to see a woman, to speak to her, to simply take delight in her nearness.

The nights were even worse, as the moment he closed his eyes, she invaded his dreams. He had no sleep, no rest, no peace. She had banished them all without even knowing it, and without intending to. She had never sought his good opinion, but she had won it nevertheless, and in that battle, he had lost his self-confidence and his tranquillity. His time in Hertfordshire had become distressing and he knew he should leave. But he could not sever the link that tied him to Elizabeth. Not yet. He was not prepared to depart from her so soon. He had not enough memories to comfort his heart in the months to come. Perhaps if he danced only one set with her, it would be enough and would induce him to return to town.

His thoughts were soon interrupted by Bingley's entrance. For a moment, Darcy panicked that his sisters might join him, but his friend was alone and carefully closed the door behind him.

"May I come in? Am I bothering you?"

"Not at all. Besides, it is your house. You do not need permission to enter," Darcy smiled.

Bingley sat. "I can see you can hardly bear Caroline and Louisa lately. I am afraid our company gives you little pleasure these days."

He replied after a short hesitation. "I am not a social person, and my conversational skills are limited."

"It is generous of you to take the blame, Darcy. I am aware they are rude and pretentious, but I cannot change them, as much as I would like to. They have a tendency to force their will on everyone. They are trying to make you declare yourself against the Bennets."

"You are the master of the house and the head of the family. You should demand the kind of behaviour that satisfies you. No less. You should make your wishes known and obeyed."

"You are right, of course. I am trying. I do appreciate you staying with me, although I assume you would rather be with your own family."

"Your friendship is valuable to me, Bingley."

"I know; and I am deeply grateful for that. There is something else I wanted to tell you. Sir William has invited me to a dinner party the day after tomorrow. In fact, he invited us all. I am not sure if Louisa and Caroline will come. Would you join me? It would be a little odd to go alone."

The question startled Darcy and chills ran down his spine. He looked at Bingley, who was watching him with obvious concern. How could he respond to such a request? To such a temptation? Elizabeth would surely be at that gathering, and that made his heart race. His previous resolution did not need much provocation to fail. He had not seen her in more than a week. But, as long as he remained at Netherfield, he could not continue to trap himself in the library, only to avoid her. That would be utterly ridiculous. He had no reason to refuse the invitation, nor did he wish to. Moment by moment, excitement enveloped him as he realised how much he missed her smiles and her sparkling eyes. He longed to be in her presence again– and a room full of people was safe enough.

"Of course I will join you, Bingley," he replied, much to his friend's delight.

"You will? This is excellent news. I am very glad to hear that! Very well then. I will let you finish your letters now. If you write to Georgiana, send her my best regards."

"I will convey her your best wishes on half a page," Darcy answered in jest, amused by Bingley's outburst of joy.

He prayed to be wrong in judging the lack of depth in Miss

Jane Bennet's feelings. Bingley was obviously so smitten by her that all his arrangements, all his actions were somehow related to her. Darcy had not discovered Bingley's plan, nor did he insist upon the matter. Bingley might want to propose, or something else entirely. But nothing was strange about Miss Jane Bennet and his strong affection for her. If he were to be deceived or betrayed, Bingley's happiness would be ruined forever. But the fear for failure did not allow Darcy the liberty to assume Miss Bennet's dishonesty and plot against his friend's desire. The risk of being wrong and turning his good intentions into the main object of his friend's misery was too dangerous to be acceptable.

For the time being, there was little he could do but support Bingley for the rest of the time he remained in Hertfordshire.

It would not be for long, but there still might be a chance for a little glimpse of happiness. A strange sense of joyfulness raised his spirits too, as he thought of the moment he would lay eyes on Elizabeth. She would likely gaze at him, challenge him with the charming raising of her right eyebrow, smile at him while finding a reason to tease him. If there was some music, he would ask her to dance again and she would probably refuse him one more time. Then, with the power of his sound deduction, he would struggle to read beyond her alluring presence and guess what her feelings for him were; how much she enjoyed or loathed his company, and how much more she expected from him. He knew he could not offer anything more, but the mere thought that she might wish for more was invigorating.

∞∞∞

The dinner at the Lucas's was the only event that broke the tedium for the Longbourn ladies. With the poor weather that kept them inside and prevented them from walking into Meryton at all, they were eager for fresh company and recent news. Also, both Mrs Bennet and her eldest daughter secretly hoped to meet Mr Bingley again–except that one of them was more vocal than the other in expressing her anticipation.

"This rain will be the end of my nerves!" Mrs Bennet complained as she entered the carriage. "It will ruin our appearance completely! And while for the rest of you that is of little importance, Jane must look her best. But then again, she is more beautiful than any other woman in the county."

Elizabeth looked at her father; cramped into a corner, bored and irritated already at being forced from the comfort of his library. They smiled and shrugged at each other. When Mrs Bennet wished for something, there was no use opposing her. And when she complained about something, the wisest reaction was to listen and nod silently.

The road was in a rather poor condition after so many rainy days and the carriage drove carefully through the mud.

"Can you remind me again why on Earth I allowed myself to be convinced to leave the house?" Mr Bennet asked bluntly.

"Come now, my dear. The entire town will be there. And I am sure Mr Bingley will attend too," Mrs Bennet responded.

"That I understand. But it means little to me. And yet, your insistence has defeated my will one more time. Even worse, fool that I am, I agreed to come so early! What shall I do all evening?" the gentleman asked in earnest.

His wife dismissed his complaint with a gesture.

"Do not whine, Mr Bennet. Once we have at least one daughter happily married, we will have plenty of time to rest."

"Mrs Bennet, if you promise you will not bother me with balls and parties again, I am ready to chase a few husbands for them right away. I am sorry Mr Collins left; he would have been a good start and without much effort," Mr Bennet replied in jest, winking at Elizabeth.

She did not enjoy the joke though and she frowned.

"Well, if you can find at least one good husband for our daughters, or if you can induce Mr Bingley to propose sooner, I will never trouble you further," Mrs Bennet declared.

"Mama, please do not speak of Mr Bingley in such a way," Jane interjected with despair.

"Oh, hush Jane; he cannot hear us! And if he does, so much the better. It is time for him to decide. He cannot expect the most beautiful woman in the county to wait for him forever!"

"Mama, please!" Jane whispered, blushing with embarrassment.

Mrs Bennet, however, was no longer listening as the carriage stopped in front of the Lucas's house.

The rain did not keep Sir William from displaying the proper skills of a host, greeting and welcoming his guests. He invited them in, gibbering about the party, and Lady Lucas, and the times he had attended gatherings in town.

In the dining room, there were more people than Elizabeth expected. Aside from over fifteen families from Meryton, there were several officers who were entertaining the ladies with what appeared to be an amusing conversation. Mr Bingley and his family were nowhere to be seen and Jane appeared slightly disappointed. Her beauty could not conceal the sadness in her eyes, just as Mrs Bennet's curious glances could not disguise her own displeasure.

While she looked for Charlotte Lucas, a silhouette suddenly brought Elizabeth's attention to the middle of the crowd. Surrounded by good-looking officers dressed in neat uniforms, she singled out a gentleman with handsome features and an amiable smile that grew as he took part in an animated conversation. The ladies nearby appeared delighted by his story, trying to catch his attention. Charlotte was one of them and Elizabeth smiled to herself. A pleasant face and some interesting narratives easily beat a path towards any lady's heart.

Charlotte waved to her and the gentleman turned. The moment their eyes met, he smiled at Elizabeth and bowed his head in a discreet greeting. Elizabeth was impressed by his air and she liked him immediately. She returned the smile, wondering who he might be, content that Charlotte would surely enlighten her.

As she hoped, her friend came in her direction, followed by the gentleman himself and by their old acquaintance,

Lieutenant Denny.

"Miss Bennet, what a pleasure to see you," the lieutenant addressed her directly. "Please allow me to introduce my friend, Mr Wickham."

She politely curtseyed, while Mr Denny continued.

"I met Wickham in London and we returned together. I am happy to say he has accepted a commission in our regiment."

"Miss Bennet, it is a privilege and a delight to meet you," Wickham bowed with great consideration and apparent pleasure.

"I am happy to meet you too, sir. And even happier to hear that you will not leave our little town very soon," Elizabeth responded.

"No indeed. I just arrived and I am already charmed. I look forward to knowing everyone better and to enjoying many such lovely gatherings," Wickham declared, holding her gaze.

The rest of the Bennet ladies joined them and Charlotte performed the remaining introductions. Mr Wickham was equally charming to each of them and led them in a perfectly correct and unassuming conversation. Elizabeth was delighted by the newcomer, even more so as he showed an immediate inclination towards her. He spoke to her, looked at her, smiled at her, asked for her opinion, and responded to her questions– proving that the brief acquaintance was equally agreeable for both. Elizabeth's sisters were also enchanted by him and Mrs Bennet herself welcomed the young man and expressed her wish to have him as a guest at Longbourn and see more of him soon.

Soon, Mr Wickham was unanimously admired and everything was in his favour: his appearance, his fine countenance, his good figure and enjoyable address. Elizabeth mused that Mr Wickham had succeeded in gaining everyone's admiration in such a short while, just as Mr Darcy managed to lose it at the Meryton assembly two months ago. Contrary to the other gentleman, Mr Wickham talked to each person who happened to be near him and made every effort to make himself likeable to his audience.

She quickly became irritated by her own thoughts. Why on Earth was she thinking of Mr Darcy and even comparing the two? There was no connection and no resemblance between them.

She was surprised to see Jane's face suddenly lightening and glowing with delight. She searched for her sister's point of interest, quickly betrayed by Sir William's rush towards the entrance. There were Mr Bingley and Mr Darcy finally arriving, long after all the other guests.

Elizabeth looked for Bingley's sisters and was relieved to see no sign of them. Mr Bingley appeared somehow troubled, but his spirits immediately revived as he caught sight of Jane.

Mr Darcy was his usual self–standing still in the doorway, scrutinising the people in attendance with a superior gaze, his expression stern and cold. His appearance distressed Elizabeth just as it had on previous occasions, stirring strange chills inside her. He made her uncomfortable like no other man ever had before and she could not be at ease anywhere near him.

All the noise, all the laughter and all the conversation ceased as everyone greeted the two gentlemen. Mr Bingley quickly moved toward the Bennets; Mr Darcy remained behind and for a moment Elizabeth's glance met his. Then his glare travelled beyond her and stopped on a point of interest that startled and darkened his countenance. A deep disdain marred his face and his eyes narrowed into a fury he could hardly conceal.

Astonished, Elizabeth turned and noticed Mr Wickham staring back at Mr Darcy over her shoulder, crimson and obviously nervous, his mouth wide open, his eyes blurred by distress. Darcy stepped forward, while Wickham took a step back, as if he was being pushed by Mr Darcy's increasing ire.

Elizabeth remained still, glancing from one to another, ignored by both, feeling like a useless barrier attempting to stop a flooding river of rage.

Chapter 6

*A*s Sir William turned all his attention towards the most important guests, Elizabeth saw Mr Darcy send another glare at Wickham, then move in the opposite direction from him. To her surprise, he stopped in the proximity of her father. She was uncertain if it was on purpose or a mere coincidence. Her father greeted him; he appeared startled, but quickly recovered to bow to him. They exchanged a few words, until Mr Bingley and Sir William joined them.

Elizabeth looked at Wickham and caught his eye. His countenance had completely changed in the few minutes since Darcy had entered. He tried to smile, but it was more of a grimace that twisted his lips. Elizabeth watched him with increased curiosity and puzzlement. The short meeting had surely affected both Wickham and Darcy enough to ruin their dispositions. They were obviously well-acquainted but not cordial to each other. What could they have in common? In what way were they connected?

She had barely met the man an hour earlier and did not dare enquire further. He too seemed willing to approach her but hesitant to do so. From across the room, Darcy's gaze was burning her face with its dark intensity and she wondered if he was looking at her or at Wickham, who was standing behind her. Even from such a distance, she could feel the discontent that distorted his usually handsome face. Immediately she felt herself blushing. Why on earth had she called his face 'handsome'? Even to herself it sounded silly. Not because it was not true, but because his unpleasant manners obscured any agreeable aspect of his features.

"Lizzy, did you see?" her mother unexpectedly whispered in her ear, grasping her arm.

"What is it, Mama?" She whispered back, startled.

"Mr Bingley went straight to your father! And Mr Darcy too! Is this not a sign that he intends to propose to Jane? Perhaps he is trying to befriend Mr Bennet, to ensure his success?"

Elizabeth breathed deeply to calm herself. "Mama, I do not think that is the reason. And please let us not speculate more; it will only distress Jane."

"I will not speculate, except to you. I do not want to trouble Jane. She must keep her serene beauty and her light expression. Men like women with a sweet disposition."

Elizabeth did not reply, as Mr Wickham and Lieutenant Denny were only a few feet away.

"I am sure I am right, Lizzy. Why else would they go to your father?"

"Mama, I believe both Mr Bingley and Mr Darcy enjoy Papa's company and I know the feeling is mutual. I would not be surprised if Mr Bingley mingles with other guests, but Papa and Mr Darcy will stay in the corner to speak of books. I think they rejoice in their common dislike of this party."

"Well, I will tell your father to be prudent in what he says to Mr Darcy. That man is rather frightening at times, and we do not want to upset him, at least not until Mr Bingley proposes. Did you see how he looked at all of us the moment he entered? Mr Darcy, I mean. So much disdain! I wonder what was on his mind–he would likely make all of us disappear if he could!" Mrs Bennet continued in a low voice.

"Mama, I am sure you are mistaken. Mr Darcy had no reason to look at us with disdain. If that was the case, he would not have come tonight–just like Mr Bingley's sisters. He might be in a poor disposition, that is all. And look–he seems engaged in a conversation with Papa."

"Indeed. Then again, your father has a favourable opinion of him. And we must admit that Mr Bennet is a good judge of character. So perhaps Mr Darcy is not as bad as we think. Oh dear God–look! Mr Bingley is moving towards Jane. Praise the Lord! If only someone would play something so they can dance. But they are talking–how lovely! Oh, for Heaven's sake, why is Sir William bothering them?"

Mrs Bennet's nervousness increased, then mixed with contentment and anticipation while she mingled with the other guests. Things appeared to settle down: Mr Darcy remained in the corner, with Mr Bennet, while Mr Wickham retired to the opposite side of the room, talking privately with his fellow officers.

Several glares were exchanged between Mr Darcy and Mr Wickham, but nobody seemed to notice except Elizabeth. The party grew more animated, joyful voices and laughter filled the room. Whatever tension might have existed between the two young men remained unknown to the others.

Mr Bingley seemed determined to spend his time in Jane's company, giving Mrs Bennet the greatest satisfaction. His admiration for the beautiful Miss Bennet was openly displayed and easily read by everyone. The evening went better than she had hoped, and Mrs Bennet could not remember when she had last been so happy.

But then tragedy struck: less than half an hour after his arrival, Mr Darcy had a private conversation with Mr Bingley, then he excused himself to Sir William and Lady Lucas, and left. On his way out, he sent a dark look towards Elizabeth, who caught it briefly. His glance stirred her nervousness and chills ran along her skin. She sensed that he wished to tell her something, but no words had been exchanged and she knew him too little to read his silence.

Mr Bingley remained only long enough to take his farewell; minutes later, he followed his friend, leaving the other guests completely puzzled and the Bennet ladies deeply disappointed.

Immediately, rumours and speculation filled the room. What could have possibly induced the two gentlemen to leave so abruptly? Mr Bingley's sisters did not attend. Was it something related to them? But the decision came from Mr Darcy–that was beyond a doubt. Had he received some unexpected news? Very unlikely, since no stranger and no letter had arrived.

Being a small party among old acquaintances, the astonishment was openly expressed, and questions without answers shared. In the middle of the din, Mrs Bennet played an important role. Along with Mrs Phillips and Lady Lucas, she debated all the possible scenarios. She was relieved that both her companions agreed with her regarding Mr Bingley's admiration for Jane. Anything else was bearable.

Jane looked as demure as usual, but the slight shadow in her eyes did not go unnoticed by those who knew her well. She sat with Elizabeth against the wall, with a cup of tea. The looks filled with questions, doubts, speculation and even pity were annoying. Elizabeth would have gladly returned home, taking Jane with her, as the party was ruined for them anyway.

Lydia and Kitty, however, were in excellent spirits. They spoke and laughed loudly with other girls as well as some officers. Mr Wickham was also one of those whose spirits rose immediately after the two gentlemen's departure. Elizabeth watched him attentively. The previous tension had all vanished from his expression and his large smile and conversational skills quickly charmed his audience again.

Now, she had no doubt that something of great importance had occurred between their new charming acquaintance–the town's new favourite–and Mr Darcy. Something so grave that it did not allow Mr Darcy to even be in the same room as Mr Wickham, but did not permit him to make a direct confrontation either. He chose to leave; was this proof of faulty behaviour, of an unreasonable disdain, or of some painful recollections?

"Lizzy, I cannot imagine what might have happened," Jane whispered. "Mr Bingley showed no intention of leaving so soon, but I believe he did not want to abandon his friend. Mr Darcy must have had a real problem...I hope he is not ill...Mr Bingley's gesture of returning home with him was very generous. Would you not agree?"

"I do agree, Jane."

"People are asking me why Mr Bingley left but I truly have no answer or explanation."

"How could you know that? This is ridiculous! The gentlemen left the party. Is it a tragedy? Should we cry in despair? Should we mourn over their absence?"

"No...but I can understand that our neighbours are curious..."

"I am curious too, Jane. But it is of little consequence. No matter the reason for their decision, the gentlemen are allowed to do as they please."

"Indeed. But if they came and then left, it must be something that occurred here, at the party. If Mr Darcy were opposed to this evening, he would not have come at all."

"True. Dearest, it is difficult to make sense of all this. But whatever Mr Darcy's reason might have been, I am sure it is in no way related to you," Elizabeth tried to calm her sister.

"Indeed it is not, I can assure you of that," Wickham unexpectedly interjected, startling both sisters. Jane paled, then her cheeks coloured with embarrassment while Elizabeth tossed him an enquiring look.

"Miss Bennet, Miss Elizabeth, I beg your pardon. I am terribly sorry that I unwittingly heard some of your conversation. But I am happy to be able to put you at ease. I am the reason why Darcy left so unexpectedly. He cannot stand to be in the same room as me." Wickham's tone was kind, even caring and Jane blushed even more at his obvious attempt to dissipate her so intimate fears.

Wickham's interference and his sudden confession disturbed both sisters. Jane was distressed and slightly ashamed while Elizabeth felt suddenly irritated. How much of their conversation had Wickham heard and why was he standing so close to them? Even if he had overheard them by mistake, a gentleman should have departed immediately without acknowledging his error and furthermore should never interrupt such a private conversation. However, Elizabeth's curiosity was stronger than her annoyance.

"What could you possibly mean, Mr Wickham? As for putting us at ease, I assure you there is no need," Elizabeth said with a sharp smile.

"I have a long and rather unpleasant history with Darcy. In fact, our past was quite pleasant, the present not so much, since he chose to end our relationship in a most unfair way."

"I am very sorry to hear that," Elizabeth answered.

"Oh, you must not be. I have no reason to complain, although he did me a great injustice," Wickham replied. "However, without his unfair treatment, I would not be here today, in such delightful company, and that would have been a tragedy indeed," he concluded, bowing to Elizabeth with the most charming smile she had ever seen in a man.

Elizabeth returned the smile. "If you are content, so are we, sir."

"Indeed I am. I have heard all kinds of rumours and your youngest sisters also talked about why Mr Bingley left. So I thought it was my duty to dissipate any doubts and not to allow anyone to feel guilty for Darcy's departure. He does that to people."

"He does what to people, sir?" Elizabeth asked further.

Wickham replied with a grin, "Makes them feel uncomfortable. And guilty. He always watches people, judging and measuring them. And very few meet his ridiculous expectations."

Elizabeth recognised Wickham's description. She too had that feeling when Darcy stared at her. Wickham recognised her hesitation and continued, with a little meaningful smile.

"I understood from your Miss Lydia and Miss Kitty that you too had the misfortune of feeling a piece of Darcy's usual rudeness. I heard that he is not one of your family's favourites, which is not surprising to me. Therefore, I was worried..."

Wickham's insinuating tone irritated Elizabeth despite his charming features and caring words. He seemed to assume a familiarity that was equally impolite and disturbing. Despite her dislike of Darcy's manners, the notion that a man whom they barely knew was so openly sharing his private affairs with them and interfering in private family matters displeased Elizabeth even more. And to add to all that, Jane's distress was too obvious to be neglected. How did the man believe he could put Jane at ease by such improper intervention?

"We appreciate your concern, Mr Wickham, and we regret any inconvenience you might have suffered due to any unfair treatment," Elizabeth said. "As for us, there is no reason to worry. Mr Darcy might not always be the most amiable person, nor easy company, but he is a good friend of Mr Bingley. And Mr Bingley, whose opinion we value, is a good friend of our family. My father holds both Mr Darcy and Mr Bingley in high regard and he is usually a good judge of character, so we trust his opinion."

Wickham took a step back and bowed. "I apologise if my intrusion was inappropriate. I meant well."

He looked sincere and Elizabeth smiled slightly, softening her tone. "I am sure you did, sir. And, as I said, your concern is appreciated."

"Indeed," Jane approved. "We thank you for being so considerate."

"It is easy to be considerate, when you enjoy someone's company so much. I hope this will not be a singular occasion," Wickham continued.

"That is no reason for concern either," Elizabeth laughed. "Meryton is a small town and Longbourn is only a mile away. You should be warned that we will surely meet more than you might want."

"That would not be possible, I assure you," he concluded.

This final exchange eventually put Jane truly at ease and caught the attention of others. Mrs Bennet, together with Lydia and Kitty joined them, asking what they were talking about. The conversation grew, then changed from one subject to another, skillfully conducted by Mr Wickham and supported by his fellow officers.

Elizabeth's opinion of their new acquaintance was uncertain. She did enjoy his company, his manners, and his readiness to make himself accepted by people. He was very handsome too, but something in his air left Elizabeth wondering. The subject of Mr Darcy was not opened again, but even his reluctance to mention the name increased Elizabeth's curiosity. She was tempted to find a proper moment and ask more, but surely it was neither the time, nor the place for such an attempt.

An hour later, Mr Bennet declared he wished to return home and asked his family to join him.

Lydia and Kitty objected, but they were left with no choice. To compensate for her youngest daughters' distress, Mrs Bennet invited the officers to have tea at Longbourn the next day, and they readily accepted.

"Well, that was a long enough visit to not have to repeat it for at least a month," Mr Bennet said in the carriage.

"What a lovely time we had," Lydia cried and Mr Bennet rolled his eyes.

"Do you know that Mr Wickham grew up with Mr Darcy? Mr Darcy's father was Mr Wickham's godfather–can you imagine? It seems the late Mr Darcy was a very good man, but the young Mr Darcy is cruel and resentful. He mistreated poor Mr Wickham very badly, but he did not say in what way! I am sure that is why he left!" Lydia cried when they finally arrived at Longbourn.

"How astonishing that Mr Wickham chose to tell you the story of his life only minutes after he met you," Mr Bennet declared suspiciously. "This is quite an unusual behaviour for an officer. I hope he will not be as outspoken with our country's enemies."

"My dear Mr Bennet, you should not mock a man's suffering. Mr Wickham looks like such a good-natured young man, so handsome and sincere! Why is it wrong that he is trusting enough to share his history with us?" Mrs Bennet interjected.

"I am sure there is some misunderstanding, somewhere," Jane interrupted. "Mr Darcy cannot possibly possess any of the aforementioned faults. Mr Bingley always speaks of him as one of the finest gentlemen of his acquaintance. He praises him and is very fond of him and grateful for his friendship."

"I am sure there is some misunderstanding," Mr Bennet declared. "Whenever there is an argument between two men, a young woman should not interfere. There are always two sides to the story, and each party is tempted to tell only as much as is to his advantage. Especially when he wishes to impress a lady. So I would suggest you all remain prudent and not encourage the spread of such tales."

"Your father is right, girls! Be careful of what you speak, as we do not want to upset Mr Darcy. At least not until Mr Bingley proposes!"

"But Mama, can we still like Mr Wickham?" Lydia asked.

"He is truly the most charming man I have ever met," Kitty insisted.

"Of course you may like Mr Wickham! There is nothing better than a handsome man in uniform with pleasant manners and an amiable nature!"

"What if Mr Darcy, who hates Mr Wickham, demands Mr Bingley not invite him to the ball? Dear Lord, that would be a tragedy," Lydia said with distress.

"Surely Mr Darcy cannot do that?" Kitty responded with equal concern.

"Mr Bingley told me that he has already invited all the officers to the ball," Jane explained.

"Oh, he did? How kind of him to share his thoughts with you," Mrs Bennet immediately changed her interest. "And what else did he say?"

The subject held the family's interest for the rest of the evening, and long after dinner ended they were still talking about Mr Wickham and Mr Darcy.

Elizabeth added little to the conversation. From the two gentlemen's reaction, she was certain their past dealings had been harsh and unpleasant. And most likely Mr Wickham was somehow deprived in some way by Mr Darcy, otherwise he would not have had so much to say. But to speculate further was difficult. Jane was still troubled and lost in her thoughts, so Elizabeth had no one with whom to debate the matter further. She had little else to do but wait for time to provide her with more information.

∞∞∞

From the moment he left Lucas Lodge, Darcy's anger grew by the moment. During his short stay at the gathering, he had fought the temptation to take Wickham by the collar and throw him out of the house, demanding an explanation regarding his presence in Meryton, of all places.

He could not stand to see him any longer, so he simply had to leave before a scandal arose.

Once at Netherfield, he locked himself in his room, desiring not to be bothered by anyone but he opened the door an hour later, when Bingley knocked.

"What happened? Are you ill?" Bingley enquired, looking at him quizzically.

"No."

"Then you are very angry."

"I am."

"Would you tell me why? What or who upset you so much that you left a party? You should know that everybody was surprised and puzzled."

Darcy paced the room and hesitated briefly.

"Wickham."

Bingley looked at him in astonishment.

"Wickham? The new officer? Why? What did he say?"

"He said nothing. Just being there. He is the lowest kind of human being. I cannot believe he is joining the militia, and precisely this regiment. I wonder if he knew I was here and did it on purpose."

"But Darcy..." Bingley watched him as he moved around the chamber. "Did you know him before?"

"Yes; I have known him since he was born. His father was Pemberley's steward and my father was Wickham's godfather."

"Really? Was he? I did not know that!"

"Well, it is not something I share with many people, since Wickham turned out to be so unworthy of my father's affection. He paid for Wickham's schooling, he supported him in every way, and even asked me to offer him a living when one should become available."

"Really?" Bingley listened with increasing astonishment.

"Yes. And as I long suspected, Wickham had no other interest but drinking, playing cards, easy women and questionable friends. He demanded money for all kinds of reasons. He pretended to be studying the law, and for a while I complied with all his demands. But I will not bother you further with this story. It is enough to say that he was the reason that I was away all summer and I hoped to never see him again. And yet, here he is."

Darcy poured himself a drink and stood staring out of the window.

"So... what should we do now? What do you want to do?" Bingley asked.

"Do? Nothing. It might be a mere coincidence. I should not have allowed his presence to upset me so. After all, he has the right to choose his profession. I still pray that he will come to his senses and will embrace a decent way of living. My father was very fond of him and we grew up together. I wish him well, although I have lost all hope."

"So you will allow his presence to trouble you for as long as he stays in Meryton?"

"What other choice do I have? Besides, I will not stay long

in Hertfordshire. I wish to spend Christmas with Georgiana in town. I can bear Wickham for another fortnight."

"But Darcy… you will leave?"

"Of course I will," Darcy smiled. "I cannot stay with you forever."

"I spoke more with Miss Bennet today," Bingley said and Darcy's smile warmed.

"And? What is new in this? You always speak to Miss Bennet when you meet."

"Indeed I do. She is so easy to speak to. So gentle and sweet. She seems to understand me so well."

It was Bingley's turn to pour himself a drink. "So, what do you think? About her feelings for me?"

"Come now, Bingley! I hardly saw or talked to Miss Bennet at all today. My estimation could not have changed from yesterday. But if you are certain, why do you need my opinion?"

"I am certain of my feelings for her. I believe I am. Such affection, such thrills, such desire I have never felt for another so far. But I wonder–since you said you have seen me in love many times–am I steady enough for her? Am I worthy enough for her? And more importantly–are her feelings strong enough to last a lifetime?"

Bingley's nervousness increased, as well as his pacing. Such distress made Darcy calmer, forcing him to take charge.

"Do you have any reasons for doubt?" Darcy asked. "Genuine reasons?"

"No. I just worry and wonder… More than my feelings, I am worried about hers. I know I will be devoted to her all my life, if I marry her. But if she does not truly love me, if she will only settle for me, if she will only accept me to please her family, I will feel that. You know I will. Every time I am close to her, every time I touch her, or share a bed with her… I would feel it. Would I not be selfish if I forced her into such a union, if her heart is not genuinely engaged?"

Darcy sat and filled his glass again. His friend's torment seemed deep and powerful, so his own disturbance appeared insignificant by comparison.

"Bingley, I have listened to your words, and I can honestly say it is the least selfish statement I have ever heard. Your thoughtful consideration of Miss Bennet's sentiments proves that you have no reason to doubt the depth of your affection for her. Of her wishes and desires, you must search for evidence. Nobody can do that better than you. But if you need my honest opinion, I will declare that she cannot possibly find a better husband than you."

"I do need your opinion, and I thank you for it. It truly makes me feel better."

"I am glad to hear that," Darcy smiled at his friend's enthusiasm. For the first time since they arrived in Hertfordshire, he wished for Miss Bennet to return Bingley's affection and to accept the upcoming proposal that seemed inevitable.

And immediately, his thoughts flew to Elizabeth's wishes and desires. And his own–which he knew to be as strong as they were impossible to fulfil.

∞∞∞

The following morning, the excitement began at Longbourn immediately after breakfast. Lydia and Kitty counted the hours until the proper time for a visit, hoping that the officers would call, while Jane glanced outside occasionally, with apparent calmness but inner nervousness, for a glimpse of Mr Bingley.

Elizabeth was the most silent in the family, still preoccupied with the previous day's events, thinking of Mr Darcy more than she would like to, struggling to sketch his character and to decide how much of Mr Wickham's story was worth asking about in earnest. Her unusual disposition drew Mr Bennet's mockery.

"Lizzy, my dear, you seem out of spirits again. I hope you

do not miss Mr Collins' carefully chosen compliments."

Elizabeth directed a sharp glare at her exceedingly amused father.

"Well, she should miss the opportunity she so thoughtlessly rejected," Mrs Bennet immediately cried. "She might have ruined her only chance for a safe future. Truly, we cannot expect her to receive any other marriage proposal anytime soon."

Elizabeth cast another upset look at her father. "This is truly a useless discussion, Mama. Papa is making sport of me and I am unwilling to argue further over Mr Collins."

"Well, I imagine that," her mother interjected. "I know you think Mr Collins is not the most charming, nor the brightest man, but he is handsome enough, clever enough and is in a far better position to support a wife than the better looking and more amiable officers. Not to mention he is also willing to marry, unlike other men who only wish to preserve their liberty and avoid any engagement."

"Mama, can you imagine how wonderful it would be if I should marry Mr Wickham? Or someone as handsome as he?" Lydia interjected, beaming with anticipation.

"You are too young to even walk alone into Meryton, let alone to think of marriage," Mr Bennet replied severely, rolling his eyes. "And yes, with your lack of wisdom and spendthrift nature and with his limited income, you would make a perfect couple."

"I would like to see at least one of my daughters married to an officer," Mrs Bennet declared, then quickly became silent when the servant announced Mr Wickham, Lieutenant Denny and Lieutenant Reeves.

"My dear gentlemen, what a pleasure to see you! Do come in," Mrs Bennet readily invited them.

"It is our pleasure to be here, ma'am. We were grateful for your invitation and took the first opportunity to respond to it," Mr Wickham said.

They bowed to the ladies, who curtseyed most graciously.

"We wondered if you would keep your word and call today," Lydia admitted.

"How could we not have come, when we were so eager to see all of you again?" Wickham replied, looking deliberately at Elizabeth. She was surprised and slightly uneasy at such a direct insinuation, so she averted her eyes.

They all sat and the conversation started, then grew more animated by the minute. All the officers were pleasant company, but Mr Wickham was easily singled out from among his colleagues.

"Mr Wickham, I told my parents about how poorly Mr Darcy treated you," Lydia suddenly announced.

An uncomfortable moment followed and Mr Wickham looked embarrassed but not as much as might be expected.

"Miss Lydia, I am sorry I distressed you and anyone else by even mentioning my past dealings with Darcy. I shall kindly beg you to forget everything for as long as Darcy and I are in the neighbourhood. My respect and affection for my godfather forbids me from saying a single bad word against him," Wickham responded with apparent remorse.

"Well, it might be a little too late for such a resolution," Mr Bennet whispered mostly to himself. Elizabeth did not miss her father's words, nor his displeased countenance.

"I will only say that, if Darcy had respected his father's will, I would now be making my living as a parson, in the parish of Kympton. That would have suited me greatly, but it would have deprived me of the pleasure of being here, with you," Wickham continued, glancing at Elizabeth again. "So all in all, I have no reason to repine."

"Parson? Oh, I truly do not believe you would have liked making sermons! I am sure you will enjoy being an officer far more. And the uniform is so much better looking," Lydia declared.

"Lydia!" Jane immediately censured such an improper statement, but the young girl ignored the scolding.

Mr Wickham laughed.

"I am glad to have your approval of my present situation, Miss Lydia. This is just further proof that we must ignore my unpleasant past dealings with Darcy and only speak of the present and future."

"We are certainly very happy to have all of you here," Mrs Bennet strengthened her youngest daughter's statement.

"Yes, we are," Kitty and Lydia added, while Elizabeth and Jane only looked at each other, intrigued and silent.

"And so are we," the other two officers offered.

"So, Mr Wickham, did you study to become a clergyman?" Mr Bennet asked.

The question seemed to find Mr Wickham unprepared. "Well, not exactly... not yet... but I would have studied, if I were offered the living."

"It is good that did not happen; I am not sure how you would have handled such a boring position," Lieutenant Denny laughed.

"Well, it is fortunate that being an officer needs no special knowledge. And it is not boring either, I imagine. Let us have a drink to easy, entertaining professions," Mr Bennet concluded. "Should we go to the library, or would you rather stay here with the ladies?"

"You should stay a little longer," Mary unexpectedly said, staring out of the window. "Mr Bingley and Mr Darcy have just arrived; they will enter any moment now."

Chapter 7

*T*he appearance of the last two gentlemen fell like thunder in the drawing-room. The bewilderment was so generally felt that nobody said a word for several long moments.

Darcy's first glance was towards Elizabeth and, being caught unguarded, she met it with concern, so he frowned, worried that their unannounced call was unwelcome. Bingley had insisted on briefly checking up on the Bennets, after their disappearance the previous day. He did not wish to let Jane believe he had left because he did not enjoy her company. Darcy had opposed such a notion, although he too would have liked to see Elizabeth. Fighting his wishes, he suggested they send a note to Mr Bennet.

But since they were engaged to meet Colonel Forster and other officers in Meryton, Bingley prevailed. They arrived at Longbourn intending to stay less than a half hour.

When they entered and saw Wickham pleasantly conversing with the Bennets, a heavy burden fell on Darcy's shoulders. He knew Wickham noticed his distress for the smirk on his face betrayed his satisfaction. Wickham had not changed and he likely never would.

Darcy sensed a new sort of danger in Wickham's presence at the Bennets. He looked at the young women, wondering if Wickham could find a victim among them. The younger ones were obviously the picture of his usual target. However, he soon chased away his own worries–the Bennets' lack of fortune and connections would be their best protection against Wickham's rapacity.

"Mr Bingley, Mr Darcy! What a lovely surprise! Please come in!" Mrs Bennet finally uttered. Bingley glanced at Jane–who blushed–then at their hosts, then at the other guests.

"Thank you, ma'am, but we cannot stay," Bingley answered. "We are expected by Colonel Forster. We only stopped to greet you briefly."

His superfluous explanation demonstrated one more time how unwilling he and Darcy were to be in Wickham's presence.

Wickham did not miss the opportunity to point it out. "Mr Bingley, I hope you are not in haste to shorten your visit because of us. We can leave if necessary, so you can stay," Wickham said. The tone of his apparently polite words was so rude and patronising that Jane, Elizabeth and Bingley paled, glancing at each other. Behind Bingley, Darcy's visage darkened with ire and the struggle to control his fury put a grimace on his face.

Whatever had occurred between the two in the past, Wickham's audacity and his repeated attempts to offend Darcy were glaringly obvious. The younger sisters and their mother, together with the other two officers, were oblivious to any hidden meaning in his statement, but Mr Bennet's eyes narrowed with anger.

"Well, how fortunate that we have you to organise the schedule of our visits, Mr Wickham. I truly appreciate your care in arranging our daily programme, but please do not burden yourself with such a responsibility," Mr Bennet replied sharply. "Now, are any of you gentlemen willing to drink something?"

The sharp rebuke perturbed Wickham, whose expression changed again.

Bingley was confused for a moment, looking at Jane again. Darcy watched Mr Bennet with silent contentment.

"We would be happy to–on another day," Bingley finally responded. "If that is convenient to you, sir."

Mr Bennet only shrugged. "It is convenient whenever you like. I rarely leave my library."

"Then we shall return soon. Good day to you all," Bingley bowed, his glance lingering on Jane a moment longer.

Darcy followed his example, but instead of taking with him a last glimpse of Elizabeth's eyes, he met Wickham's stern glare. The visit had been a failure and only left him with more worries and no indication of Elizabeth's opinion of him or of Wickham. Perhaps it was time to put aside any restraint and to enquire directly. With Wickham, any subtlety was both useless and hazardous.

"Would you rather have stayed longer?" Bingley asked once they resumed the ride towards Meryton.

"Not at all; I am grateful for the way you handled the situation, Bingley. I am sorry you did not have more time with Miss Bennet," Darcy answered.

"It is fine; there will be plenty of time later. Hopefully, with no disturbance around," Bingley concluded.

At Longbourn, as soon as the two gentlemen had left, Wickham turned to his hosts with equal concern and distress.

"Mr Bennet, Mrs Bennet, I deeply apologise if my intervention sounded inappropriate to you. My genuine intention was to avoid any unpleasant circumstances, therefore I offered to leave. As you all saw, it is obvious that Darcy cannot stand my presence, so it is my duty to be certain we shall never be in close company again."

"Mr Wickham, you should not distress yourself to accommodate Mr Darcy's preference," Mr Bennet said, still with sharp mockery. "If he does not wish to be near you, he will surely find a means to avoid it."

"Indeed," Mrs Bennet interjected. "From what I observed, your behaviour was beyond reproach."

"Oh, I hope you will not miss the ball, only to avoid Mr Darcy," Lydia exclaimed. "We are all counting on seeing you at Netherfield!"

"You are too kind," he replied, with a lovely smile and proper bow. "That drink is still waiting," Mr Bennet repeated and finally the three officers followed him into the library.

Half an hour later, with a brief farewell, they left, leaving the ladies with more subjects for discussion and speculation.

∞ ∞ ∞

"Papa, what do you think of this story about Mr Darcy and Mr Wickham?" Elizabeth asked her father later that day when they were alone in the library.

"What do you think of it, Lizzy?"

"I do not know what to believe... Their past dealings must have been harsh and painful, as they obviously have strong and uncordial feelings towards each other."

"Well, on this we all agree, I am sure," Mr Bennet jested. "But... which one do you think is telling the truth? Did Mr Darcy say anything at all?" Mr Bennet asked.

"No... what I mean is ... do you believe Mr Wickham has been honest with us?" Elizabeth enquired, with equal curiosity and distress.

"What do you believe, Lizzy?" her father repeated the question, raising his eyebrow in challenge. "From the little I have seen, it is clear that Mr Wickham favours you over the other young women in the village."

She rolled her eyes. "Papa, stop teasing me... I must confess, however, that Mr Wickham is the most pleasant man of my acquaintance."

"Yes, he is. A very fine fellow; he seems to love us all, just as much as we love him back."

"Papa, do be serious! Are you not interested to know if Mr Darcy is as cruel as Mr Wickham describes him? Or if Mr Wickham has tried to deceive us?"

"Which one do you think is the truth, Lizzy? Let me hear your opinion and afterwards, I will share mine too."

"Well, Papa, I believe the late Mr Darcy left his godson a living ... however, since Mr Darcy chose not to give it, could it have been only a recommendation? If such a wish was put in a will, I doubt Mr Darcy would have disobeyed it. Am I correct?"

"Most likely, my dear."

"So, from this point on, we only have two paths to take. Either the living was left under some condition that Mr Wickham did not fulfil and he purposely has concealed it from us, or Mr Darcy is truly a cruel, dishonourable man who ignored his father's wish out of contempt or resentment," Elizabeth concluded.

"My child, I would say that your examination is quite accurate and I totally agree with it. So toward which one do you lean?"

"I am still very puzzled, as I do not know enough of either gentleman. But there could also be a middle ground; perhaps both have a share of guilt and innocence. However, what troubles me…"

"Yes?" Mr Bennet asked her to continue despite her hesitation.

"I wonder why Mr Wickham would share such a private story with us, on such a brief acquaintance. And even more so, he shared it with Lydia and Kitty even yesterday. That was very…unwise of him," Elizabeth admitted.

"Yes, that is what disturbed me too. He sounded like Mr Collins, praising Lady Catherine only minutes after we met. Wickham did the same–only in the opposite way. The annoying result was similar, though."

"Papa!" Elizabeth laughed and embraced her mocking father.

"Now, now, Lizzy–here is a most perfect scenario: Mr Collins will return soon and he will talk about Lady Catherine, while Mr Wickham will talk about Darcy. And all along, both Collins and Wickham will fight to gain your favour. Perhaps we will even have a duel; wouldn't that be just wonderful?"

Elizabeth narrowed her eyes in reproach. "Papa, you are simply impossible. How can you make sport at my expense? Do not mention Mr Collins gaining my favour ever again, or I will tell Mama that you insisted on me rejecting Mr Collins!"

Mr Bennet stared at his favourite daughter in disbelief. "Surely you cannot be serious!"

"I can and I will! If you are decided to use Mr Collins to torment me, I can easily do the same! After all, everybody knows I take after you," she declared fiercely.

They faced each other in challenge, both on the edge between laughter and anger. Eventually, Mr Bennet rolled his eyes and opened his book.

"You are wild and insolent, Lizzy. No man would want such a disrespectful wife so you will remain a spinster. Ask your sister to let you teach her children to play the pianoforte as ill as you do! Now go and leave me alone, I have had enough distractions in the past few days to last me an entire month."

Elizabeth laughed, kissed her father's cheek and left.

$$\infty \infty \infty$$

Over the following two days as the ball was approaching, the weather took a turn for the worse. Rain, wind, hail, cold, clouds–kept spirits low and the girls indoors.

Mr Bingley was greatly missed and often mentioned. Mrs Bennet debated several times if he might propose before or after the ball, while Jane tried very hard to keep her mother's speculations reasonable. They had no evidence to justify such hopes, but Mrs Bennet cared little about anything else except her plan.

Jane was distressed by such unreasonable fantasies. She spoke to Elizabeth, confessing her hopes and her worries, wondering every minute if Mr Bingley would call.

Elizabeth was quite at ease after the conversation with her father; she did think of both Mr Darcy and Mr Wickham on several occasions, but she succeeded in satisfying her reason and reaching a sensible conclusion about the two. She decided to wait before making any more assumptions and to put all her strength into comforting Jane.

One morning, with the ball approaching, the weather eventually took pity on them, and the sun broke through the clouds. A lovely, cold but sunny November day greeted them, brightening their dispositions.

"Mama, could we go to Meryton and see if our bonnets and gloves have arrived?" Lydia asked animatedly. "Mr Crawford ordered them a week ago! I cannot wait any longer! Besides, I would like to see Maria Lucas too!"

Everybody knew that it was not the bonnets, which could easily be delivered to Longbourn, that were drawing Lydia to Meryton. Her mother hesitated only briefly, glancing at her eldest daughters and at her husband to meet their approving nods. Elizabeth and Jane were both desirous for some time outdoors, while Mr Bennet looked forward to a peaceful, quiet morning.

"We can all go! It will be a lovely afternoon walk," Mrs Bennet agreed. "Besides, I can call on Mrs Phillips too; she had a nasty cold last week and she is just now improving."

Mary preferred to stay at home and practice the pianoforte, so the other five Bennet ladies walked together into Meryton, enjoying the fresh, crisp air.

More than one among them hoped to catch a glimpse of a certain gentleman but such wishes remained undeclared. As they approached Meryton, a gentle yet cold breeze started to blow.

The village was rather empty, as it was getting very cold again. They entered the bonnet shop and were happy to receive the news that their purchases had arrived.

"Would you like to take them now, or should I deliver them to Longbourn?" Mr Crawford asked.

"Oh, do send them, please!" Mrs Bennet answered. "We walked here, and will return home soon, before it starts raining again."

"Very well. I imagine you are waiting for the ball with much keenness. The entire town is looking forward to it," Mr Crawford said, with a meaningful look at Mrs Bennet.

"Oh, yes we are. I do not doubt that it will be the finest event that has taken place in the neighbourhood in a long while.

Mr Bingley is hosting it at my daughters' special request," Mrs Bennet added.

"Mr Bingley invited the entire town! To be honest, we all know that we owe this lovely ball to you," Mr Crawford whispered meaningfully and Mrs Bennet smiled with the deepest contentment.

"You are too kind, Mr Crawford. Mr Bingley is such an amiable and generous man! I look forward to seeing you at Netherfield." Mrs Bennet exclaimed with affability.

"I will send the package to you tomorrow. I know the young ladies will want to try them as soon as possible."

"Excellent, Mr Crawford! Come now girls, let us visit my sister quickly and then return home," Mrs Bennet hastened them.

Outside, the wind blew stronger, freezing their faces. The clouds were already gathering and it was getting dark, although it was still early in the afternoon.

When they were close to Mrs Phillips' house, a familiar voice called them and they all turned to face Mr Wickham and Lieutenant Denny.

The pleasure of meeting again was mutual and friendly greetings were readily exchanged.

"We are going to our aunt Phillips' house. Will you not join us?" Lydia asked animatedly.

"We do not want to intrude," Wickham replied with friendly politeness.

"No intrusion at all! I am sure my sister will be very pleased to see you," Mrs Bennet replied.

Wickham looked at Elizabeth for a moment, then at her mother again. "If you believe we will not bother Mrs Phillips, we would be happy to join you."

"How fortunate that we met!" Lydia laughed as she took Wickham's arm. "We thought this would be a boring stroll to employ our time. But I did hope we might meet."

"I hoped that too," Kitty added.

"You are too kind, ladies," Wickham uttered with another

glance at Elizabeth.

Elizabeth was less enthusiastic than her sister about the impromptu encounter, but it pleased her to have some company while visiting her aunt Phillips. Perhaps having the gentlemen around, the conversation would not revolve entirely around Mr Bingley and would not embarrass Jane so much.

As Lucas Lodge was close by, Kitty invited Maria and Charlotte Lucas to join them; Sir William and Lady Lucas came too, so the party was large enough to become an animated gathering.

Although it was planned as a brief call, refreshments were ordered and the conversation began, while time flew.

As had happened before, the discussion quickly moved to Mr Wickham; he seemed to know many things, to have extensive knowledge of the world and to be able to relate his stories in a universally appreciated manner.

Elizabeth employed her time with Charlotte but occasionally her glance met Wickham's. He showed her a particular interest, which intrigued her and made her the recipient of Charlotte's teasing.

With so much good food and good conversation, Jane was the only one who paid attention to the time and the weather outside, which had turned for the worse.

"Mama, we should leave soon. I am afraid it will start raining. It will take us a while to walk back home."

Jane's statement interrupted the animated discussion and caused Mrs Bennet to glance outside. "Oh dear, it is dark already! How did we stay so long? We should leave now; it looks so cold outside!"

"It is not so late, but the clouds are so heavy that they have turned day into night," Lady Lucas said. "Did you walk to Meryton?"

"Yes, we did; the weather was wonderful when we left and we thought we could benefit from a little exercise. But now, we should send a servant to ask Mr Bennet to send us the carriage."

"I would be happy to loan you my barouche," Sir William

offered. "It is large and comfortable, although, if it rains, you will get wet. Fortunately, Longbourn is very close so you will be there in no time."

"You are very kind, but we cannot possibly drive a barouche," Mrs Bennet replied. "Jane, what do you think? Should we walk or send a note to your father?"

Before Jane had time to answer, Wickham bowed to them and kindly provided the perfect solution.

"Mrs Bennet, Lieutenant Denny and I can accompany you to Longbourn, if this is acceptable to you; we will drive the barouche and then bring it back to Sir William."

The ladies' faces brightened in a moment and the youngest cried with delight. Mrs Bennet even clasped her hands together at her chest, in thanks for such generous care.

"My dear Mr Wickham, you are simply the best! What a lovely idea! That will be perfect indeed!"

"We are entirely at your disposal, ma'am. It will be our pleasure to take you safely home," Wickham answered. He glanced at Elizabeth again and she returned a smile of gratitude to him.

"The barouche will be ready in no time," Sir William offered, sending a servant to inform his coachman.

"You are such a considerate gentleman!" Mrs Bennet responded.

"I am only doing what I learned during my stay in town and especially on introduction at St. James'," Sir William responded and readily received even more praise and appreciation.

The party continued cheerfully for a little while, until the barouche was brought in front of the house. Farewells were exchanged in haste and the two officers helped the ladies into the carriage. The wind was blowing quite strongly and a few claps of thunder reverberated across the sky.

"Mama, we will get wet!" Lydia cried, squeezing between her sisters.

"We should have left earlier," Kitty complained, trying to

sit comfortably.

The gentlemen sat in the front seats, with Wickham taking the reins.

In the back, the ladies held each other's arms tightly, as the carriage began to move.

"Mama, it is so cold! I will freeze," Lydia cried out.

"Stay still, child. You will have no time to freeze before we reach Longbourn."

Moments later, another crash of thunder startled them and the horses neighed.

Then, the sky seemed to break, and a heavy, dense, freezing autumn rain started to fall over them while the horses rode on at a fast pace.

The Bennets had taken that path countless times–on foot, on horseback, by carriage–and they knew it by heart. That day, however, it looked different. There was nothing ahead of them but darkness and a dense curtain of rain. They soon became soaked, wet and frozen, just as Lydia feared. But Longbourn should have been very close, as Elizabeth knew.

More thunder was followed by lightning illuminating the sky. Frightened, the girls screamed, and the horses neighed again.

Wickham pulled the reins, and the horses stopped, then rose up on their back legs. Another clap of thunder shook their surroundings, and the horses started to run on at a gallop, jolting the carriage. The girls embraced each other tightly, wet, scared and lost in the dark storm.

"Mr Wickham!" Mrs Bennet yelled. The horses were running blindly, unrestrained. Wickham was pulling the reins with no success, trying in vain to control the stallions.

Long moments passed and Elizabeth struggled to see something– anything. She was sitting on the floor of the barouche, holding her sisters and mother together.

"Mr Wickham!" Mrs Bennet screamed again.

"I cannot stop them!" Wickham shouted through the rain, pulling the reins with all his strength. The jolting of the carriage worsened, and Elizabeth wondered how it had not broken yet, fearing what would happen to them when it eventually did.

Only minutes had passed since they had left the Phillips's house, but it felt like hours. Frightening, cold, dark hours. Elizabeth looked at her family, desperate to find a way to protect them and herself.

"We should jump, the carriage will break!" Lieutenant Denny yelled to them.

They were all thrown to one side as a wheel cracked and Elizabeth screamed in horror.

"Jump? Jump?" Mrs Bennet repeated in disbelief.

"We will help you," Wickham said, releasing the reins and trying to move towards them. The horses were running, and the barouche lurched so badly that Wickham almost fell. The horses continued to run, and cries of despair cut through the rainy obscurity.

Then a powerful jolt threw them all down onto the floor, amid cries and screams, grabbing any support they could find to protect themselves from falling from the carriage. They were trapped in a nightmare; they held hands, hopeless, powerless...

And then the carriage slowed down and eventually stopped, with the ladies sobbing in pain and fright.

Over the noise of the rain, a voice called them repeatedly but no one answered until a strong hand grabbed Jane's arm.

"Miss Bennet? Are you hurt? Miss Bennet?"

They finally opened their eyes but could see little. However, Jane immediately recognised Bingley's voice and the grip of his hand. She turned, and without thinking, she fell into his arms.

"Are any of you hurt?"

Another voice sounded and Elizabeth was shocked to see Darcy, looking at them with worry, his hat lost and his coat splattered with mud.

"No, I do not think we are hurt," she answered, and Darcy took her hand to help her down from the carriage.

"We did not know that it was you," Bingley explained,

mumbling. "We were caught in the storm, and we heard the carriage. Darcy stopped the horses–he actually jumped from his horse to yours and stopped them. The wheel is broken… Are you hurt?"

The ladies listened in shock, staring at Darcy, then at each other. He brushed his fingers through his hair.

"It is good nobody is hurt," Darcy replied. "Can you climb down?" Wickham and Lieutenant Denny seemed even more shaken than the women, so Darcy and Bingley helped all the Bennet ladies to the ground.

"Thank you, sir," Mrs Bennet addressed Darcy. "You stopped the horses? How extraordinary indeed!"

"Ma'am, I am glad you are all well," he responded briefly.

Elizabeth looked around to assess their surroundings. She felt dizzy and could hardly stand. The danger they had just overcome had frozen her more than the cold rain and the autumn wind.

Darcy had jumped on the horses to stop them? How could that be? And how did it happen that he and Bingley were there?

With her mind spinning, she struggled to catch a glimpse of something familiar, as they could not be too far from Longbourn.

She breathed in relief as she recognised the place and finally felt useful. "We should find shelter until we decide how to proceed," Darcy said, staring at her as if guessing her thoughts.

She nodded, barely seeing his eyes.

"The Talbot cottage is here, very close," she said, pointing with her hand.

It sounded like the two of them were responsible for the others' well-being.

"Let us hurry then," Darcy said, gently pushing her forward.

"It is very close," she repeated, while hastily taking the lead. She and Jane took Mrs Bennet's arms, while Wickham and Denny recovered enough to help the girls walk behind Elizabeth.

Mrs Bennet cried, grunted, and lamented at every step,

while Lydia and Kitty swore they were hurt and would die soon.

Realising what could have happened only minutes before, Elizabeth listened to them absently, allowing unseen tears to roll down her cheeks.

Darcy and Bingley remained behind, but the latter soon joined them, offering Mrs Bennet one arm and Jane the other.

After a short ordeal through the rain, walking on the slippery ground, frozen and frightened, they finally reached the cottage. Bingley pulled at the door, with Wickham and Denny hurrying to help him.

The door opened wide, permitting them to enter. It was still dark and cold inside, but the discomfort of the rain falling on them suddenly stopped, and a strange sort of silence enveloped them.

Elizabeth looked around, trying to adjust to the darkness, while Lydia and Kitty were still crying and complaining.

Bingley closed the door, and the silence became deeper. Wet, scared and exhausted, there was nothing much for the Bennet ladies to do. Elizabeth knew the cottage well enough to search for something useful, and she stepped carefully from one corner to another, but with little success.

She turned to look for Darcy, feeling that he could help her at least with some advice if not more.

As she could not see clearly, she tried to recollect where he had gone. And only then did she realise that she had not seen him since he helped her out of the carriage. He was not with them.

Chapter 8

"*D*ear Lord, it is freezing in here! If the storm does not stop soon, we shall all die, either inside this horrible cottage or outside in the rain, trying to return home!" Mrs Bennet whined.

Sheltered from the storm, their eyes slowly became accustomed to the gloom inside. Outside, the darkness also cleared slightly, as the clouds scattered after the wild burst of rain.

"Mama, I will give you my coat," Jane responded, taking her mother's arm.

"Your coat? What use can I have of it? It is as wet as mine. And what about you? If you die of cold, what compensation would that be for me?"

"I would gladly give you my coat, Mrs Bennet, although it is wet and dirty," Bingley offered.

"You are very kind, but I have no use for it. Can I sit somewhere?" Bingley quickly looked around–without clearly seeing–for a chair for Mrs Bennet.

Each tried to find a place and removed their coats; the ladies took off their bonnets and the gentlemen their hats, all dripping with water.

"Where is Mr Darcy?" Elizabeth eventually addressed Bingley.

"He must have found a means of escape and left us here," Wickham replied mockingly. "Probably he returned to Netherfield by horse. Let us hope he will send help so we can leave this place."

"I do not understand your meaning, Mr Wickham," Bingley replied severely. "Darcy went to release the horses from the carriage; they were still tethered and they could have been harmed in this storm. He would never abandon anyone in need."

"I apologise if it sounded disrespectful, it was only a joke," Wickham said defensively, still with a trace of sharpness in his voice.

"A poor one, I must say," the always amiable Bingley said, apparently offended.

"I find it inappropriate to mock someone who has just saved us. I fear to imagine what could have happened if Mr Darcy had not stopped the horses," Elizabeth said. She felt annoyed by Wickham's rude comment in such a trying moment and was distressed with worry for Darcy's absence.

The storm was still strong, blowing against the roof and the windows, and he was alone outside, without knowing the surroundings well enough. He might need help, while all the other men were safe in the cottage, not even considering looking for him.

"That is true! Mr Darcy was like a hero! I never expected that from him! I was certain we would die, crushed under the broken carriage! Oh Lord! The carriage! Sir William will hold us responsible for it! He will rightfully demand compensation! Why did we not send for our carriage, instead of taking his?" Mrs Bennet started to sob.

"Ma'am, I am sure nobody could hold us responsible for this unfortunate accident," Wickham interjected. "Who could blame us for the storm or for the horses' fright?"

"Who? Sir William! We have left him without a barouche! How can he not consider us responsible?"

"Mrs Bennet, I beg you do not worry about the barouche or about the horses," Bingley interjected. "I will take care of everything. Even tomorrow, I will talk to Sir William."

"You are too kind, sir," Jane whispered. "My father will surely repay any inconvenience, but we are deeply grateful for your care."

"Please do not mention it, Miss Bennet," Bingley answered.

"You are the most generous and caring man, Mr Bingley. And it is beyond kindness for Mr Darcy to put his own life in danger to save us and the horses. But all will be of little help if we freeze to death. Will you gentlemen not start a fire? There must be a tinderbox around the fireplace," Mrs Bennet suggested.

"Should we not see if Mr Darcy needs help?" Elizabeth asked. It had been several minutes since they had come inside while he remained somewhere in the rain.

"No. I am sure he can manage the situation. He instructed me to stay inside and take care of you," Bingley explained.

"Well, we can take care of the ladies very well if you wish to go," Wickham declared sharply.

"It would be an excellent proof of care if you could start the fire," Mrs Bennet insisted with increasing annoyance. "I cannot feel my feet nor my hands."

The men looked at each other perplexed, while the ladies gazed at them, hoping for help. Mr Bingley, willing to be of use to Jane, quickly looked around, in the hope of finding something to start the fire. Lieutenant Denny joined him, followed reluctantly by Wickham. There was some wood and some tinder spread out in the fireplace, all wet and dirty and Bingley's attempt failed.

"This will never ignite," Mr Bingley admitted, embarrassed and regretful.

"I agree," Lieutenant Denny offered.

"We cannot use those, they are all wet and dirty," Wickham declared.

"Well, thank God we all agree upon that matter. At least we will freeze in agreement," Mrs Bennet snapped, rolling her eyes.

"Perhaps we could at least light a candle, to be able to see something," Lieutenant Denny muttered.

Mrs Bennet's voice cut their ears.

"A candle? How can you light a candle with no fire? And if you had a lit candle, why would you struggle to make another fire? I will lose my mind soon, I am sure! That is, if I do not freeze to death beforehand!"

"Mama, there is nobody to blame for our situation. We can only try to make the best of it," Jane interjected graciously.

"Making the best from the worst is not easy. I would hope that Mr Wickham or Lieutenant Denny know how to light a fire. As an officer, you should know how to survive in the war; surely you can do so in a cottage."

"If the tinderbox is useless, I do not see what else we can do," Wickham said. "I have never dealt with this matter before. Usually there were servants around to light the fire."

"So we have the company of three gentlemen but we could better use the presence of only one servant," Mrs Bennet continued.

Wickham appeared offended. "I will give it a try and see if I have any success," he replied.

Mrs Bennet cared little for his hurt feelings and admonished him further.

"Well, you should attempt it. I doubt there will be servants in battle. And when we speak of fire, one can only succeed or fail. Trying is not enough. The fire is either burning or not and we will either catch a cold and die or not."

"Mama," Lydia intervened. "You cannot scold Mr Wickham for being nice. He is doing everything he can. Besides, you said many times that people do not die from a mere trifling cold."

"Well, we might start," Mrs Bennet concluded, irritated.

Elizabeth avoided entering into the debate, although she rather agreed with her mother. She looked at the old, ruined mantelpiece, at the wet tinderbox, then walked around the cottage, trying to find something useful. She found a kettle and an old chest of tea. In the closet she found a few towels and some sheets–all dirty but at least dry.

"Perhaps these would help us to keep warm," she said, sharing the items with her mother and sisters. Wickham also took a towel and shared it with his comrade, drying their faces and hair.

A few moments later, the wooden door opened and Darcy barged in, together with the wind whistling and the rain pattering. He was all wet, water dripping from his face and clothes. Trying to accustom his eyes to the darkness inside, he stopped in the doorway, looking around. Elizabeth stepped forward towards him.

"How are the horses?" Bingley asked.

"Safe, I trust. The carriage horses were tangled in the reins but fortunately none of them looked harmed, as little as I could see. Sadly, I could not hold any of them. I am sure they will run back home," he answered with his usual severity.

"Mr Wickham suspected you had ridden back to Netherfield," Mrs Bennet said, with obvious gladness to see him. He suddenly had become her hope for a happy ending to their distressing situation.

"I have not," he responded bluntly. "We should start the fire; it is hard to say how long the storm will last and the ladies must be freezing."

Mrs Bennet raised her hands and rolled her eyes in exasperation.

"I have been saying that since we arrived but, unless you have your servants waiting outside, nobody seems able to start the fire."

"We tried, Darcy. We are not such fools as to ignore the obvious; we all know that we need a fire; there is no need for you to teach us," Wickham said insolently. "But the tinderbox is all wet and muddy and it does not work."

"Well, if it were clean and dry I could have done it myself," Mrs Bennet said, pulling the towel around her. "We could have prayed to the Lord to stop the rain so we can go home to warm by the fire."

"Allow me, ma'am," Darcy spoke with his regular cold politeness, purposely ignoring Wickham. He took off his coat and hat and put them on the back of a wooden, broken chair, then stepped up to the fireplace. He knelt near the hearth, his back blocking the others' view.

The ladies looked at each other, while Bingley hurried to kneel by his side and offered to help. Wickham rolled his eyes with a smirk, glancing meaningfully at the others. They heard Darcy's moves, blowing upon the tinder and knocking some stones together to ignite it; after a few long minutes, a flame and a welcoming red light brightened the frozen chamber and met equal joyful cheers and gaps of disbelief.

Darcy stood up, dusted his clothes and brushed his fingers through his messy hair. He briefly glanced at Elizabeth, then turned to Mrs Bennet.

"You should sit by the fire to warm yourself, madam," he said.

"Oh, what a lovely surprise! Mr Darcy, you are a magician. I would have never expected that! Oh, I could really kiss you! You speak so little and do so much! What a man!"

With utter delight, she even stepped towards Darcy as Elizabeth watched in dismay, fearful her mother would truly kiss him. He stepped back, smiled with embarrassment, then bowed and put himself at even more of a distance, pulling a chair closer to the mantelpiece.

"I believe here would be a good spot," he said to Mrs Bennet, who received his attention with enough satisfaction to put any other gush of affection aside. Then Darcy, followed by Bingley, put two more chairs near the fireplace, but there were no more. Therefore, they chose a few bigger logs and put them down so the other girls could sit. Wickham and Denny did the same, and soon everyone was seated comfortably around the fire.

"I will look for some candles–there must be a few," Elizabeth said.

"And–curiously–now that we have the fire, the candles might actually be of some use," Mrs Bennet returned with barely hidden reproach. She was obviously angry with Wickham and Denny and blamed them for not handling the horses and for breaking Sir William's carriage.

Elizabeth returned with four old candles. Darcy took

two from her hands and lighting both, placed them around the room. There was a silent, mutual understanding between Elizabeth and Darcy that stirred them both in a strange and most pleasant way, despite their difficult circumstances.

"Oh, what a pleasure that someone saved us from freezing to death in Talbot's old cottage. I declare there is nothing better than a good fire on a cold, rainy day," Mrs Bennet continued. "Mr Darcy, you are simply the best man I have met in a long while."

"You are too kind, ma'am; I surely do not deserve such praises, for doing what any other man would do. I am glad I could help. You should stay close to the fire, you look very cold. Miss Elizabeth, perhaps you could find a kettle to boil some water to make some tea? We can fill it with rainwater."

She nodded and rose. "I have actually already found one."

"Please sit and warm yourself. You look cold too," Darcy said. "I will take it out to clean it and fill it with water.". Bingley hurried to help him once more, following him around the room. Darcy held the kettle and Bingley took a large jar; they exited into the storm, closing the door behind them.

"Mr Darcy did not even take his coat; he will get all wet and cold," Jane muttered.

"Well, we should not worry too much, he never falls ill. He is too proud to allow anyone to see any weakness. So he would rather die than keep to his bed," Wickham pronounced.

"That is a very ungenerous statement, Mr Wickham. We should all be grateful to Mr Darcy for his care, not make jokes at his expense, while he is showing us so much consideration," Elizabeth said coldly, disturbed by Wickham's words and even more by his impertinent manners.

"I apologise, Miss Elizabeth. I am only trying to lighten our disposition and I am only speaking the truth. I believe we all have had to put up with Darcy's pride and his disdainful manners since we met him. Even his helpful gestures are due to the pride of showing he can do what others cannot."

Mrs Bennet frowned and her lips twisted in a grimace of displeasure.

"It is true Mr Darcy's manners are not as amiable as other men's, nor is he the most pleasant company most of the time. And I do not doubt he does loathe our company as much as we do his. But upon my word, in times of need, he seems to be everything a man should be! Pleasant manners, nice speeches and charming smiles are only useful in a ballroom. When one is about to die in a runaway carriage or in a storm, one needs a real man, not the appearance of one," Mrs Bennet said severely.

Wickham and Denny startled at such a severe reprimand but were forced to bear it silently. Wickham obviously struggled to censure his reply and only whispered something to his friend. Elizabeth and Jane blushed with embarrassment, attempting to calm their mother, who felt angrier with every passing moment.

It took a while until they noticed Darcy and Bingley watching them from the doorway. They handed the kettle to Elizabeth, who tried to find a place to put it to boil. Unexpectedly, Darcy knelt next to her again and assisted her until the kettle stood steadily. A strange sensation that she had never felt before warmed Elizabeth's skin more than the fire's heat. Although she was grateful for his help, she was becoming uncomfortable with his closeness and with her unconscious brushes against him. They were both wet and cold, and their frozen, clumsy fingers reached each others' as much as the kettle, while their knees touched too.

"There; I think this will work," Darcy said when the kettle was safely placed. He then rose and moved back to Bingley's side, while Elizabeth sat next to Jane. The sudden silence in the room was broken by the fire, the rain, and the wind. As if mesmerised, they all stared at the fireplace and the kettle, waiting for the water to boil.

"Mr Darcy?" Mrs Bennet finally spoke.

"Yes, ma'am?"

"Thank you for the fire, sir. Without you, we would have surely frozen to death."

"I doubt it," he replied with a trace of lightness in his voice. "But you are very welcome."

Elizabeth looked at him and their glances met briefly; suddenly, she felt warm.

For the next few minutes, the ladies stayed around the fire, while Wickham and Lieutenant Denny sat on one side of the fireplace, talking mostly to Lydia and Kitty. Elizabeth, Jane and their mother gathered together, with Bingley and Darcy on the other side. Despite the fire, they were all becoming colder and a state of tiredness and weakness slowly enveloped them. The tea they drank using the only three available cups, one by one, did not help much. Outside, it was getting darker.

"I am going back to Netherfield to get help," Darcy suddenly said. "We cannot stay here any longer and surely we cannot spend the night in our present situation."

"I am coming with you," Bingley declared.

"But it is still raining," Jane interjected with concern. "You cannot walk three miles in this weather, with no light!"

"And it might rain for a long while still," Darcy replied. "Three miles is not such a long distance. And we will keep to the main path–there cannot be any danger."

Elizabeth watched them intently, met Darcy's gaze above all the others, and then stood up and walked to him.

"I am coming with you. Nobody knows these grounds as well as I do; in this storm you will need my knowledge of the easiest shortcuts through the woods."

"Absolutely not! I cannot allow that!" Darcy answered hastily.

Elizabeth frowned and glared at him.

"It is not for you to allow it or not, sir. I am doing what is best for my family. If I come with you, we will save time."

"Miss Elizabeth, this time I must agree with Darcy. You cannot go out in such weather. I am sure someone will look for us and help will come soon. It is safer to wait here, where we have fire and shelter," Wickham interjected.

"I cannot count on what the others will do. I am going! With you or by myself. Shall we?" she spoke to Darcy and Bingley, while taking her coat and tidying her bonnet. They were all cold and wet and shivered at the unpleasant sensation.

"Lizzy, sit down! You are going nowhere," Mrs Bennet said. She pulled the towel closer around her while her teeth were chattering from the cold.

"I am going, Mama. You look very ill and you need help as quickly as possible. My decision is made. Let us not waste precious time," Elizabeth said, moving to the door, ignoring the opposition of her mother and sisters.

Another clap of thunder shook the cottage and the door opened, pushed by the wind and rain. In its frame, Darcy's valet and four other men appeared, protected by raincoats.

The ladies startled and jumped to their feet, while the men all moved towards the newcomers.

"Stevens!"

"Thank God, we found you!" Stevens cried at his master.

"Thank God you did," Darcy approved. "At a perfect time too," he said, glancing at Elizabeth, whose eyes held his briefly.

"Your horses returned to Netherfield by themselves so I knew something had happened. We did not know you were so many ... We saw the smoke coming from the chimney and we found the carriage with the wheel broken and we assumed you must be nearby."

"How did you get here? Can you take us all from here?"

"With your carriage, sir. It is raining too heavily to ride."

"Very well," Darcy approved.

Cheers of joy sounded in the cottage; the saviours entered and pushed the door closed, while a tumult of voices made any understanding impossible.

"Let us speak reasonably, so we can understand each other," Darcy commanded, raising his voice over the din. "Would you allow me to suggest how to proceed further?" he asked and Mrs Bennet readily nodded, silencing her daughters.

"First thing, the ladies should return to Longbourn immediately. Stevens, I need someone to drive them by carriage, safely."

"Very well, sir. John will do that. Or I can."

"Let John go; he is more accustomed to driving the carriage. Where is it?"

"Near the broken one, sir. Should I bring it here?"

"No, it would be too dangerous. Ladies, we will help you to the carriage. You will have to bear the rain again, but fortunately you will be home in a few minutes," Darcy concluded.

"Oh, that is wonderful! Excellent!" Mrs Bennet cried with joy.

"Can we go with the ladies? Wickham asked. We can sit down on the floor if there is not enough room. A few minutes will be no problem."

Darcy threw him a brief cutting glare, which Elizabeth did not miss.

"Oh, yes, of course you can," Lydia cried. "We can squeeze together so there will be room for you too! Is it not so, Mama?"

"Of course! We can all fit in the carriage, for a short while," Mrs Bennet approved.

"As you wish, ma'am," Darcy accepted, looking at Elizabeth one more time. "Then let us go, there is no time to waste," he concluded, opening the door and showing the ladies out. Lydia took Wickham's arm, while Denny helped Kitty. Bingley immediately offered to support Jane. Darcy remained behind with Mrs Bennet and Elizabeth and, after a brief hesitation, he offered one arm to each.

"May I help you, Mrs Bennet?" Stevens also offered and Mrs Bennet took his arm too, stepping carefully across the muddy ground.

Wet and cold, their faces stinging from the freezing wind, Elizabeth and Darcy walked side by side, without looking at each other but strongly aware of their nearness. They reached Darcy's large carriage and quickly entered, happy at the thought of being safe soon. Even with six people, it was not as crowded as they expected.

"Dear Lord, thank you! Mr Darcy, we are very grateful for your help!" Mrs Bennet said, and Darcy only bowed. It was so dark that they could barely see each other.

"Please ask Mr Bennet to send a note to Sir William. He must be worried if his horses arrived home alone," Darcy addressed Elizabeth. She nodded, impressed by his ability to think of everything.

"I might go to Longbourn to be sure everyone is safe... And I will speak to Mr Bennet... There is still some room in the carriage," Bingley unexpectedly offered as if asking Darcy's permission. His concern and willingness to assist the ladies was obvious.

"I believe that is a good idea," Darcy approved.

"Then I will go," Bingley responded joyfully, quickly entering the carriage. "I will return in no time. You go back to the cottage and keep the fire burning, you are very wet," Bingley told his friend.

"Just leave. I will be fine. Take the ladies safely home, Bingley," Darcy uttered and the carriage moved forward slowly, while he walked back to the cottage, followed by Stevens and the two other servants.

Inside, it was silent and warm enough. The light from the fire and the candles made the old little cabin rather friendly. He sat on a chair, close to the fire, lost in his thoughts.

That afternoon's events had been so utterly unexpected that he still needed time to muse over them. As dangerous as it had been for the ladies, in those strange circumstances a strong connection was born between him and Elizabeth. Although they barely spoke to each other, their bond had grown in an alarming way. Alarming and delightful. Heart-warming. He felt she trusted him with her well-being and her family's. And she worried for him; Bingley told him she had repeatedly enquired after him while he was out in the rain. In fact, they trusted each other to keep their sense and their strength when both were needed.

Earlier that afternoon, he and Bingley had gone for a short ride and—as usual—Bingley insisted on stopping at Longbourn briefly. Even if he had not admitted it, Darcy accepted gladly.

They were welcomed by Mr Bennet, who informed them the ladies were in Meryton and invited them for a drink. They spent an hour together, hoping for the ladies to appear. When the weather worsened and the clouds darkened the sky, they decided to leave. It was assumed the ladies would remain in Meryton until the rain stopped and return home in a carriage.

On the way back to Netherfield, they were trapped in the unforeseen storm and caught in the rain in between Longbourn and Netherfield. And they were stunned to hear the sound of frightened horses and a runaway carriage, as well as screams of fear. He hurried to stop the horses, with no indication who the people were who were trapped in the barouche. When he finally saw the Bennets–with Elizabeth lying on the floor, holding her sisters' hands–his heart raced with worry, considering the danger they had been in. Then he saw Wickham and his concern was overtaken by anger. He constantly sensed that Wickham was purposely trying to annoy him. He was proven wrong shortly after; in the end, Wickham showed to everyone that he was only an idiot unable to drive a carriage with two horses.

Regardless of the fabrication he might have related to the Bennets, Mrs Bennet and her eldest daughters did not seem very partial to Wickham. On the contrary, Mrs Bennet's repeated rebuking of Wickham for not handling the horses and not starting the fire was probably the most amusing thing Darcy had heard in a long time.

With a smile, he recollected how Mrs Bennet was ready to kiss him for lighting the fire and laughed at the thought. The woman was completely lacking in decorum and was annoying most of the time, but her poor manners seemed rather diverting. So long as he did not have to bear them too often, of course.

And, in the end, she had raised two remarkable daughters in Miss Bennet and Elizabeth. She must have done something right, after all.

No. Jane Bennet was handsome and lovely in manners and appearance. Elizabeth was remarkable. Stunning in her powerful, self-confident beauty, even when she was wet, dirty, and cold. Her appearance even in that dirty cottage was more alluring than the most fashionable women he had seen in a ballroom.

He shivered at the memory of Elizabeth's fingers touching his and her worried gaze seeking his own. She was frightened and looked to him for help and support. And she was ready to forget her own comfort and safety to help others, willing to walk through the storm with him and with Bingley. In the end, her sacrifice was not needed, but that did not diminish her worthiness and her praiseworthy character. She was brave, outspoken, decided, lively, strong, and honest. She was everything he had hoped for in a woman but had never found before. She was his perfect match in everything except a few insignificant aspects. Of that, he had no doubts.

But was he worthy of her? Was he brave enough to admit his desires and fight for them, despite everything and everyone? Was he her perfect match or only a pompous fool, blessed with fortune and connections he had done nothing to deserve?

Leaning back in the chair by the fire, Darcy was slowly warming, forgetting the wet and cold clothes that he still wore. He had spent many times by the fire, warming himself after being caught in storms, mostly at Pemberley. And he could spend so many more—perhaps with Elizabeth. Alone, embracing, on a couch placed before the hearth. She would love Pemberley, he knew that. And Pemberley would love her too. And Georgiana, Mrs Reynolds...His relatives would not accept her, he was certain of that. Most likely London society would not either. At least not in the beginning. But should he be preoccupied by the opinions of others? And yet, could he afford to disregard them?

He remained the only male descendant of the Darcys. He knew his family's expectations, his late parents' wishes and hopes for his future and his own duty toward his name and his legacy.

Just as he knew Elizabeth could fulfil the role of Mrs

Darcy perfectly. But her family's situation and poor connections, her mother and sisters' ill manners, her uncles and aunts, and so many other obstacles were impossible to dismiss. But not impossible to overcome. He needed to think thoroughly about everything. Some other time–when he was less tired and less dizzy.

For the moment, he closed his eyes and brought to mind Elizabeth's image, to comfort him.

"Darcy, are you well?" a voice startled him.

Darcy staggered to his feet, staring at Bingley.

"I am fine; I believe I fell asleep for a moment. Should we go now?"

"Yes. You look very flustered," Bingley said.

"I was warming, but now I am truly very cold. I do not remember being so cold in a long while, if ever. Let us go. Stevens, please douse the fire and the candles carefully, this cottage could burn down in no time. We will wait for you in the carriage. Do hurry," Darcy ordered.

Bingley and Darcy left the cottage, walking through the rain that had almost stopped. Occasional drops fell but they did not even sense them; more bothering was the freezing wind that blew in their faces. They finally entered the coach. On the bench was a blanket and, shivering, Darcy put it around himself.

"Are the Bennet ladies well?" Darcy asked. Stevens arrived and took the front seat with the two coachmen and they finally began moving slowly.

"Yes. I hope so. Mrs Bennet gave me these blankets. One for you, she said. I did not enter, but I was delayed by Wickham and Denny. They asked me to take them to Meryton by carriage and I could not refuse them. I am telling you, if all the officers are like those two, God protects us from enemies!"

Darcy laughed, tightening the blanket around himself closely, then responded earnestly. "Do not let yourself be deceived by Wickham. He is a dangerous scoundrel, who would do anything to gain an easy advantage. He cannot be trusted for a single moment. And he seems to have already charmed the youngest Misses Bennet. He would lie, cheat and betray you in the blink of an eye, if that serves his purposes."

"I am sure he would, but he looked rather pathetic to me. He did try to criticise you several times when you were away, but he was readily rebuked by Miss Elizabeth and by Mrs Bennet. In the carriage back to Longbourn, he tried to be charming and protective, repeating how happy he was that the ladies were safely home. Like he had done something to accomplish that happy outcome. If not for you... dear Lord, they all could have been harmed."

"Do not mention it, Bingley. Everything turned out very well."

"But Darcy, I must ask...how did you jump from your horse onto theirs? That was astonishing!" Bingley asked in amazement.

Darcy dismissed the praise with a wave of his hand.

"It is not as spectacular as it appears. It was a trick I learned from our stable man when I was very young. I never thought it would serve me, except when I competed with my cousins. To be honest, I did not even think of what I was doing. I heard screams and I could not see clearly, but I knew I had to stop the carriage."

Bingley shook his head in disapproval at his friend's perfect calmness.

"It was spectacular. And you did put yourself in great danger. But do you know what astounded me the most?"

"What?" Darcy smiled at his friend's embarrassing awe.

"The fact that when you stopped the carriage you did not know who was in it. It could have been complete strangers, peasants, anyone..."

"Yes. But the people were still in danger, and the carriage still needed to be stopped," Darcy replied simply. Bingley only stared at him, but said nothing, as their carriage finally reached Netherfield's front door.

"Bingley, I hope you do not mind, but I will have dinner in my room tonight. I want only warm food please. And a very hot bath."

"Of course!" Bingley whispered while Darcy ran upstairs, trying to escape Bingley's sisters' curious and intrigued exclamations.

Chapter 9

*T*he joy of being safe from such a dangerous adventure increased Lydia and Kitty's appetites and kept them animated for the rest of the evening.

They repeated the story, in great detail, several times over dinner and after it. Mrs Bennet interjected briefly, while Elizabeth and Jane spoke little. There was so much for them to consider that words failed them.

Jane was impressed by Mr Bingley's care and generosity, while Elizabeth was astounded by Mr Darcy's behaviour, in every respect. Every gesture was so unexpected, so different from what she imagined it would be, that her estimation of him changed entirely.

After spending more time in his company and observing her father's good opinion of the man, her old grudge was already forgotten and she had long begun to see him in a more favourable light. She had sketched him as a difficult man, proud and at times resentful, but well educated, loyal to his friend, and most likely very skilful in taking care of his family and his estate business. Bingley had talked of it countless times. Every time he had called he had behaved politely towards her family – although his disapproving looks towards her mother and younger sisters were impossible to miss. To her, after the initial offence at the assembly, his manners were almost friendly, in a respectful and considerate way.

But that afternoon, in the cottage, she met a man of extraordinary generosity, deep thoughtfulness and power that still overwhelmed and flustered her. He seemed to be in control of everything, he missed nothing, he knew what to do and did not hesitate to jeopardise his own safety for their well-being.

And his small gesture when he helped her put the kettle on the fire still made her quiver. His strong rejection of her walking with them to find help, she took as his concern for her safety. She did not know if that was so, or if he considered her a good friend and held her in special regard, or he only treated her as the sister of the lady Bingley admired.

"So how on earth did Mr Darcy jump onto the running horses?" Mr Bennet asked, startling Elizabeth.

"Upon my word I do not know. But if not for him, we would be lying injured on the ground and you would have found us when it was too late, I am sure," Mrs Bennet responded.

"Well, he is a brave man, I grant him that. And quite astonishing–rich men are not usually accustomed to putting themselves in danger," Mr Bennet continued.

"I am sure he did so because he knows Mr Bingley intends to propose to Jane," Mrs Bennet declared.

Jane blushed and dropped her teaspoon. "Mama, do not say that! We cannot know what Mr Bingley's intentions are. Besides, Mr Darcy stopped the carriage without even knowing who was in it! Mr Bingley told me as much!"

"Did he?" Mr Bennet enquired, even more puzzled.

"You see? Mr Bingley always tells you more than he tells us! Besides, he offered to take care of the carriage! He said he will speak to Sir William himself! Why would he assume such an expense, if not for you? This is the best proof he intends to propose," Mrs Bennet concluded readily. Jane blushed, but could not contradict such a strong argument. Indeed, no one would take upon himself the trouble of repairing a barouche for which he was not responsible, if that person did not possess a peculiar interest in the matter.

"Proof or no proof, this is a generosity I can only applaud. Otherwise, I would be forced to offer Sir William my own carriage in return," Mr Bennet confessed.

"We should never have listened to Mr Wickham! We

should have sent for our carriage, and John would have taken us home safely," Mrs Bennet said.

"Mama, Mr Wickham was only being kind and now you are blaming him!" Lydia objected and Kitty supported her most energetically.

Mrs Bennet dismissed them with a wave of her hand, rolling her eyes. "I shall not start this debate again. I am going to sleep now. I am very tired and I am afraid I have already caught a cold. Just days before the ball! Jane, take some more herbal tea! It would be a disaster if you fell ill, when Mr Bingley is giving this ball specifically for you! You may say whatever you want, I shall not change my opinion!"

Once Mrs Bennet had left, exhaustion quickly overcame the other girls too. Mary joined Lydia and Kitty to listen to more details about their adventure, declaring it was a good subject for a story. Elizabeth and Jane remained with their father a little longer, had some more tea as their mother had instructed them, and finally retired to their chamber.

They spoke less than usual as they prepared for bed, and soon fell asleep. The rain started again and the sound, so relaxing at other times, now took Elizabeth's mind back to the cottage. She felt that she had been caught up in a storm of feelings, confusion and assumptions–and Darcy was there all the time, staring at her, touching her fingers with his and walking by her side to keep her safe and warm.

∞∞∞

The rain persisted for three more days. At Netherfield, the preparations for the ball involved all the staff. Louisa and Caroline did not miss any opportunity to express their disapproval, but Bingley put much effort and interest into hosting a flawless event.

Darcy kept himself away from the chaos, spending most of the time in his chamber or in the library. He felt in low spirits, had little appetite for food or conversation, and his head was cloudier than ever. He found some comfort writing to Georgiana and relating to her–in a light, amusing way–about their little escapade. Wickham's name was never mentioned. His sister responded immediately by express and her letter pleased him as always.

He missed Georgiana dearly and looked forward to seeing her, but a sharp pain gripped his chest as he realised that meeting his sister would mean leaving Hertfordshire.

His thoughts turned to Longbourn all the time, wondering what Elizabeth was doing. Some notes were exchanged between the two houses, and they found that the Miss Bennets were all well, but Mrs Bennet was struggling with a nasty cold–no surprise after the distress she had had to bear.

The more he thought of Elizabeth, the more confused he became. He felt pulled apart between his heart and his mind, between his desire and his reasoning. He was undecided how to proceed further; he feared he might hurt her if he showed more of his admiration but did not pursue her further. He could not allow himself to raise any expectations for her or her family until he was confident he could fulfil them. His torment was much easier to bear than the notion that she was suffering from his thoughtless behaviour. Therefore, the rain was his ally, as it offered him the best excuse to stay inside, away from her for the time being.

"Darcy, what are you doing here in the dark?" Bingley asked, barging into the library, carrying some papers.

"I am reading Georgiana's letter."

"In the dark?" Bingley repeated.

"I have a slight headache, and more light is rather disturbing. And what are you doing, Bingley?"

"I just received a letter from my solicitor, Mr Hayward. It is very strange. Look," Bingley said, handing Darcy the paper in an anxious state.

Darcy took it, intrigued by his friend's apparent nervousness and read it carefully. His eyes were hurting, and he had to narrow them to read.

"Your mother received an inheritance from an aunt?" Darcy asked minutes later. "Did you know of that aunt?"

"No! I never heard of her! It seems she has lived in France since before my parents married. And she has no other heirs. She must have been rather old."

"Fifty thousand pounds is a significant amount," Darcy observed. "Is there something that troubles you with regard to it?"

"No...Yes...Not about the amount. Mr Hayward wants me to go to London as soon as possible, together with Louisa and Caroline. The inheritance will be split between my mother's children, so Mr Hayward writes."

"As is usually the case," Darcy confirmed.

"Indeed. But I am distraught that I had an aunt and never met her! I wonder why my parents did not even mention her! I have not said anything to Caroline and Louisa yet. I have only just received the letter. I was certain I did not have other living relatives and now... now, indeed I do not have any left," Bingley concluded with grief.

"I am truly sorry for your pain," Darcy comforted him warmly. "Please let me know if I can help you in any way."

"No, no. Thank you. I shall inform Louisa and Caroline. We should return to London after the ball. I am not sure how long this business will take, but I hope it will not be too long. I would like to return to Netherfield by Christmas."

"It should not last long if the documents are clear. Besides, you only have to declare whether you accept or reject the inheritance. The rest is Mr Hayward's job. I will recommend he talks to my solicitor, Mr Moore, if necessary."

"Very well. I shall send my answer right away. I had no intention of leaving Hertfordshire; this comes most unexpectedly," Bingley declared.

"You should not be upset for receiving fifty thousand pounds, even if that means it takes you away from Miss Bennet," Darcy laughed. "I am positive that she will understand and will wait for you to return."

"Yes, yes, I know she will wait. It is just–I did not expect this," Bingley insisted. "Will you come to London with us?"

"Of course. I intended to return to London after the ball anyway. I must spend a little time with Georgiana," Darcy said, embarrassed for telling his friend only half the truth.

He wished to leave to clear his mind regarding Elizabeth. And maybe he would be brave enough to speak to Georgiana and gain her opinion about the prospect of him marrying someone from a family below theirs. He had never spoken of such matters to Georgiana, as he always considered her too young and too delicate for disturbing subjects. But perhaps it was time to rely more on her wisdom, since he could not fully trust his own judgement.

"So, will you not return to Hertfordshire? At all?" Bingley asked in panic.

"I probably will, if you invite me again," Darcy smiled, rubbing his temples. "I have no fixed plans yet, except visiting my uncle and aunt and enjoying some time with Georgiana."

"When do you intend to go to Pemberley?"

"I am not certain of that either. I shall speak to Georgiana and will inform you. I hope you will have time to visit us while you are in town."

"Of course! I look forward to seeing Georgiana too. Would you not consider bringing her to Netherfield if...some important event takes place in my life? Do you think she would dislike Netherfield? Or Miss Bennet and her sisters?"

Darcy frowned and rubbed his forehead, as pain filled his entire head.

"I am sure she would like Netherfield, as well as Miss Bennet and Miss Elizabeth very much. Probably the other sisters too, as she is so kind and friendly. But bringing her here is out of the question. I do not want her to meet Wickham. She was deeply disappointed in his behaviour, after growing up together and trusting him with her genuine affection. I cannot allow her to meet him again, under any circumstances."

"Very well," Bingley admitted reluctantly. "I accept your decision, but I hope Georgiana will have an opportunity to become acquainted with the Misses Bennet."

"That will not be too difficult, Bingley," Darcy smiled again. "If a certain event takes place, I am sure they will come to London very soon."

Bingley's face coloured and a broad grin appeared on his face. "Darcy, would you like a drink?"

"Very, much so," Darcy answered. "A large brandy, please. And then I will retire to rest a little. I believe I have been sleeping poorly lately."

Bingley handed him the glass, staring at his friend with great interest.

"I have never known you to rest at noon," Bingley said. "Are you unwell? You look pale."

"I am well, do not worry," Darcy replied, gulping some brandy.

"I hope you will not pretend to be ill so you can absent yourself from the ball," Bingley mocked him.

Darcy laughed. "Not at all, I assure you. I plan to be very present and even to dance."

Bingley stared at him in disbelief. "Dance? Now I am sure you are truly ill; you absolutely must rest!"

∞∞∞

A day before the ball, with the rain continuing to fall, tragedy struck at Longbourn with Mr Collins' return. Although he had mentioned before his intention of attending the ball, nobody took it seriously and nobody recollected it. So, when he knocked on the door in the late afternoon, he was received with surprise and reluctance.

"My dear Mr Bennet, my dear Mrs Bennet, my fair cousins, I cannot tell you how much I have missed you and what joy overwhelms me at seeing you again!"

"My dear Mr Collins, we are here to please you!" Mr Bennet mocked him in reply.

"We are surprised that you chose to travel in such weather," Mrs Bennet added. "The roads can be hazardous. I caught a very bad cold myself a few days ago, but I thank God I am strong and I quickly recovered."

"I am very sorry to hear that, ma'am. But a man should be brave enough to gather his courage when he wants to accomplish his goals," Mr Collins stated. Elizabeth rolled her eyes while Mr Bennet took up the challenge.

"I see. And was your goal to attend the ball, or is there a higher purpose in your endeavour?"

A grin spread over Mr Collins' face. "The answer would be yes to both your questions, my dear sir. I could not miss the chance of dancing with my lovely cousins. And Lady Catherine recommended that I do not return to Kent without news of my engagement. Therefore, I have hopes that this ball will be the opportunity to finally please her ladyship."

Mrs Bennet's eyes widened in delight. "Indeed, sir, this might be the perfect chance! My daughters will be delighted to dance with you, I am sure. And what better place and time for you to choose a wife?"

"Do you think so, ma'am?" Mr Collins asked, and Mrs Bennet took his arm, as they walked around the drawing room.

"Absolutely. Do tell me, what are your most important expectations in a wife?"

They paced around for a while and the girls excused themselves and retired, each appalled by the implied danger. Kitty, Lydia, and Mary whispered and chuckled in the hall at Mr Collins' stupidity, Elizabeth grew angry with her mother again, as she could easily guess the conversation between the two. She gathered her strength to wage another difficult battle, praying that her mother would not expose them all to ridicule at the ball.

The night before the ball was restless and disturbing for

Elizabeth but exciting for Jane. They had not seen Mr Bingley since he brought them home, but they knew he had settled the matter of the carriage with Sir William. He refused to provide more details to Mr Bennet–that way saving him from expenses–but they all knew the meaning of his actions. Jane did not dare assume too much, although her heart spoke loudly enough; but she did look forward to thanking him in person.

The day of the ball was one of true chaos at Longbourn. Lydia and Kitty raced around the house, searching for dresses, reticules and gloves, continuously debating how many of the officers might attend.

"Lizzy, do you think Mr Wickham will come? I surely hope so! And I hope we will all dance with him! I am certain he is a wonderful dancer! He must be, since he is so handsome!"

"How could I know Mr Wickham's plans, Lydia?"

"Oh, and Mr Collins told Mama he will dance with each of us! How horrible!"

"Lydia, keep your voice down. And please do not walk around undressed. Do you wish me to help you with your gown?"

"No, I am fine. Kitty will help me. You look very pretty, Lizzy. That dress is very becoming on you, and I like how you have put flowers in your hair," Lydia said.

"Thank you, my dear," Elizabeth smiled. "Now go and prepare yourself. Mama insists we not be late."

"Mama hopes Mr Bingley will propose to Jane tonight. I hope so too; otherwise, she will force one of us to marry Mr Collins. I heard her saying that. I am afraid you will be the one, Lizzy."

"I doubt that very much, Lydia. Both matters are very unlikely to occur, at least tonight," Elizabeth concluded.

Despite her confident tone, Elizabeth felt rather nervous. She could think of nothing else but Mr Collins showing a ridiculous preference for her and Bingley's sisters amusing themselves at her expense. Perhaps Mr Darcy too. And likely the entire village.

The family gathered in the main hall, and Elizabeth's nightmare began when Mr Collins bowed to her and smiled from ear to ear.

"My dear cousin Elizabeth, you must allow me to tell you how charming you look tonight! And to ask you for the favour of the first set, if you are not otherwise engaged, which I hope you are not!"

Elizabeth paled and looked towards her father–who seemed utterly amused–and to her mother, who was glaring at her.

She breathed deeply and responded. "Thank you, sir. I am not engaged."

"How fortunate! I am sure it will be a lovely night. I consider a proper ball to be a most acceptable diversion for a clergyman," Mr Collins declared as they entered the carriage.

"Mr Collins, did I tell you that we broke Sir William's carriage and Mr Bingley generously paid for it?"

"No, you did not, ma'am! This is extraordinary! How did that happen?"

"Mama!" Jane attempted to stop her, but Mrs Bennet continued to relate the details of their accident, insisting on Darcy's bravery and Bingley's care, all as proof of the gentlemen's consideration for the Bennet family.

It was a relief for both Elizabeth and Jane when the carriage eventually stopped at the main entrance. Netherfield was lit by many torches, looking impressive and festive, as Mr Collins observed and Mrs Bennet readily agreed.

On the morning of the ball, Darcy woke up with his head pounding and barely able to breathe. It had been another sleepless night, in which he only thought of Elizabeth. After all the torment and struggle, he realised it was in vain to conceal his feelings and to reject his desires. When the dawn broke the darkness, he reached a truce–a peace within himself.

He was determined to go to London and talk to Georgiana, then return to Netherfield, to be near Elizabeth. He needed more time to know her better and to allow her the chance of knowing him better too.

When they first met at Oakham Mount, her behaviour towards him was rather cold and distant. She was still carrying a grudge for his offensive remark at the assembly. At that moment, he was only a strange man who had offended her undeservingly. But since then, their acquaintance had improved and grown. However, of the depth and the nature of her feelings, he could not be certain. He had reasons to assume she recognised his attraction and welcomed it; yet much more was needed for him to decide to take the most important step of his life.

He was also aware that it was his duty to warn her about Wickham. As discreetly as possible and without many details. She needed to know he was not to be trusted. Darcy secretly planned to take a ride early in the morning, if the weather allowed it, in the hope she would go for her usual walk. Unwilling to leave everything in the hands of fate, he intended to mention to Elizabeth his hope for a short private meeting before his departure, to discuss something involving her family. After all, they had met before in similar circumstances, and it could have happened again at any time.

Equally important, he planned to dance at least one set with her. Perhaps even the first one, if she did not oppose it. Any set she preferred would do for him, he thought, delighted at the mere notion of holding her hand.

After a strong coffee, the pain diminished slightly, but the tiredness overwhelmed him. He could barely move and any noise, any voice, disturbed him as much as too much light.

He spent most of the time in bed, while Stevens packed his luggage. It was decided he would leave the next morning, straight after breakfast.

"Darcy, may I come in?" Bingley asked, standing in the

doorway. "Forgive me, I did knock."

"Do come in; I did not hear you."

"What are you doing in bed?" Bingley enquired with deep concern. "Darcy, you truly look very ill. I will send for the apothecary."

Darcy shot him a sharp glare. "Do not be ridiculous. I am fine, only a headache. And I have been sleeping terribly lately."

"You keep saying that... but you have headaches, and you look either pale or flushed, and you have stayed in bed during the day more than I have ever known you do since we first met. I am very worried! I am sure you have a bad cold!"

"Either way, the apothecary cannot help much. He will come to the ball later, I assume. But I cannot bother people on the day of the ball for a trifling cold."

"So what? Will you come to the ball as you are?"

"If you will allow me," Darcy joked.

"I will order some soup and some tea right now! And tomorrow, once we arrive in London, you will see your doctor. You must promise me that!"

"I promise I will see Dr. Cooper. And yes, I would like some soup. And some tea, if you insist."

"I do insist! So, I came to talk to you about a very delicate matter. Sir William's barouche needs time to be fixed. Until then, I have offered him my carriage. He insists he needs one and he was truly vexed about his being broken."

"I imagined as much," Darcy replied.

"So, you will have to bear us all the way back to London. I tried to purchase another one, but I could not find anything appropriate at such short notice. So, we will have to travel in your carriage. All of us," Bingley explained, slightly uneasy.

"Of course," Darcy responded. Then, a moment later, he startled.

"I actually planned to ride... You may take the carriage and the luggage."

"Ride?" Bingley cried angrily. "Have you lost your mind? You cannot ride!"

"But I cannot travel with your sister for so many hours either," Darcy mused to himself.

"Come now, Bingley! Take the carriage. You are four, I am alone. I might even catch you on the road. If I am tired, I will stop and sleep at an inn. I will meet you the day after tomorrow in town–come and have dinner with me and Georgiana."

"But Darcy!"

"Bingley, you are doing me a favour, trust me. Let us not have a debate in front of your sisters. I shall talk more with Stevens about the travelling arrangements."

"Very well. I know I cannot win an argument with you."

"Very wise decision," Darcy laughed. "By the way, did you invite Wickham to the ball?"

"I invited all the officers. Should I ask him to leave?"

"Dear Lord, no. You must not start a scandal. Leave him be. If I ignored him at the cottage, I can surely do so in a ballroom. Now be so kind as to send me that soup and let me sleep a little."

Bingley did as requested, leaving the chamber with increasing worry. He could see Darcy was not well, and his decision to ride was frightening, even though he knew Darcy had done it before, even over longer distances. He was determined to open the debate again later and to make Darcy see reason, eventually.

Late in the afternoon, after some rest, more tea and soup, Darcy's state improved. He felt much better and was pleased with his resolution. He had planned everything carefully, and nothing could go wrong. When he joined Bingley downstairs, dressed for the ball, Darcy looked like his usual self and Bingley was happy to see him thus.

They had no time for much conversation, as the Bennets' carriage–which Bingley had been expecting for a long time–

arrived.

Bingley almost ran outside to greet them, much to his sisters' disapproval. Less voluble but equally nervous and eager, Darcy followed him at a steady pace and arrived at the carriage as the ladies descended. Just in time to be bewitched by Elizabeth's beautiful face, brightened by her sparkling eyes. And the smile she offered him was the best medicine for any illness that had troubled him these past few days.

Chapter 10

B ingley welcomed the Bennets enthusiastically, smiling at Jane,
who flushed under his admiring gaze.

As soon as she stepped down, Elizabeth observed
Darcy standing behind Bingley. She caught his gaze and
shivered, blaming the cold weather. He leaned his head slightly
towards her and she replied with a little smile.

"Mr Bingley, I cannot thank you enough for inviting me,"
Mr Collins bowed low, grinning widely. "And Mr Darcy, how
fortunate to see you! I am in the favourable position to inform
you that I left Rosings yesterday and Lady Catherine was in
perfect health."

"Thank you for informing me, sir," Darcy replied briefly.

"It is my pleasure, I assure you. Her ladyship was surprised
that you were still in Hertfordshire," Mr Collins added.

"As I am surprised to see you returned so soon, Mr Collins.
Did Lady Catherine not need your assistance?"

"I truly hope she does, Mr Darcy, but she generously
allowed me to come. In fact, she insisted on my doing so..."

"We should enter. It is very cold," Mr Bingley stopped
Collins' effusions.

"Yes, yes, let us go inside. I could easily catch another cold!
Mr Collins, come. What do you think of Netherfield? Is it not a
handsome manor?" Mrs Bennet asked.

"Is it indeed, ma'am. It does not have quite as many
staircases as Rosings, but it is very handsome!" Mr Collins
declared.

"Well, too many stairs can be tiresome," Mrs Bennet said and Mr Collins quickly argued with such a preposterous notion. Nothing related to Rosings could ever be tiresome!

The group entered, led by Bingley and Jane.

Darcy remained behind, maintaining as much distance from Collins as possible. To his utter surprise, Elizabeth slowed her steps, waited for him, then walked by his side.

"Mr Darcy, I must take this brief moment to thank you again for saving us," Elizabeth said.

"Miss Bennet, I am glad we are all well after that... escapade. Nothing else matters," he replied. She glanced at him and smiled.

"And we owe that to you."

"Please do not mention it again," he pleaded with embarrassment.

By that time, they were already in the main hall, where Caroline and Louisa greeted the Bennets loudly and most insincerely.

"Very well, I shall do as you wish. But be warned that my mother is not as easy to convince and she looks forward to thanking you. You must allow us to repay you somehow," she teased him in a low voice.

He sighed with mock despair and she released a peal of laughter as their eyes met briefly.

Seeing Darcy in full light, Elizabeth's smile turned into a frown. He was pale and dark circles surrounded his eyes, making his countenance cold and severe, opposite to the warmth in his gaze.

"My mother has felt rather ill from a cold in the past few days; she only recovered yesterday. You are well, I hope?" Elizabeth attempted the delicate question.

"I am well, thank you for your care. And I am glad that Mrs Bennet is recovered," Darcy replied.

"My dear Mr Bingley, what a lovely house you have," Mr Collins' voice startled them. "Miss Bingley, Mrs Hurst, I deeply appreciate you inviting me. I can already see it will be a wonderful ball!"

"Thank you, sir. Please do enter. I can see other guests are coming," Caroline said with barely concealed rudeness.

The Bennets moved towards the ballroom, while Mr Bingley remained with his sisters to greet the new arrivals.

More guests came in a short amount of time and soon the ballroom was crowded and noisy. Colonel Forster arrived with all the officers, much to the ladies' enjoyment. Small groups were formed, conversations started, and the musicians took their places.

All the families of consequence in Meryton were there, and even some from beyond.

Soon enough, Mr Bingley joined them again and asked Jane for the first set and Elizabeth for the second. Darcy still kept away, searching for a comfortable spot in a secluded corner of the room. Caroline Bingley attempted to speak to him but he cut her short. Then Sir William, Mr Collins and Colonel Forster all greeted him and attempted to converse with him, but he only replied briefly, changing his spot to avoid the company.

While Bingley engaged Jane in small talk, Elizabeth allowed them privacy and retired, leaning against the wall. She looked for Charlotte and spotted her across the room, talking to Mr Collins. Charlotte seemed strangely preoccupied with the discussion, and Elizabeth wondered if it was about Rosings or Lady Catherine.

She walked along the wall, looking around, until she passed Darcy, who stood alone and lonely by the window. Their eyes met and she slowed her steps; he looked pale and distant as always, and she was sure he was employing his time criticising people and despising the ball itself. Hero or not, friendly or not, his pride and haughtiness were not easy to change. He unexpectedly smiled at her; she flushed, smiled back and stopped.

"Miss Bennet."

"Mr Darcy." As they were now facing each other, he looked even paler and she watched him with concern. "Sir, are you well?"

"I am, thank you. I am only looking for a bit of peace and solitude," he replied. "But it is not easy to find in the middle of a party."

"True. Forgive me, I shall leave. I did not mean to interrupt your solitary reverie."

"You did not; quite the contrary. I am grateful for your concern but it is not needed."

"I am glad to hear that. Forgive me, but you look unwell."

He forced a smile. "I am sorry you think so. I was hoping to look dashing enough to convince you to accept my request. But I am afraid I will have to face another failure."

His attempt at teasing surprised Elizabeth and made her cheeks turn crimson.

She stared at him in disbelief.

"What request would that be, sir?"

"Well, I have given much consideration to our earlier conversation and I have decided how you can thank me, if you truly want to," Darcy said in a teasing tone that surprised and exhilarated Elizabeth.

"Indeed? Do tell me!"

"Would you do me the honour of dancing a set with me? Perhaps the first one, if you are not otherwise engaged? Or I would be happy with any other set that is preferable to you."

The invitation surprised Elizabeth even more, and its implication left her silent and bewildered. That Darcy asked her to dance was astonishing enough. But the first set? Surely he must be aware of the implication of such a request. Was he being serious or was he still teasing her? She stared at him for a long moment and in her hesitation, frowned at him. He had been sure of her acceptance and suddenly it appeared he had to face rejection.

"Miss Bennet?"

Lost in shared misunderstanding and amazement, neither noticed Wickham approaching, until he called Elizabeth's name for a second time.

"Miss Bennet?"

"What?" she asked in an unladylike manner, then quickly gathered her composure.

"Mr Wickham..." She smiled and curtseyed.

"Forgive me, I hope I am not disturbing you?" he continued, with a most charming smile. Both he and Darcy were struggling to ignore each other.

"Actually, Mr Darcy and I were in the middle of an important discussion," she said, hoping Wickham would leave. Instead, he grinned.

"I came to ask for the favour of the first set. And perhaps another one later," Wickham continued with self-confidence.

Elizabeth breathed deeply; she had imagined the purpose of Wickham's approach, but his friendly manners made her uneasy. There was no hesitation in his tone, as he surely expected a ready acceptance.

She put a proper smile on her face. "I would be glad to dance the third set with you, if that is agreeable."

Wickham was slightly surprised but he reluctantly replied, "Excellent, thank you." And yet, he remained near her, prolonging the awkward situation.

"If you do not mind, Mr Darcy and I must finish our earlier conversation before the dance starts," Elizabeth addressed Wickham, with determination combined with such sweetness that she left him no choice.

"Oh...I see...Yes, of course," he mumbled, then took a few steps away, joining his fellow officers.

Only then did Elizabeth turn to Darcy, who had been a silent spectator to the whole scene.

They looked at each other. His expression was severe, his eyes darkened and his pallor had increased. Wickham's nearness appeared to be disturbing for him and his efforts to bear it were obvious.

"I am already engaged for the first two sets. The first one to my cousin, Mr Collins, the second one to Mr Bingley," Elizabeth explained.

Their conversation was perfectly proper in a room full of people, but a strange nervousness stirred Elizabeth inside.

"I see," Darcy responded with such apparent disappointment that Elizabeth's heart raced.

"Would the supper dance be convenient?" she offered, feeling her cheeks burning at such a bold attempt. Had another woman already proposed the set to Mr Darcy, she wondered?

His face brightened immediately.

"Perfect," he replied briefly. He hesitated to speak further, and she was again puzzled by his apparent uneasiness.

"Miss Bennet, there is another thing… I do not know if Bingley has informed your sister yet. Tomorrow morning we are all leaving for London. I am not sure about the length of our stay in town, but I suspect Bingley will return before I do."

Again, she was caught entirely unguarded. She looked around the room for her sister and saw her talking to Mr Bingley and his sisters. Jane looked as serene as always and Mr Bingley full of joyful awe.

An icy hole developed in her stomach, and she searched for something to say to conceal her unexpected dismay. Why would Mr Darcy's departure upset her so? She was being completely unreasonable and absurd.

"It is not an unpleasant situation that takes you back to London so suddenly, I hope," she replied.

"No, not at all. I have long planned to return to London to spend Christmas with my sister, although my previous plan has changed significantly lately," he said. He was avoiding her eyes and Elizabeth thought she noticed a trace of redness on his neck. Was he embarrassed by something?

"I see…but you intend to return, you said?" she continued, tormented by her own inquisitive boldness.

"Yes."

"And Mr Bingley?" She knew she had no right to ask so many questions but he did not seem to disapprove.

"Bingley has some important and unexpected business. Forgive me but I am not comfortable providing you with more information. I am sure he will tell your sister all the details," Darcy answered.

"Of course. As long as all is well," Elizabeth agreed. To her surprise, he continued.

"I will leave later than the rest of the party and I was wondering… Is there any chance that you still enjoy walking early in the morning?"

This time, her amazement was complete. "Yes, I do … every morning, when the weather allows me…"

"I am glad to hear that… If we happen to meet tomorrow morning, there is something that I would like to speak to you about. Something related to a common acquaintance. Please, do not worry, it is nothing grave. But I thought it would be fair for me to provide you with some information that you and your father may find important and useful."

Elizabeth was now lost; her mind spun, trying to guess what he could tell her that would require a private meeting in the woods. It was clearly not in regard to her. But who could be the common acquaintance about whom he possessed private information? Mr Bingley? Mr Wickham? Mr Collins?

"I hope I have not disturbed you," he whispered.

She startled and looked at him. "A little," she admitted. "But a long walk in the morning would be beneficial in any circumstances," she concluded.

He looked so content that Elizabeth was left with even more questions. Why was the meeting so important to him? She had no time to enquire further though, as the music started and Mr Collins walked towards them, bending over and grinning with satisfaction.

"My dear Miss Elizabeth, I have come to claim your hand… for the first set. Mr Darcy, I heartily thank you for keeping company with my cousin."

"It was my pleasure, I assure you," Darcy replied, exchanging a glance with Elizabeth as she departed with Mr

Collins. His mind, still foggy from tiredness and the ill state that had troubled him for days, started to speculate.

What was in that ridiculous man's mind? Surely he could not consider pursuing Elizabeth! Was he completely irrational?

The musicians tuned their instruments and the music cut through Darcy's temples. It sounded so loud that he could hardly bear it.

Bingley and Miss Jane Bennet led the dance. Couples took their place in line and his eyes met with Elizabeth's annoyed glance. He tried to smile at her but she looked utterly uncomfortable.

Wickham was dancing with Mary King, a young lady whom Darcy had seen for the first time that evening. Darcy planned to watch him closely, but his headache allowed him little strength for such intense scrutiny. He would speak to Elizabeth the next morning and she would know what to tell Mr Bennet to avoid any danger from Wickham's disgraceful behaviour.

The first set started. With the impressive number of officers, all the young ladies were engaged for the dance, while the married ladies were sitting by the wall, enjoying tea, sweets and a bit of gossip.

Darcy retired to a corner with a glass of brandy. His head felt sore and his temples were burning, his neckcloth restricted his breathing. His gloves felt like a trap on his heated hands. His entire body was warm, unbearably warm.

He watched people lost in noisy discussions. The music sounded so loud that his head felt pierced by knives. The light was so powerful that his eyes could hardly bear it. He wondered if there were too many candles or simply his disposition was inappropriate for such an event. He had never found a ball more tiresome and disturbing than this one. He wished for nothing else but peace and silence and darkness but he was there for her, for Elizabeth. For that half hour when he would dance with her. And he had already been rewarded by their short encounter earlier, when he felt alone with her in the room filled with people, by her smiles and teasing and by her generously offering him the supper set.

It was worth bearing the crowd, the noise, the discomfort, for the opportunity to see her, to fill his mind with her image, to carry with him as many memories as possible for the time he would be in London. He was delighted by her easy acceptance at meeting him in the morning. He could see she was surprised, but not displeased. Just as she was taken aback by him asking her to dance. Had he been so ungentlemanlike in manners that she did not expect even a simple dance request? Or was she stunned by him asking for the first set? It was always a meaningful one and people would have surely gossiped about it, just as they were now talking about Bingley and Miss Bennet, and about Elizabeth and that Collins man.

Elizabeth's uneasiness seemed to increase during the dance and he felt the need to protect her. It was a silly, but strong impulse, against which he had to fight. And only inches from him, Mrs Bennet was discussing the future of her daughters with Lady Lucas and Mrs Phillips.

"If I could see Jane at Netherfield and one of my other daughters married to Mr Collins as the future mistress of Longbourn, I would wish for nothing more. Seeing my daughters well married is my only desire and all I pray for."

"But sister, I believe you must not worry about Jane any longer," Mrs Phillips replied. "And Mr Collins seems to favour Lizzy, which is only right. She is the second in age and beauty."

"My dear sister, if only Lizzy would not be so stubborn. I worry about her constantly. I saw her talking to Mr Darcy earlier and I pray she did not say something to upset him. I know Mr Darcy's opinion carries much weight with Mr Bingley," Mrs Bennet said.

Lady Lucas whispered something to her companion and all the ladies turned to look at Darcy. They nodded to him, he responded, and the ladies continued to speak in a lower voice.

Another thought caused Darcy a slight panic. He was about to leave the following day. Was there any chance that

Elizabeth would accept a marriage proposal from that man? But could she afford to reject it?

He realised that the situation was not favourable to any of them. Bingley was leaving the next morning without any arrangement between him and Jane Bennet. Therefore, a future engagement, though desired and presumed by all parties, was still uncertain. Under those circumstances, if the man to inherit Longbourn and to be responsible for their fate proposed to any of them, who would dare refuse and jeopardise the family's safety?

But still–could any parent force a woman like Elizabeth to marry someone like Collins? What parent would want such a tragic fate for a daughter? He glanced at Mrs Bennet–who was talking and gesticulating wildly, pointing at the dance floor. There was the answer–in front of his eyes.

The notion of seeing Elizabeth married to Collins–or to any other man– made him nauseous. His head ached so badly that he had to close his eyes to seek some relief.

"Mr Darcy? Are you well, sir?"

He startled, looking around somewhat confused.

"Mr Bennet. I am well, thank you. Why would you presume otherwise? Forgive me, but Miss Elizabeth asked the same thing earlier. I am starting to worry about my appearance," he joked.

"Forgive me for saying so, but you look rather ill. However, since you are amused, I might be wrong."

"I have a slight headache. It might be because I am not very fond of balls," Darcy replied in jest.

Mr Bennet nodded in agreement. "I can well understand that. Sir, I want to express my gratitude for your heroic rescue of my family. It was as generous as it was brave. My wife and daughters would have been in serious danger without you."

"Please do not mention it, sir. I did no more than any other man would have done."

"If only he had been able to. If it was I who happened to be with them, I would have been of no use, as I have no knowledge of calming a wild horse, nor how to start a fire from nothing. But in my defence, neither of the two officers–the ladies' favourites–were in any way better. Admittedly I did not expect such skills in a gentleman who does not need them," Mr Bennet said.

"I used to spend much time outside with my father, uncle and cousins. We learned many things that we might not need on a daily basis but would be helpful in dangerous situations."

"So you did and we were happy to benefit from them. To Mrs Bennet, you are more of a hero than if you had won a battle!"

"I am happy to see Mrs Bennet recovered. I know she has been ill."

"Well, thank you, it was only a trifling cold."

"I am glad. And all the Miss Bennets seem in good health."

"They are. All thanks to you."

"I am glad I could be of help."

Each took a sip of wine, while watching the dancers.

"I noticed you watched Mrs Bennet earlier," Mr Bennet eventually spoke. "I know you disapprove of our family's manners and I am aware you rightfully do so. Mrs Bennet's public discussions of her daughters' marriages seem especially appalling to you and I cannot blame you."

Darcy startled, staring at his companion. He did not expect such an open approach to such a delicate matter.

"Mr Bennet, I do not..."

"Come now, Mr Darcy. It is obvious that you loathed hearing about Jane marrying your friend or Lizzy marrying Mr Collins. Just as I am sure you despise hearing about Mrs Bennet arranging husbands for our daughters. You cannot deny that, and I admit my own personal feeling is not far from yours."

"Mr Bennet, my opinion means little to anyone. What I think I am keeping to myself," Darcy said.

"Not quite," Mr Bennet laughed. "I do not wish to be impertinent, but your expression is quite open and apparent. I imagine it is not just I, but everyone else who is able to read your thoughts."

"My thoughts should be private and I will keep them that

way. I apologise if I was not careful enough."

"You seem to disapprove of everything and everyone, Mr Darcy. And yet, you were generous enough to jeopardise your own life to save some unknown people. If I were bold enough, I would ask which one is the real Mr Darcy? The proud and arrogant one or the hero? The one who criticises my family's behaviour or the one who seems to enjoy spending time in our company?"

"I am certainly not a hero, Mr Bennet. I did what was required under the circumstances, and I would do it anytime if needed. And I surely do not despise everyone. In fact, the better I know Miss Bennet and Miss Elizabeth the more I come to admire them. And I have enjoyed the time I have spent with your family."

"I am glad to hear that. But I think it would be more accurate to say you enjoy spending time with some of my family."

"I believe very few of us enjoy everyone's company," Darcy declared.

Mr Bennet smiled and approved. "True. And I am one of them. In this, we are very much alike."

The music soon stopped and the couples joined their families and friends. Mr Collins was holding Elizabeth's arm and continued to talk close to her ear while she was obviously trying to keep some distance. He frowned, forgetting that Mr Bennet was watching.

"Mr Collins is surely not one of those whose company any of us enjoy," Mr Bennet said.

Darcy startled and looked at him.

"And yet, your aunt, Lady Catherine de Bourgh, granted him her good opinion and her protection. His position, his situation in life, her patronage, would surely make him a desirable husband. Would you not agree?"

Darcy could not decide if Mr Bennet was being genuine in his statement or only mocked him, so he replied politely.

"I believe it depends on the lady who will be his wife.

Mr Collins has a steady income, he seems to be serious about his duties and I assume he will be careful and attentive to his family."

"Indeed. Sadly for him, he seems to have chosen in such a way that he will face a severe and painful rejection. I almost pity him," Mr Bennet continued, offering Darcy the relief he needed to ease his fear.

He should not have doubted either Elizabeth or her father. One would never accept such a marriage proposal, and the other would never force her to make such a sacrifice.

Now, he had time to act according to his desires. He had to arrange his plans carefully, so he did not delay his return too much.

By that time, Elizabeth and her sisters were in a group surrounded by officers. Wickham's closeness to Elizabeth displeased Darcy even more, although he had little reason to worry in that regard. But Lydia and Kitty, as well as Maria Lucas, seemed to have forgotten their manners under the officers' charms.

"Forgive me, I must have a word with my youngest daughters," Mr Bennet said, excusing himself from Darcy.

"Mr Bennet!" Darcy called after him and the gentleman turned. "In case we do not have another chance to speak tonight, I want to inform you we will all depart for London tomorrow morning."

"Really? That is unexpected. You will not be away too long, I hope," Mr Bennet responded with obvious concern.

"Bingley intends to stay away for as short a time as possible. I plan to spend Christmas in town with my sister, so I am not certain of my plans yet. But if I may be of some use, if there is a certain book you would like to acquire or anything else from town, just let me know."

That mere statement was enough for both to understand that his return, although not established, was beyond doubt. Mr Bennet bowed to him.

"You are too kind, Mr Darcy. I wish you a safe journey and

we will anticipate seeing you again at Netherfield when your plans allow it."

"Likewise, Mr Bennet."

Elizabeth's father left and the music started again. The pairs returned to the dance floor; voices and laughter were all around and Darcy's headache increased. He gulped a little more wine, but he felt even warmer and could hardly breathe. He exited into the hallway, hiding from anyone who could approach him and rested against a wall. A moment later, he decided to retire to the library for a little while but was startled by Mr Collins repeatedly calling his name. He had no other choice but to stop and bear the boredom.

Chapter 11

"**M**y dear Mr Darcy, there is an extraordinary favour that I dare beg you grant me!"

"What is it, Mr Collins?"

"It is a delicate matter that I would never dare to bring to you if it did not have Lady Catherine's support."

"If it is delicate, it should probably remain private," Darcy said, eager to be left alone.

"It would usually of course, but your opinion is too important to me, and I cannot miss this opportunity since God has placed you in my path."

"Mr Collins, please be more specific. I have a slight headache, and it is difficult for me to follow you."

"I deeply apologise, sir. The favour I am asking you is in regard to my cousin, Miss Elizabeth Bennet."

The pain in Darcy's head and chest grew. "What favour can I possibly provide regarding Miss Bennet?"

"You see, Lady Catherine has advised me to marry, and she suggested I choose one of my cousins. After much discussion with Mrs Bennet, I understand the eldest cousin is no longer available, therefore I have shifted my interest to the second one. I believe Miss Elizabeth will be the perfect wife, with her enchanting presence, lovely smiles, and her delightful liveliness. I intend to propose tomorrow."

"I see," Darcy said, surprised by how cold his own voice sounded. "And how may I help you in this endeavour? I am rather uncomfortable speaking about a young lady who is not even my relative. I cannot see why my involvement is desired."

"I would very much desire your opinion, Mr Darcy. I have seen you talking to Miss Elizabeth, and I know you are somewhat familiar with the Bennet family. Do you think she is a proper choice for me? Would Lady Catherine be pleased?" Mr Collins enquired pleadingly.

Darcy breathed deeply, careful to select the appropriate words. He knew he could easily be honest and simply say no! Lady Catherine would loathe Elizabeth's wit and her stubbornness that he admired so much. And he was already confident that Elizabeth would reject Collins's proposal in any case, so the entire conversation was useless and tiresome.

"Mr Collins, I can easily admit that Miss Elizabeth Bennet is one of the most remarkable women I have met. And, if your affection for her is strong enough and if you are certain that she shares the same feelings, you should not worry about Lady Catherine or anybody else's approval."

Mr Collins stared at him with his eyes wide open in disbelief. "I beg your pardon, sir, what do you mean? There is nothing more important to me than her ladyship's appreciation, and I could never make a decision that would not meet with her approval."

"Then it appears an unhappy alternative is before you, Mr Collins. And I am puzzled as to how I can solve this dilemma," Darcy responded severely.

"But...what do you mean, sir? Would Lady Catherine not approve of Miss Elizabeth?"

"I do not know Miss Elizabeth well enough to make a sound judgment, but I do know Lady Catherine. She does not like stubborn, obstinate people and does not tolerate any opposition. So if you believe Miss Elizabeth is a modest, obedient, docile person, one who would always accept Lady Catherine's suggestions and never contradict her, then you have nothing to worry about."

"Oh..." Mr Collins mumbled, glancing back to the ballroom and spotting Elizabeth talking and laughing with the officers. "I see...so...do you think I should..."

"Mr Collins, I am in no disposition and have no desire to continue this conversation. I am sure you are able to decide what is best for you. Now, you must excuse me," Darcy said and departed hastily, leaving Collins to stare across the crowded room.

Once in the library, Darcy slumped down on the sofa, closing his eyes. To himself, he could not deny he was ill. He needed a doctor, but he had no time for that. He only had to bear it for one more day. By tomorrow evening he would be in London, after he had talked to Elizabeth.

He rang and asked for tea and for his valet, waiting with his eyes closed. He was still warm, so he opened the window. The air was cold but refreshing, and he could breathe more easily.

As he rested, he heard the music from the ballroom and wondered which set it was. Elizabeth was probably dancing with that scoundrel.

He would have to dance a couple of other sets too, or at least one with Caroline Bingley. Otherwise, he would never hear the end of it. Besides, dancing only one set with Elizabeth would be rather impolite and strange enough to raise all sorts of rumours while he was away.

His valet arrived with his tea.

"Mr Darcy, are you well?" Stevens asked with concern. "I have been worried about your state for days now. Sir, forgive my boldness, but we should delay our return for a day or two and talk to the apothecary. You cannot travel in such a condition, and certainly not alone!"

Darcy dismissed him with a small gesture. "I thank you for your care, but I will be fine. I have some significant business to finish tomorrow morning, and I cannot delay it. But I have not lost my mind, I know I cannot ride to London in this weather. Here is the plan–I have already informed Bingley about it."

"Very well, sir," Stevens replied, surprised and attentive.

"You will leave with the others but stop at the first inn–I do not recall its name."

"The Red Horse Inn, sir."

"Yes, yes. Stop there, take two rooms and wait for me. Hire a carriage to take us to London. Bingley will inform Georgiana that we will arrive later, maybe even the day after tomorrow. I will only have to ride for less than an hour."

"Oh, I see. That is a relief, sir. Mr Bingley sent for some medicine from the apothecary earlier today. May I bring you a herbal drink now?" Stevens tried prudently. Darcy was too tired to oppose him.

"Yes, go and fetch it. But quickly, as I am engaged for a set soon," he said to his dumbfounded valet. In his many years in Darcy's service, he had never known his master preoccupied with having to dance a set.

Stevens returned minutes later, and Darcy drank the medicine in one gulp, then dismissed the valet. He took a few moments to rest before summoning the courage to return to the noisy ballroom.

His peace was shattered as voices sounded through the window.

"I am telling you, Miss Elizabeth Bennet is one of the most fascinating women I have met. And I meet plenty."

Wickham's voice and laughter startled Darcy and he rose immediately, approaching the window. A group of officers was gathered outside, enjoying their cigars and amusing themselves.

"She is too sharp for my taste," someone replied. "I much prefer the sweet, docile type."

"So do I, but I am always intrigued by a challenge, and Miss Elizabeth is surely one," Wickham said sarcastically. "I have never met a woman who could resist my charms, and I cannot allow it to happen now."

"What sort of challenge? You cannot consider pursuing her; I heard they have a very small dowry, if any," another voice said. "Why waste your time?"

"Conquering a beautiful woman is never a waste of time," Wickham laughed. "And I am considering pursuing her, just not marrying her."

"You should not play with fire if you do not wish to burn your fingers. Miss Elizabeth does not seem the kind of woman to trifle with."

"And speaking of fire, I heard you didn't excel in starting one," another man mocked Wickham, and more laughter flew around.

"Yes, yes, very amusing," Wickham responded. "Why would I have bothered with such a task? Even more so, when I could watch Darcy acting like a servant, kneeling at the fireplace? It was too beautiful a picture to miss, one that I will vividly remember for a long while!"

"Dear Lord, do not start talking about Darcy again," someone demanded. "You may say whatever you want, but I heard he jumped on a running horse that you could not handle."

"Shut your mouth, Davidson. You still owe me some money from the last card game," Wickham ended the conversation sharply.

"Come, let us go back; the next set is about to start!" Darcy heard, then the sound of footsteps indicating the last suggestion was quickly followed, and then silence fell outside again, as the music started.

Darcy's discomfort was now mixed with profound anger and a trace of panic. That crook appeared to have taken many liberties in speaking to his companions. That Wickham sullied Darcy's name was no surprise, but did he dare mention something about Georgiana?

Darcy needed only a moment to decide to talk to Colonel Forster the following day, before his departure. He was not sure what and how much he would disclose to the colonel, but a fair warning about Wickham, including his inclination for drinking, incurring gaming debts, and seducing innocent young women was necessary.

Darcy reluctantly returned to the ballroom. His headache had diminished, but his stomach was hurting now–and he was increasingly warm. The light and the noise hit him, and he paused in the doorway.

It was the fourth set and Elizabeth—as well as her sisters—was still dancing. Mr Bennet was talking to Sir William, while Mrs Bennet remained with the same company she had been in earlier.

Mr Collins was now dancing with Charlotte Lucas and both seemed to be enjoying their time. Darcy had come to consider Miss Lucas a sensible young lady, but he knew nothing much of her. Seeing her standing face to face with Mr Collins, he wondered if she would willingly trade her sense and sensibility for a safe and comfortable future.

Bingley and his sisters were also on the dance floor, while Colonel Forster spoke animatedly with a group of ladies. Wickham joined them, much to the ladies' enjoyment. That man was not to be trusted anywhere around respectable young women, Darcy mused, pleased with his decision to talk to the colonel.

The half an hour passed painfully slowly for Darcy. It was almost midnight, and he wondered how long the ball might last. Bingley and his sisters tried to engage him in conversation, but he was not in any disposition for any kind of discussion.

To his relief, the music stopped and started again and finally it was time for him to claim Elizabeth's hand for the supper set.

Although the headache was gone, his head was spinning. He moved towards Elizabeth—she was with her family in the opposite corner. She saw him and smiled, their eyes locked.

It seemed days since he had asked for a set and she had offered one that pleased them both. She was slightly flustered and he thought it was because of the heat in the room. His own cheeks were burning.

His feet were unsteady but brought him closer to her. He was finally there, bowing to her. Her sisters and mother looked at them with puzzlement. Mrs Bennet's eyebrow rose in wonder.

He bowed to her slightly. "Miss Elizabeth?"

"Mr Darcy..."

Elizabeth stretched her hand out to him and he took it.

They walked towards the dancefloor holding hands and their eyes met again when they faced each other. Then the orchestra began to play, the music filled the room and they followed it with harmonious moves. Their fingers touched each other again from time to time, their eyes met and lingered an instant too long, both astonished by the strange feelings that enveloped them— feelings that one of them had already admitted and accepted, yet the other had only just begun to struggle with, wondering about their nature and strength.

Near the wall, Mrs Bennet watched in disbelief, staring at the couple for a long while. And she was not the only one–not by far.

With the prospect of an upcoming meeting, Darcy and Elizabeth found little to speak of. But, during the second dance, Elizabeth was already troubled and found the courage to speak openly.

"Mr Darcy, forgive my boldness, but you are truly pale, sir. I admit you are one of the most skilful dancers I have had the pleasure of standing up with, but you do not look well," she said, trying to keep a trace of a joke in her voice.

"I am sorry that you are displeased with my appearance, but I find some comfort in your compliments regarding my dancing skills," he smiled in reply.

They continued to dance, speaking a little about the number of pairs and about the arrangements for the ball but mostly looking at each other in silence, each preparing what they had to say for the next morning. That little secret, that small conspiracy, made them gaze at each other in a certain way, indefinable but not unnoticed by the others.

Mrs Bennet continued to talk to Mrs Phillips, never taking her eyes from her second daughter and her companion. Wickham and Bingley's sisters were staring at the couple with equal curiosity. Mr Darcy dancing with Elizabeth Bennet–of all ladies–quickly became the talk of the ball.

As soon as the music ended, Darcy offered Elizabeth his arm and they walked towards the supper table, with all eyes still on them.

"Mr Darcy," Elizabeth whispered, "I will tell you this and then I shall not speak another word on the subject."

He looked at her, puzzled by her seriousness.

"Sir, your hand is very warm. You must have a high fever. I know it is not for me to give you advice, but you should rest and take some medicine."

Their eyes met briefly. Her concern was genuine and he did not attempt to deny or to joke about it. "Thank you, Miss Bennet. I will do just that," he answered.

Darcy was having the most pleasant time he ever remembered having at a ball. Since the evening had started, a bond between him and Elizabeth had slowly grown. There was no special gesture, no particular conversation, just many small things together that gave him a feeling of completion and enjoyment he had never sensed before with any other woman.

Elizabeth was in the centre of a tumult of thoughts and feelings, all spinning around Darcy. She had come to enjoy his company exceedingly and to seek out opportunities for small conversations and meaningful glances. He undoubtedly had singled her out, not only by dancing with her but also by talking to her in a private way, seeking to be close to her, smiling at her in a peculiar way. Had he behaved the same before and she had missed it, or had his behaviour changed in recent days? She was delighted by his warm, friendly manners and wished for more–without knowing what more she could hope for. Her regret for his pending departure had turned into sorrow by the end of the ball, and she was grateful for having one more chance to talk to him, whatever reason he might have for that private encounter.

At the supper table they sat opposite one another. Looking at each other was an easy task, but conversation proved to be rather difficult. Bingley was near Elizabeth, opposite Jane, who sat between his sisters.

The officers were seated at one end of the table, around Colonel Forster. Closest to them were Mr Bennet and his youngest daughters. Conversations carried on across the table became rather chaotic. Above it all, Mr Collins' voice could be heard from time to time, as well as Mrs Bennet's.

The rest of the evening passed with little excitement. Some of the ladies sang for the guests–including Mary–some card games were played by several gentlemen and officers, and more dancing was performed.

Elizabeth barely spoke to Darcy at all. He refused to retire early, but he remained silent and did not dance again. She danced a couple more sets but her attention and interest did not reside with her dancing partners.

Late in the night the ball ended and the guests left after expressing much praise and gratitude for such a wonderful evening.

The Bennets–together with Mr Collins–were among the last to leave. Mr Bingley and Mr Darcy both took a formal farewell, as they planned to travel to London immediately after breakfast. Wishes for a safe journey and hopes for a speedy return were expressed and finally they separated.

In the carriage, Mrs Bennet voiced her approval for the evening repeatedly and insistently, mentioning Mr Darcy singling out Elizabeth. She was certain it had been his way of apologising for offending her at the previous assembly, his consideration for the family, and his support for his friend's upcoming engagement to Jane.

An hour later, silence fell over Longbourn. It was already time for the servants to wake up, and tiredness should have defeated Jane and Elizabeth but they remained awake, talking under the sheets, exchanging opinions. As always, Elizabeth was more voluble than her sister, but she was careful with her words, worrying she might say more than she wished to.

"Lizzy, I am afraid Mr Bingley will not return," Jane suddenly said and Elizabeth startled, dumbfounded.

"What do you mean, Jane? Why would you say that when Mr Bingley mentioned even at the end that he planned to return in a fortnight?"

Unexpectedly, Jane began to sob, much to Elizabeth's

despair. "Dearest, look at me! Why would you say that? What happened?"

"Oh, Lizzy...Caroline told me they have some important business in town but they are also eager to see Miss Darcy. She suggested Mr Bingley is very fond of her and he misses her dearly. Even he told me as much–he said he planned to spend much time with her and with Mr Darcy while he is in town. He said Miss Darcy is one of the most accomplished ladies he has ever met. He even said I would surely like her. And Caroline said the entire family hopes and prays for such a union to take place and that it would have surely occurred by now if Miss Darcy was not so young!"

Jane spoke through gulping sobs and her suffering was so deep that it broke Elizabeth's heart.

Caressing Jane's hair, she thought of everything that had happened that night, of her discussions with Darcy, of the small things he had mentioned or shared with her.

"Lizzy, please believe me that I am happy for him. I wish him to find the woman who is best suited to him and who will make him happy. And I am sure Miss Darcy is a perfect choice. I cannot blame him or his family for preferring her. But it hurts so much, it is so hard to bear the pain."

Elizabeth held Jane tightly while her sister cried in her arms. Hurt on her sister's behalf, angry at anyone who could harm Jane, Elizabeth needed a while to see reason. Eventually, she managed to calm herself enough to comfort her sister.

"My dear, let us be reasonable. Please think carefully if Mr Bingley said or did anything to suggest that he would prefer another over you. He is an honest man and would never deceive you on purpose. Why would he host such a ball without Miss Darcy, if she is his choice?"

"I do not know, Lizzy. I cannot understand it. He was so kind, so gentle...he said he would call on us as soon as he returns and that he wishes to speak to me about something important. Maybe he intends to tell me about his engagement to Miss Darcy...Maybe...I do not know."

"Or maybe this is all just Miss Bingley's attempt to separate her brother from you! I have no doubt that she wishes him to marry Miss Darcy, but I cannot believe she will succeed. Everybody who sees you together can testify to his affection for you!"

Elizabeth struggled to calm Jane and help her find some rest. She would soon discover the truth and all this torment would be gone. In a few hours, she would meet Darcy and would ask him directly, even if he took it as an offence and breach of propriety. She refused to allow her sister to suffer out of consideration for him or his sister.

She would only have to wait a little while. Her reason told her such a scenario was impossible, but then, all sorts of thoughts broke her confidence. Perhaps this is what Darcy wished to tell her, and she had misjudged him and his intentions completely.

Eventually, Jane's crying ceased but Elizabeth's torment increased. And so it happened that, while one of the sisters fell asleep in exhaustion and despair, the other one remained alert and distressed, staring out of the window waiting for a glimpse of light.

As the darkness was still deep and heavy, tiredness eventually defeated Elizabeth too. The dawn came and went, and, unlike other mornings, she did not wake up from her deep rest until a rumble of thunder and a gust of wind rattled the window.

Startled, Elizabeth jumped from the bed, meeting Jane's astonished gaze. "Lizzy, what happened?"

"Nothing...It is just..." She looked around–it must already be breakfast time.

Panicked, she hesitated a moment, looking outside. It was cloudy and the weather had seemed to worsen. Had she missed the chance to meet Darcy?

She started to dress, while Jane still looked at her with puzzlement.

"It has been raining all morning, this is such unpleasant

weather! Breakfast is not ready yet. Everybody in the house is still in their chambers," Jane explained.

"I see," Elizabeth answered absently, putting on her gown. Had he left already, or was he still waiting for her? After all, it was his desire to speak to her. He could not expect her to walk before dawn! And why did he not call at Longbourn? Surely her father would not have opposed him talking to her, even privately. What was his strange decision, she wondered, as she tied her bonnet and put on her gloves.

"The party at Netherfield has left," Jane continued. "Very early this morning; Hill told me that. They seemed eager to arrive in town as soon as possible."

"It is a long drive to London, so it is wise that they left early," Elizabeth agreed.

"Yes, you are right. But Lizzy, where are you going?" Jane asked, suddenly realising her sister's intentions.

"I need to walk, Jane. I have a headache and some fresh air will help me. If I am late, please do not wait for me with breakfast. I am not hungry at all."

"What do you mean, not wait for you? Mama will not accept it."

"Then I shall try to return before breakfast."

"But Lizzy, it has rained all morning and it looks like it is raining again. And it is very cold. You cannot walk by yourself. May I join you?"

"Dearest, please stay at home. It is cold, and you do not even like to walk. I would much rather go by myself. I will not be out long," Elizabeth said, embracing Jane and then leaving the room in haste.

She left the house, and the cold air blew in her face. It smelled like winter and it felt the same.

Elizabeth stepped carefully, her shoes unsteady on the slippery ground. Leaving the garden, she took the main path. It was cloudy, and the sky darkened again. She briefly wondered how Darcy could ride to London, once the rain started. He surely could not feel much better than the previous night, and his apparent state would not allow him to ride such a long distance in such weather.

She walked on decidedly, determined to convince him to see reason. Perhaps he could stay one more day. After all, Netherfield was empty but not deserted. One day would make no difference to anyone, except him, his health, and his safety.

Elizabeth started to climb the path to Oakham Mount. Longbourn was behind her; in front, only trees, sad and desolate, leaning in the wind, and above, an ominous, dark sky.

She tried to scrutinise the road, but there was not much to see. Everything was grey and foggy and windy and a few drops of rain fell.

She heard a horse whinnying from between the trees, but, as there was no rider visible and no carriage in sight, she hastened her steps. She wished to avoid any meeting that would delay her even more and, whoever it was, she had no time and no patience for a polite encounter.

Curiosity was the main reason for her eagerness, but, although reluctant to admit it, there were other feelings, stronger and more distressing, that pushed her to meet Darcy, despite the cold and threatening clouds.

She knew the rain could start even before she reached Oakham Mount, but, once she was with him, they could return to Longbourn together.

So she continued to walk, shivering inside and out with chills, until she reached the spot where they had met some weeks ago. Once there, she breathed deeply, looking around and down into the valley, her heart racing from the effort and from anticipation.

But there was nothing and nobody waiting for her. She was alone, in the middle of the unfriendly weather, surrounded by bare trees, her own tormenting thoughts and disappointment.

The party had already left Netherfield hours ago. So he either was there and did not wait, or did not even bother to come.

If he wished to talk to her and could not wait he surely would have sent a note to Longbourn. He would have found a way to reach her, instead of letting her walk like a simpleton, in freezing weather, putting her health in danger. She worried so much about his health and he cared nothing for hers.

Clearly the suggested meeting was only a whim, perhaps induced by having one too many drinks. Why was she such a fool to accept it? She should have told him to come to Longbourn, as any honourable man would do.

Or perhaps he wished to confess about Bingley's engagement to his sister?

Could Caroline have been right and Darcy such a deceiving scoundrel?

After minutes of turmoil, pacing around furiously, Elizabeth's agitation took a turn for the worse, just like the weather. The wind blew stronger, the cold was now sharp, and drops of rain fell relentlessly.

Growing angrier, amid the sound of thunder echoing around her, Elizabeth turned her back on the place where her hopes had been so utterly ruined and almost ran back home.

Step by step, moment by moment, the meeting she so eagerly awaited remained behind her, while Longbourn appeared in her sight. Tears of anger rolled down her face, combined with the drops of rain.

What a ridiculous, gullible fool she was! What did she expect Darcy had to tell her? What extraordinary secret had she expected? What other reasonable woman would have walked impetuously to meet a man in the middle of nowhere, with the threat of a storm looming?

How stupid, ridiculous and thoughtless she had been!

When she descended the slope towards Longbourn, the rain intensified as much as her rage–against Darcy and against herself. She startled only when, even through the sound of rain and wind, she heard the same horse whinnying again.

She stopped and listened carefully, looking around. What horse would stay in the same place for such a long while? Was it caught on something? What could the poor animal do? She briefly recollected Darcy's care for the horses when they had been caught in the storm, but quickly dismissed the memory.

Stepping carefully off the main path, she glanced around, calling. "Hello? Is anyone there? Hello?"

She shouted a few more times, entering further into the grove of trees. The whinnying sounded closer, and she finally spotted the horse, with the reins hanging loosely from its neck.

She moved closer, her eyes narrowing to better see what was happening.

The horse shuffled its feet a little but did not move.

Fighting her fear of horses, Elizabeth approached carefully, talking to the animal. With horror, she noticed a man lying on the ground, with the loose end of the reins tightly knotted around his leg. The rain continued to fall, and her heart beat wildly.

"Sir? Are you hurt?" she asked in a low voice, and the horse neighed again. She stepped closer, still talking to the animal, then fear froze her still, as she stared at the stallion. She did not recognise it, but she needed only an instant to distinguish Darcy's motionless body lying in the mud.

"Oh dear Lord," she cried, then covered her mouth, to avoid scaring the horse. "Come, my dear, let me help you," she coaxed the horse. "Only a moment, my sweet beauty, only a moment," she said, kneeling and approaching carefully. She finally reached the body and with trembling hands and frightening thoughts spinning in her mind, untied the reins.

"There, you are free now," she said. The stallion whickered and took a few steps but still did not move from his master.

Panicked, frightened, quivering, praying and calling his name, she gently turned Darcy.

There was no answer, no movement, only weak breathing warmed her face when she leaned towards him.

She could not see what was wrong with him and did not dare move him too much, only wiped the dirt from his cheeks.

Desperate, she looked around. Longbourn was close

enough, but she could not move him. Helpless she sobbed, powerless, lost as to what she should do.

What was he doing there, so close to Longbourn? For how long he had been on the ground? Did she hear his horse when she began the stroll toward Oakham Mount? Was he already hurt then? Had he lain on the ground all that time? How badly was he harmed? Could she have found him there earlier if she had paid more attention to her surroundings? Such useless questions made her dizzy and increased her tormenting panic.

Moments passed until she made a desperate decision. She took off her coat–still wet and dirty–and put it under his head, then with a last glance she started to run towards the house, faster than her thoughts, than her fears, than her sorrow, than her despair. She ran for his life.

Chapter 12

*E*lizabeth *entered the house breathless, water dripping from her clothes and hair, crying out frantically.*

"Papa! Jane! Hill! Jane!" She raced from one door to another and found her family in the drawing room. They looked at her, astounded and desperately worried by her frightening state.

"Lizzy, what happened?" Jane ran to her. "Are you hurt?" She shook her head in denial, leaning on the back of a chair for support.

"Mr Darcy has fallen in the grove! Behind the house! Just where the path starts to climb towards Oakham Mount! He does not speak, nor move! He needs help! We must go now!"

Everyone rose in haste, looking at each other, then at Elizabeth, panicked and desperate.

"But how...? Why...?" Mrs Bennet cried.

"Mama, I just ran to ask for help! I am going back now! Elizabeth yelled. "Bring the carriage, send for Mr Jones! Send John and Tom and Hill after me! I must go back now! He is alone on the ground!" she shouted, turning to leave.

"Lizzy, wait!" Jane called her. "You are all wet! You must change!"

"Jane, he will die alone if I do not return! Can you not understand?"

"We will come after you," Jane said tearfully but Elizabeth did not hear her, as she left the house running. Every step was heavy and painfully slow. The rain, the mud, the wind, all seemed to slow her down. As if she was in a nightmare, she wished to hurry, but something was holding her, pulling her back. She put all her strength into her feet, moving one after another, again and again.

Eventually, after minutes as long as years, she finally returned to the spot where she had left him. The horse was still there, but Darcy had moved, crawled to a tree, in an apparent attempt to rise. He was now leaning against the tree, on the ground, her coat close to his chest.

Elizabeth sat next to him, calling his name, but he did not respond. She took his head and put it in her lap.

"Mr Darcy," she called him again. "Please open your eyes... please...I am sorry I left you alone...I just went to get help. They will be here soon. Do not worry; we will take you to Longbourn in no time. Please talk to me..." She continued to speak, and for an instant, her hopes rose, as he opened his eyes and looked at her. She breathed in relief, while more tears rolled down her cheeks, falling onto his face. She wiped his face first, then hers but without much success, since the rain continued to fall steadily. She took his hands in hers, and he tightened his fingers around her own. She removed her wet, dirty gloves, then his and held his hands again.

"Miss Bennet..." she heard him whisper, and the pain in her chest loosened its grip.

"Mr Darcy...I am so happy you are awake! Sir, are you hurt?"

His eyes were still half closed. "My head hurts...and my leg...and my chest...and my back...Oh, my horse is still here. Please ask someone to take care of him. I cannot stand..."

"Do not worry...we will take care of everything," she assured him.

"You should not be here...it is very cold, and you are wet... You will catch a cold," he mumbled, barely coherent.

He seemed to fall asleep again, and she called to him repeatedly, with no response.

Fortunately, she soon detected the sound of a carriage

approaching, then several voices calling for her and there were her father, John, Tom, and Hill, all getting down from the carriage and hurrying to her. John was carrying several blankets, while Tom took the reins and tried to bring the horses and the carriage closer, slowly moving through the trees.

"Mr Darcy spoke," Elizabeth explained to her father, trying to move. "But he cannot stand. He has hurt his head and his leg... I do not know how we can move him."

"We should put him in a blanket and carry him with it," Mr Bennet said. "I have seen that done several times. This way, if he has broken anything, we will not increase the damage. Jane has gone to fetch Mr Jones, but I am not sure when they will be here. I am not sure if we would be better to wait here or take him to the house."

"Papa, we cannot wait any longer. He has been out in this weather for a long time...I believe even before I left for a walk," Elizabeth pleaded.

"We will try, my dear. But it will not be easy to carry him to the carriage."

"We will find a way, sir," John said. "Miss Lizzy is right, we should not wait. Mr Darcy looks truly ill."

"And you look very ill too, Miss Lizzy. You should hurry back home and change your clothes right away! We will do fine without you," Hill insisted, but Elizabeth refused and dismissed the notion with a gesture.

With infinite care, they put a blanket down on the wet, muddy ground, then rolled Darcy onto it; each held a corner, carrying it step by step to the carriage. While they struggled, the sound of another carriage and voices interrupted them. Mr Jones arrived in his phaeton, with his assistant Peter, followed by Jane. The men put their efforts together and eventually managed to settle Darcy on the floor of Mr Jones's phaeton. Then they all drove towards Longbourn, which was only half a mile away.

Elizabeth rode in the carriage with her father and their servants, her arms wrapped around herself and her gaze following the carriage carrying Darcy. Her mind kept wondering about the circumstances of his present state, and she imagined he had come to Longbourn precisely to be close to her, to avoid her walking such a long distance. And she had accused him of indifference and lack of consideration! She had accused him of so many things, and probably she had been wrong in most cases. He remained behind because he wanted to talk about something private and important to her. Otherwise, he would have left with the rest of the party, and he would have been safe and sound now. But instead he was lying there, with only a glimpse of life in him, which could vanish at any moment.

Despite being thoroughly wet and exhausted, her senses were frozen. She felt nothing else but worry for Darcy and overwhelming fear for how this dreadful situation would end.

They arrived at Longbourn's gate, and the effort of carrying Darcy started again until he was finally brought into the house. There, in the main hall, under Mrs Bennet and her daughters' astounded stares, the party stopped again.

"Where should we put Mr Darcy?" John asked and a short moment of confusion followed. Mr Jones offered some incoherent suggestions, more distressed than the family had ever seen him.

Mrs Bennet moved closer, looking at Darcy, who lay on the blanket, still, wet and dirty. Her hand covered her mouth to stop a gasp.

"We cannot take him upstairs; it would be too hard to carry him such a long distance. We will put him in my chamber, here, on the ground floor," Mr Bennet declared.

"No, in my room! It is larger and has two beds. He will need constant attendance. I will move until he recovers," Mrs Bennet interjected with such perfect logic and utter determination that the others stared at her in silence. "Hill, bring some hot water! And some dry clothes from Mr Bennet's closet. Come, follow me," the lady continued to give precise orders that were immediately followed.

Mr Bennet only nodded, remaining in the hall with his daughters, helpless and troubled. They looked at each other, lost for words and action.

"Lizzy, go and change yourself this instant. And you, Jane! I do not need you to fall ill as well," Mr Bennet eventually commanded his eldest daughters.

Elizabeth protested weakly, wishing to stay and wait for news from Mr Jones, but Jane grabbed her arm and pulled her to their chamber. Kitty, Lydia and Mary remained in the hall, disconcerted, looking at their father.

"Come, girls, let us go to the drawing room and think what we should do," the gentleman said. "Although there is little to do, except wait."

In their room, Elizabeth and Jane threw their wet clothes on the floor and wrapped themselves in dry towels. Elizabeth washed her face and Jane helped her dry her hair beside the fire.

They assisted each other with hasty moves and few words. Elizabeth started to shiver, and her lips turned blue, as she began to feel the coldness her body had suffered. Then her thoughts flew to him again. How long had he been in the cold and how might his body recover after such suffering?

"Jane, I am fine, thank you. Let us go downstairs; Mr Jones must have news by now."

"Lizzy, wait, dearest. Let me arrange your hair, it is still very wet. And you must have some herbal tea; you look truly ill."

"I am well, Jane. You should take care of yourself—you rode in that terrible weather. Thank God you did not suffer an accident. Mr Darcy is an excellent rider, and he still fell from his horse," Elizabeth said, hurrying out of the door and down the stairs.

Jane struggled to keep pace with her, but Elizabeth barged into the drawing room, where their parents and sisters were gathered and talking animatedly.

"How is Mr Darcy?" Elizabeth asked.

"Lizzy, come and sit by the fire! Have a cup of hot tea! You too, Jane! Lord forbid that you catch a cold too! Lizzy, you have not eaten anything today! Have some biscuits!" Mrs Bennet demanded. Jane hurried to pour two cups of tea, but Elizabeth ignored her mother's requests.

"What did Mr Jones say? How is Mr Darcy?" she repeated, glancing from one to another.

"Mr Darcy is still unconscious. He has been washed and changed but he is badly hurt. Mr Jones seems…a little overwhelmed," Mr Bennet answered gravely. "He and Peter are still with Mr Darcy. We expect them to give us more details soon."

Mr Bennet appeared distressed too; he was barely able to find the proper words to express his concern.

Elizabeth paced the room and refused the cup that Jane handed her. "So–what should we do?" she asked. "We must do something."

"We will take care of Mr Darcy, of course! We expect some happy times to occur when Mr Bingley returns, and he surely cannot be happy if his best friend is ill."

"Mama, we should not make plans about Mr Bingley's return for the time being," Jane said in a trembling voice. "He has barely arrived in London, I imagine. I am sure returning to Hertfordshire is the last thing he has in mind."

"Let us not discuss Mr Bingley's schedule and instead concentrate upon Mr Darcy," Mr Bennet interjected. "We must wait for Mr Jones and decide how to proceed further. Mr Darcy is certainly in no condition to be moved, and his family must be informed of the situation. But I do not understand why he was here? On a horse? Why did he not leave with his friends?"

Elizabeth paled, then turned red. She gulped some tea from the hot cup. "He did not look well at all, even last night," Mr Bennet spoke further.

"Did he not? I did not notice. What do you think, Lizzy? You danced with him, did you not? He looked a marvellous dancer, despite his usual haughty manners," Mrs Bennet said.

Elizabeth ignored her, so her mother continued. "I say, everybody was astonished that he danced with you–and only with you! You appeared to be almost friends! Upon my word, if it were not the proud and unpleasant Mr Darcy, I would say he favoured Lizzy over everybody else!"

"Mama!" Elizabeth interrupted with an anguished cry. "How can you be interested in such frivolous things when a man is in danger of death?"

Her mother glared at her, while her father nodded to her to keep her temper.

"Mind your words, Lizzy; these are not frivolous things!" Mrs Bennet rebuked her. "I was only curious to know if you noticed something peculiar, or he told you something since you talked for half an hour. He might have caught a cold that day he saved us. He stayed in the rain for so long, he went to unleash the horses, then we all left, and he remained in the cottage. Any man, even as strong as he is, would fall ill. That was my concern, missy!"

"Forgive me, Mama; I spoke thoughtlessly. I know you are concerned, like all of us. It is just that I found him there on the ground and I thought he was dead. I have never seen anyone in such a situation," Elizabeth replied holding the cup that burned her fingers.

"Well, for once in my life, I thank God for your wild habit of walking across the fields like a hoyden! No other young lady I know takes pleasure in such an endeavour, but this time you might have saved Mr Darcy's life. If not for you, Lord knows when and if he would have been found or would have recovered by himself."

Elizabeth found nothing to respond, only moved towards the window, staring outside in tormenting silence.

A little while later, Mr Jones appeared. He looked more distressed than they had ever seen him and he was shifting from one leg to another, clasping his hands together while the Bennets gathered around him.

"Well?" Elizabeth asked.

"Mr Darcy is badly wounded…I would say his ribs are badly bruised, maybe even broken. He has a bad cut on his leg and he seems to have lost blood; his trousers were all dirty from it…"

"Did he recover at all? Did he speak?" Mrs Bennet enquired.

"No. Not at all. He has a very high fever too. He is burning, truly."

"And? What is to be done? You have hardly told us anything more than we already observed!"

"I confess I am not certain, Mrs Bennet. My knowledge as an apothecary is not enough for his needs. I have cleaned the wound with some aromatic vinegar and I have bandaged it; for the fever, we gave him some medicine that he barely swallowed. But there has been no improvement in his state so far. And we are talking about Mr Darcy. I am afraid I do not feel confident making decisions about his health in such a grave situation."

"But if you do not, who will?" Mrs Bennet demanded.

"I...I do not know, ma'am. His family...They must be informed at once; we have not a moment to lose."

Elizabeth's heart skipped a beat. What was the meaning of such a statement? Surely it could not imply what she feared to admit?

"But his family is not here! What should we do now?" Mrs Bennet continued in a higher voice.

"I will show you what you can do for his fever, ma'am. But Peter and I will not leave the house either, at least for tonight. If you would be so kind as to host us, we would rather stay," Mr Jones said with obvious concern.

"I shall write to Mr Bingley urgently, by express, and ask him to inform Mr Darcy's family. I am sure they have a family doctor too," Mr Bennet decided. "I will send John to Netherfield to obtain Mr Bingley's address."

"I know it, Papa. It is 23 Grosvenor Street. I heard Mr Bingley talking about it. And Mr Darcy's house is 12 Park Lane," Jane interjected.

"Good. Good. Let us write to both addresses, and I will mention that we sent two letters, to avoid raising more panic than necessary."

"Papa, for a man like Mr Darcy to be so ill, I believe panic is not unjustified," Elizabeth said. "Jane, please write the letters with Papa; Mama and I will go with Mr Jones, and see what we can do for Mr Darcy."

They walked down the hallway, with Mr Jones leading them, and entered the chamber. From the doorway Elizabeth's eyes fell on the bed and she gasped: Darcy was lying still, pale, and undressed. His shoulders and neck were exposed from the sheets and his bandaged, injured leg appeared from beneath the covers. The fire burned steadily, lighting the room. At each side of the bed, a candle was burning.

"Dear Lord, he looks almost dead," Mrs Bennet murmured, as they approached carefully.

"The most important task is to keep his fever low." Mr Jones told them. "It is already very high, and it will increase during the night. If it grows too high, he might…"

"Oh, for heaven's sake, do something to lower the fever, do not tell us what will happen if it grows! This is why we called for you," Mrs Bennet interrupted the apothecary. Already distressed, the man looked at his assistant and at Elizabeth, as though asking for help.

"Mama, let us stay calm," Elizabeth pleaded gently. "We are all worried. So, Mr Jones, what should we do to help you?"

"As I said, we have given him some medicine, and we will cool him with some cold water and vinegar. Can you bring us another large bowl and one more sponge?"

Mr Jones was less and less confident, and his lack of coherence brought nothing but more panic.

"He looks so pale," Elizabeth whispered, gently touching Darcy's hand and his forehead. "But he is rather cold…"

"We should cover him in blankets, then. Perhaps his temperature has dropped too abruptly," Mr Jones offered, wrapping the blankets around the patient.

"Oh dear, high fever, low fever! Let me check," Mrs Bennet demanded, annoyed and impatient. She pushed her companions away and, under their astonished gazes, she bent over the bed and touched her lips to Darcy's temples.

"Mama!" Elizabeth cried. "What are you doing?"

Mrs Bennet silenced her with a wave of her hand. "I am checking his fever. It is what I did with you girls when you were little. If I touch the forehead with my palm it may be misleading but touching the temple with the lips is always accurate. The old Dr. Benson taught me when Jane was an infant."

Elizabeth was still dumbfounded, and for some strange reason, she blushed. "In fact, that is very true," Mr Jones approved. "However we should not let Mr Darcy know that someone took such liberties with him while he was unconscious."

"Well, considering how unpleasant and haughty he is most of the time, that might be the closest thing to a kiss he will ever get," Mrs Bennet declared in earnest. "Although, he is handsome and wealthy enough to have women kissing him anyway. If only we can keep him healthy too!"

"Mama, please!" Elizabeth cried, filled with embarrassment and distress.

"He is feverish," Mrs Bennet told Mr Jones, ignoring Elizabeth. "So, what should we do now?"

"I will send Peter to bring some more medicine and teas, but I doubt Mr Darcy can swallow any. I will stay here until morning. And I hope his family will come tomorrow with a doctor from town," Mr Jones admitted honestly.

"Then–may I help?" Mrs Bennet asked.

"Not for the moment, ma'am."

"Well then, I will go and take care of dinner. I need to move some of my clothes to another room. God knows how long Mr Darcy will need to stay in my chamber. And what else? Well, let me think…" Mrs Bennet spoke to herself as she left the room.

Peter exchanged a few words with Mr Jones and left too, leaving the apothecary alone with Elizabeth and the patient.

They looked at each other, then at Darcy, then at each other again.

"Miss Elizabeth, you have nothing to do here for the moment either. You should have some medicine and some tea yourself and rest a little. You have had a hard day, and you spent so much time in the cold rain that I am worried about your health too," the apothecary said.

Elizabeth took the bottle handed to her. "I shall be fine, sir, but I thank you for your concern. I will leave now. Please send for me if I may be of any use."

"I will. But please promise me you will take the medicine and have some hot tea. And perhaps some soup, to gather your strength."

Elizabeth nodded in agreement, then glanced at Darcy again and left the room. She felt like she was abandoning him, but could not find a reason to stay against Mr Jones's instructions.

In the hall she stopped and leaned against the wall, allowing the tears to roll down her cheeks. She recollected their discussions from the previous night, his jesting answers when she suggested he looked ill, his teasing smiles, his warm hand holding hers during the dance…Did all this occur only hours ago?

Strange and unexpected circumstances had brought him to his present state and kept him to the bed.

She regretted his agony, she felt sorry for him, as she would have for any other person in such a situation. The awareness that he had suffered the accident because he came to talk to her increased her grief.

But there was much more that added to her growing turmoil and overwhelming fear, more than she was capable of recognising and of understanding. The previous night, she thought it was too soon for such considerations. Now, it could be too late.

Chapter 13

*A*t Longbourn, distress and worry were experienced in the same manner as joy and amusement: with increasing noise building from loud and silly conversations, accompanied by tasty refreshments.

Elizabeth did not doubt their genuine concern for Darcy, but she could not stand their behaviour; therefore she withdrew to her chamber.

She felt unwell–both her body and her mind were exhausted–and she wished for a little rest which was denied to her. She sat on the bed, then rose, paced the room, looked outside, then returned to the bed, gazing at the fire. She shivered from the cold, then heat enveloped her. She felt too tired to rise, but could not bear to lie down either.

Eventually, she remembered she had neglected Mr Jones' advice, so she took the suggested medicine and returned to bed, wrapping the covers around her.

Sometime later, a knock on the door startled her, and her first thought was that something had happened to Darcy. But Jane entered with a tray, followed by their father.

"Dearest, I brought you a little hot soup, some biscuits, and warm tea. We will leave you now so you can sleep," Jane said.

"No, do not leave! I am not sleeping; I just needed a little quiet. Stay and keep me company. How is Mr Darcy?"

"The same," Jane replied.

"We sent the letter by express to both Mr Bingley and Mr Darcy's town residences," Mr Bennet explained. "We were debating if we should write to his aunt too."

"His aunt?" Elizabeth asked absently.

"Yes. The famous Lady Catherine de Bourgh."

"I would not do anything until I hear from Miss Darcy. She should decide who else she wishes to inform. But I am sure Mr Collins will pass the news to Lady Catherine immediately; he probably has already done so," Elizabeth responded, annoyed.

"Mr Collins left this morning. With all this chaos, I forgot to mention it to you. For some reason, he decided to return to Kent early today. He did not share the reason for his sudden–and I would say welcome–departure, but he did mention he had some business to complete first in Meryton. Since he asked nothing of me, I was happy not to enquire further," Mr Bennet declared.

"Finally good news for today," Elizabeth rolled her eyes. "Just imagine how Mr Collins' ridiculous comments would have exacerbated this disaster!"

"Your mother is rather distracted. I suspect she secretly hoped Mr Collins would propose to one of you before he left the neighbourhood."

"Papa, I know you find great amusement in this situation, but I am not diverted at all. We all knew Mr Collins intended to propose to me, just as we all knew I would have rejected him and would have provoked a huge scandal. Thank the Lord he left and let us pray he will not return anytime soon!"

"Come now, my dear, nothing is more relaxing than making sport of difficult situations in life," Mr Bennet replied.

"Forgive me, Papa, but I am in no disposition for jokes," Elizabeth said, rubbing her temples to relieve a sudden headache.

"Yes, I have noticed that. Well, my dear, try to sleep a little bit. Perhaps that will improve your disposition."

"I cannot sleep, Papa. I will come downstairs with you, but there is something I must tell you first. I trust you will keep the secret, as it would be tragic if Mama discovered something," she declared, gathering her courage to confess her anguish. To her father and sister's worried and puzzled gazes, she replied with a nervous smile.

"During the ball, Mr Darcy told me he wished to speak to me privately, about an important matter of concern for him and for our family. We planned to meet this morning; we had happened to meet before on previous occasions, so it was nothing special. He never appeared, and now we know why; I imagine he was so close to Longbourn because he did not want me to walk far from home in such weather. Of course, there could be other reasons too."

Jane and her father were now staring at Elizabeth with the deepest surprise and curiosity.

"But what matter? And why privately? Mr Darcy has been in our house several times. I would not have been opposed to him talking to you," Mr Bennet said.

"I wondered the same, Papa. Sadly, I was not wise enough to ask that last night and to suggest he call on you instead. I do not know what was in my mind, or in his. We both lost our reasoning," Elizabeth spoke hastily, with increasing distress, rubbing her hands together.

"Lizzy, could he have something truly private to discuss with you alone? I mean–I have noticed you have been on friendly terms lately. And he danced only with you..." Jane suggested shyly.

Elizabeth glared at her, her cheeks burning instantly. "Jane, do not be silly! You sound like Mama now! We were barely on friendly terms, after hating each other for weeks. And do you imagine that after only one set danced together he decided to propose to me in the middle of the woods? This is absolutely ridiculous!"

"Lizzy, I am truly sorry, I did not mean..." Jane attempted to apologise with distress.

"Lizzy dear, calm yourself! You are being silly and ridiculous, truly," Mr Bennet scolded her. "And I too noticed the new friendship between you and Mr Darcy. He even confessed to me his admiration for you last night. But I agree that he is not the sort of man to propose in such circumstances. Now, Mr

Collins–he would surely do that if he met you in the woods…"

"Papa! Please!" Elizabeth cried angrily and almost tearfully.

"You may shout at us if doing so makes you feel better, Lizzy. But if I do not jest, how else may I help you? Tell me what you want me to do. Can you presume what Darcy intended to talk to you about? Could anyone be in danger? I do not think so, or else he would have told you immediately rather than waiting until the morning."

"I do not know, Papa. Forgive me, I am so distressed that my mind is blurry. You know, I heard the horse when I headed towards Oakham Mount. If I had looked for it then, he would not have stayed in the rain for two more hours."

"Now, you are indeed being silly and ridiculous. You could not have imagined such a situation and surely cannot blame yourself for it. As I said earlier, you saved his life! I am equally concerned for you, though. You also stayed outside in this freezing rain for a long while. Promise me you will not be ill too."

Elizabeth embraced her father and kissed his cheeks, answering in jest, "I promise I will be fine, Papa, if you promise to keep Mr Collins away."

Mr Bennet returned the kiss. "Well, my child, then I am afraid you will need Mr Jones's assistance too. Thank God your mother thinks nobody dies of a trifling cold!"

Later in the afternoon, Mr Darcy's fever increased, Mr Jones's distress rose, Elizabeth and Jane's concern and helplessness grew, and on top of everything, Mrs Bennet's nerves had another trying obstacle to overcome.

Lady Lucas arrived with Charlotte, bringing the most unexpected and upsetting news, under the pretext of enquiring after Mr Darcy's health.

"We did not expect to hear such a report about poor Mr

Darcy! How horrible indeed! Everybody is shocked in Meryton!" Lady Lucas said.

"It was shocking for us too, but we are doing our best to take care of him. I cannot imagine how a man who stopped a couple of galloping horses could fall from his own. He was lucky that Lizzy found him," Mrs Bennet replied, inviting the guests to sit.

"And although this is not the best moment, we must take this opportunity to share with you some news. Perhaps we should have waited a few more days, but considering that we are almost family, we wished you to be the first to know."

"To know what?" Mrs Bennet asked, looking from mother to daughter.

Those Lucases could be very irritating at times.

"Earlier today, just before he left the country, Mr Collins called on us. He proposed to Charlotte and she accepted!" Lady Lucas cried with such cheerfulness that Elizabeth feared she might start clapping her hands.

With astonishment and disbelief, she glanced at Charlotte, but her friend avoided meeting her eyes. Surely this must be a poor joke!

"Proposed what to Charlotte?" Mrs Bennet asked with vexation.

"Marriage, of course!" Lady Lucas answered.

Mrs Bennet dropped her cup of tea. "Marriage? To Charlotte? But how? Why? He does not even know Charlotte! How could he propose?"

"He most certainly does! He visited us a few times, and he and Sir William got along very well. Just last night he danced with Charlotte and they spoke quite enough. He was charmed and he said he could not find a better wife!"

"But...but..." Mrs Bennet could not believe her ears and she glared around the room, from the guests to her family, waiting for someone to tell her it was a joke. She had few hopes that Elizabeth would ever accept Mr Collins if he happened to propose to her. Perhaps Mary would have been a better choice for him and more easily persuaded. She did not regret so much losing Mr Collins as a son-in-law, since she expected Mr Bingley to return soon and solve all their problems. But the notion that Charlotte Lucas would one day inherit Longbourn was unacceptable.

She was about to faint, but did not wish to give Lady Lucas and her daughter the satisfaction!

"Congratulations!" Jane said warmly.

"I am sure this union pleases both Sir William and Mr Collins and indeed I am sure he could not have been more fortunate in his choice of a wife," Mr Bennet said in all honesty.

Elizabeth forced a smile to her friend, trying to conceal her disappointment. She moved towards Charlotte and took her hands.

"I wish you all the happiness you deserve, my dear," she said.

"Eliza, I know this is a surprise for everybody," Charlotte whispered. "I can imagine what you think, but I hope you understand my decision."

"I wish nothing else but to know you are happy with your choice, my dear. If you are content, so am I," Elizabeth concluded.

"We are all very content," Lady Lucas continued, while Charlotte still looked at Elizabeth with embarrassment. "Mr Collins hurried to inform Lady Catherine de Bourgh, and he will write to Sir William about his plans. We should have a wedding soon! What can be more satisfying for a mother than to know her daughter is settled with a happy, safe future?"

"Well, we should not speak of happy events when Mr Darcy is so ill. We are all too worried to think of anything else," Mrs Bennet spoke sharply, red-faced with envy.

The guests did not stay longer than half an hour, but the visit distressed Mrs Bennet so profoundly that she needed to retire and rest. She chose Mary's room, who was banished with Lydia and Kitty. None of them was content, but they did not dare to argue with their mother either.

Elizabeth checked on Darcy several times. With particular embarrassment, she assisted Mr Jones while he cooled Darcy's face, forehead, torso, and hands with cold water and vinegar. But the patient never moved, nor showed any sign of recovery, much to their mutual despair.

Almost two hours after Lady Lucas left, a more pleasant and less bothersome call was received at Longbourn: Mr Wickham and two other officers came, also brought by the news of Mr Darcy's accident.

Mrs Bennet and her younger daughters welcomed the distraction and invited the gentlemen to stay for dinner.

Elizabeth found the visit intrusive and their repeatedly expressed regrets inappropriate, but tried to remain calm and polite. She feared that every family from Meryton would come to ask about Mr Darcy, as his accident had already turned into a subject of gossip and entertainment.

Elizabeth was in no disposition to dine, but neither did she have any strength to reject her mother's insistence on having a proper meal. So she bore the lively conversations and the lengthy courses stoically for a while.

"It is very kind of you to take the trouble of nursing Mr Darcy," Lieutenant Denny said.

"Well, he took care of us too, as I am sure you remember. Besides, he is Mr Bingley's friend and Mr Bingley is like family to us," Mrs Bennet declared, making Jane blush with embarrassment.

"I wonder what could have happened to Darcy," Wickham added. "He used to be a skilful rider."

"We do not know, but it matters little," Mr Bennet declared. "Even the most proficient riders suffer accidents."

"And how long will he stay at Longbourn?" Wickham continued.

"That depends on his improvement or his family's decision," Mr Bennet replied. "We have informed them and we await their answer."

"Well, you should expect someone from his family to

come and fetch him soon. They are all proud people who loathe being involved with anyone outside their circle. My godfather was different, but the Fitzwilliams all share the same repulsive arrogance and haughtiness."

"Is Miss Darcy the same?" Lydia asked.

"Very much so. She was a sweet, gentle child but she has grown up to be more and more like her brother."

"I have heard Miss Darcy is a very accomplished lady, and exceedingly talented at the pianoforte; everybody who knows her praises her character and qualities," Jane said, with a slight pallor and trembling voice.

"I know she is very talented at music and very well educated. But that is different. She inherited some good qualities from her father, but the Fitzwilliam traits appear to be stronger," Wickham concluded.

"Well, if they do come to take him, even better for us. But I doubt he is in any state to be moved for the time being," Mrs Bennet said, taking offence as she felt her efforts were unappreciated.

The conversation became more animated, and Elizabeth found it impossible to listen any longer. She apologised, and addressed her sister. "Jane, will you come with me to watch Mr Darcy? I am sure Peter and Mr Jones need to eat properly and to rest for a little while."

"Yes, of course," Jane replied, slightly surprised.

"Miss Bennet, is it not too much trouble for you to watch Darcy? Can you not get a servant to do it?" Wickham enquired officiously.

Elizabeth turned to him. "It is no trouble at all to sit in a chair and watch a wounded man who only a few days ago put himself in danger to save us. Please excuse us," she ended, taking Jane's hand and leaving.

"He is annoying," Elizabeth whispered to Jane. "And impertinent!"

"Lizzy, I think he means well. He was only worried for you," Jane tried to temper her.

"He might have been worried for me, but I sense he is somehow content with Mr Darcy's accident."

"Lizzy! Do not even think such a horrible thing! Why would you suspect him of something so odious?"

Elizabeth knocked on the door and avoided answering her sister. She was in no disposition to contradict Jane's tendency to see only the good in people.

Mr Jones and Peter readily accepted the offered break and welcomed the invitation to join the family for dinner. They left, leaving Elizabeth and Jane standing in the middle of the room, staring at the still pale and unmoving Darcy.

Elizabeth stepped closer and sat on the edge of the bed. She looked at him as though she were seeing his features for the first time. Without his usual arrogant countenance, he looked younger and more handsome. Oblivious to her sister's presence, she touched Darcy's hands, then his forehead then took his hand in hers.

She stayed there for a few long moments, with Jane gazing at her in wonder, until she startled and gasped at a soft whisper.

"Miss Bennet…"

"Yes! I am here," Elizabeth murmured, leaning closer to his face. She squeezed his hands tighter, calling his name.

"Mr Darcy, can you open your eyes?"

"Elizabeth…" he whispered again. Elizabeth blushed and caressed his hand.

"I am here. How are you feeling? Mr Darcy?"

But he said nothing else and fell back into a deep, frightening sleep.

∞∞∞∞

Darcy felt trapped in a block of ice, shivering from the coldness that froze his senses. He tried to wrap his arms around himself, but could not move. Then, a moment later, a fire started nearby, surrounding him until the heat became unbearable. He tried to run, but his feet obeyed his will just as little as his hands. He was a prisoner, oblivious to his whereabouts or to his oppressor.

He tried to breathe, but that was no easier. He needed help but could not beg for it; was no one there to look for him, to set him free?

A final effort exhausted the last of his strength and he abandoned any struggle. He was neither too cold, nor too warm any longer. Overwhelming tiredness enveloped him and he abandoned himself to it. Until his senses stirred and he became aware of a well known and much-desired fragrance that he immediately recognised. She was there. She must be. The soft touch that warmed his skin could not be but hers and the voice which spoke through his dreams belonged to no other than Elizabeth. He had dreamed of her so many times that he could not be wrong. She was more alive and real in his fantasies than she was in reality.

He could feel her, smell her, touch her. He almost felt her flavour on his lips. If only she could come a little closer. If only he could tell her that he wanted her to come closer.

"Miss Bennet…" he heard himself saying. And she answered, but he could not comprehend the words. She kept repeating his name, so he called hers again.

"Elizabeth …"

Then the cage closed around him again and everything turned black. And his senses slowly lost the trace of her closeness: her scent, her flavour, her touch—were all gone.

∞ ∞ ∞

"Lizzy, he is sleeping again," Jane gently said, taking a chair and sitting by her sister. Elizabeth glanced at her, still holding Darcy's hand.

"I held his hand earlier in the grove, and he spoke to me. I hoped now it would happen again–and it did. But only for a short while."

"It is good that he woke up, if only for a moment," Jane replied. "Now we have greater hopes that he will recover."

"I hope his family arrives soon. I dread the notion that he might take a turn for the worse overnight, in a strange house, with no relatives around. It must be horrible."

"But Lizzy, he is not among strangers. He and Papa are quite close and you are being such a good friend to him too," Jane offered.

"He does not look arrogant and aloof at all, does he?" Elizabeth smiled. "I wonder why I thought so ill of him for such a long while."

"You cannot blame yourself, Lizzy. Your acquaintance was rather challenging in the beginning. But I am sure he knows how much we appreciate him and how grateful we were for his brave intervention when we most needed it."

"He was unwilling to accept any gratitude, Jane. He is such a strange man, so difficult to understand and to sketch. He seemed unwilling to reveal his true character."

"But his actions speak for him eloquently enough," Jane declared.

Elizabeth laughed nervously. "Yes, they do. Even when he refuses to dance with tolerable ladies at a public ball."

"Lizzy, come now," Jane's laughter escaped in her relief. "You surely have forgotten that incident, since you so deeply care for his health."

"I have not forgotten it, but I have forgiven his rudeness. He has suffered enough to compensate for it. I only wish that my care would do him some good."

"Lizzy, do you think Miss Darcy will come here?" Jane suddenly asked, hesitantly.

Elizabeth looked at her. "I imagine as much. If her affection for him is as strong as his is for her, she will come soon."

"And Mr Bingley? Will he come with her, do you think?"

"Oh, dearest, I am not sure what to say. Probably."

"Dear Lizzy, I do not think I can bear to see them together..." Jane confessed. "It will be so hard..."

"Jane, we have already discussed this. I truly believe you

have no reason for such concern. Anyone who has seen you together cannot doubt his admiration for you. Do not torment yourself over nothing, my dear. And surely not for something that Caroline Bingley said!"

"But Lizzy, I am not jealous, trust me. I mean–I might be, but if Miss Darcy is such a perfect young lady, she may be the proper wife for him. I only wish him happiness."

"You are the proper wife for him, Jane; and if he fails to see that, he does not deserve to be happy, with Miss Darcy or anyone else. And speaking of happiness, what do you think of Charlotte? Married to Mr Collins? How horrible this is!"

The sisters continued to speak and to comfort each other for a while, until Mr Jones returned.

Elizabeth hastily rose from the bed, releasing Darcy's hand and explained to Mr Jones that the patient had briefly spoken a few words.

"This is excellent news, Miss Lizzy! Excellent! You know, the guests have left already. I am sorry if you missed their company for my sake."

"Please do not apologise, sir, we are in no disposition for company anyway."

"Oh, I forgot, do you know this man?"

To the sisters' utter shock they saw Mr Darcy's valet, looking around in apparent distress.

"Yes, I have seen him several times with Mr Darcy," Elizabeth answered. "Stevens, where have you been?"

The servant explained that he had waited for his master at an inn, as they planned, and since he did not appear, he returned to search for him. Stevens immediately took his position next to his master, asking how he could help.

With so many men around, Elizabeth and Jane turned to leave, when the apothecary said, "We were wondering: John found a deep cut on the horse's flank and under the saddle. And the same cut is on Mr Darcy's leg. We just cannot imagine how that happened. The cut must have scared the horse and it threw him. Do you remember if you heard or saw anything that might help us solve this mystery? Or should we go and look around tomorrow, perhaps?"

"No, I do not recollect anything of the sort," Elizabeth replied, dumbfounded by the new details. "Do you think someone hurt Mr Darcy deliberately?"

"We do not know and cannot suspect as much. But we were wondering."

"My master would never fall from a horse for no reason." Stevens declared, and Elizabeth remembered when she first met Darcy in the woods and he pointed out that he was an excellent rider. Back then, she had mocked him for such a conceited statement. But in truth, he did not seem the sort of man to simply fall from a horse, even if he suffered from a cold. A serious, not a trifling one.

"Well, good night, Miss Bennet, Miss Elizabeth."

"Good night, Mr Jones. Please keep us informed if anything new occurs."

"We will. I only hope his family will arrive soon."

"As do I, Mr Jones. As do I," Elizabeth answered, closing the door behind her with a last glance at Darcy.

Chapter 14

*I*t was dawn when Elizabeth gently knocked on the door of the patient's room. She cared little that she was wearing only her nightgown. She had been so tormented by horrible dreams in the short amount of time that she had managed to sleep, that she needed to find out how he was feeling.

"We have no news, Miss Elizabeth," Mr Jones said. "There is no improvement but happily he is no worse either."

Elizabeth needed only a glimpse to notice that not much had changed. The three men were all seated around the bed, but the patient was still immobile.

"May I bring you something?" she asked.

"No, we have been properly attended already," Mr Jones answered.

Elizabeth wished to stay, but such impropriety was hard to justify. Therefore, she delayed for a few minutes, then left and considered if she should return to her chamber or not. At such an early hour, the house was silent and asleep.

Despite Mr Jones' caution and her own fear, Elizabeth had not caught a cold from the previous day's events. Her time spent in the rain and her desperate run through the storm had left no scars.

She eventually decided to go to the kitchen. As she expected, there was Hill, already preparing breakfast. Elizabeth's appearance was greeted with a smile of welcome. A cup of tea was offered, which Elizabeth enjoyed in the company of the long-time servant, who was more like part of the family.

"Miss, you were fearless yesterday," Hill said.

"Oh, that is nonsense," Elizabeth smiled. "I did nothing but run home to ask for assistance."

"But still. You should not walk alone in the woods–especially with all these officers around. I have heard some of them are not as honourable as they should be."

"Hill, what on earth are you talking about?"

"I say–Miss, my sister's husband works at Netherfield and she saw things at the ball. Mrs Forster was talking outside in the dark with an officer."

"What business do we have with either of them, Hill? You should not gossip at peoples' expense. Maybe they only talked. I talk with many people–men and women–all the time. Is that dishonourable?" Elizabeth scolded the servant, albeit in a friendly tone.

"Oh, you know what I mean, miss! And Mr Darcy–we believe someone attacked him! Stevens said he would never fall from his horse otherwise."

"Hill! This is a dangerous matter to speak of, if you are not certain. If you hear something beyond gossip, let me know. Otherwise, please do not involve yourself in such idle chatter. Thank God you did not say anything about Mr Darcy doing something improper," Elizabeth tried to jest, blushing.

"Oh no, ma'am. Mr Darcy is too haughty and pretentious to do anything improper. I asked Stevens if his master ever takes off his clothes when he is healthy. I cannot imagine him ever being improperly attired."

"Hill!" Elizabeth rebuked the woman with complete seriousness. "Such words are upsetting and disappointing! I did not expect such a lack of propriety from you, truly!"

"Forgive me, miss, I was only joking. I meant no offence; I was only trying to lighten your mood. I know how much you dislike Mr Darcy but Stevens said he is the finest of men."

"And if so, should we make jokes behind his back, while he is suffering? And no, I do not dislike him. Why should I, since he was the one who saved us–as I am sure you know."

Elizabeth left the kitchen feeling irritated. The rumours

that had spread so easily around the village would be hard to stop and Mr Darcy was understandably in the middle of them. But could it be true that he had been attacked? She thought quite thoroughly about the wound on his leg and on the horse. But who would do such a thing, in broad daylight, in view of Longbourn?

She spent the following hours in the library, reading, and then checked on Darcy again. The time passed slowly and it seemed forever until breakfast was eventually set. Mr Bennet, Jane and Elizabeth ate in silence, but the table did not lack animated conversation.

The distress seemed to improve the appetite and disposition of some yet ruined it for others.

Lydia and Kitty spoke mostly of Wickham and Denny, and briefly about Charlotte Lucas's horrible fate as the wife of the repulsive Mr Collins.

"I would rather die than marry a man who is not handsome." Lydia declared.

Mrs Bennet readily approved such a statement.

"My dear, sadly, not all of us can be as fortunate as Jane, to be admired by a man who is handsome and wealthy and amiable all together. But then again, not all of us are as beautiful as Jane either."

"Mama, please," Jane whispered.

"Come now, dearest, do not be modest. Everybody must agree that, if a beauty like you can gain Mr Bingley's favours, someone as plain as Charlotte is well enough settled with Mr Collins."

"Mama!" Jane repeated, flushed and embarrassed.

Mrs Bennet ignored her. "Mr Bennet, do you have any news from Mr Bingley or Mr Darcy's relatives?"

"I do not, Mrs Bennet. Rest assured that if I do, you will be the first to know."

"Well, I am sure a letter will come today."

"Very likely. With your permission, I will wait for it in the library," Mr Bennet concluded, separating from his family as soon as he finished his meal.

More hours passed and Elizabeth, together with Jane, took turns in the patient's room, allowing Mr Jones and Peter time to rest and eat. Stevens never left his master's side, barely spoke to anyone, and kept asking if any news from London had arrived. The general concern increased and the darkest thoughts invaded the family as time passed and Darcy showed no sign of recovery.

Even for the less informed among the Bennets, it was clear that the longer his state continued thus, the harder it would be to regain his strength. And Mr Jones did not help much, as his own angst was apparent.

By the afternoon no letter had come from London still, but when the daylight began to fade, a large carriage stopped in front of Longbourn.

From it, Mr Bingley hastily jumped, offering his hand to a young lady, then to an older one. Behind them was a gentleman of Mr Bennet's age, carrying a medical bag. The Bennet girls all ran to the windows, staring at the scene outside. Jane turned pale, taking Elizabeth's hand. Her worst fears had become reality, as she witnessed Mr Bingley walking with the young lady on his arm. Even for Jane's kind heart, the pain was too hard to bear.

Mr and Mrs Bennet were informed and they hurried to greet the new arrivals.

"Mr Bingley, how good of you to come," Mrs Bennet gushed, as though it were a joyous occasion. She looked at Jane meaningfully, but her eldest daughter was pale and kept her eyes down.

"Mrs Bennet, Mr Bennet...Miss Bennet..." Bingley bowed to them. The young lady clenched at his arm and he tenderly kept his hand over hers. Her figure showed delicate and flawless beauty. Her eyes were as blue as the sky on a serene summer day, but dark circles surrounded them, betraying her turmoil. She looked at them, lost, fearful, her lips dry, leaning on Bingley, searching for support.

Elizabeth held Jane's hand tighter.

"Allow me to introduce you to Miss Georgiana Darcy, her

companion Mrs Annesley and Dr. Aaron Cooper. He has been the Darcys' doctor for years," Bingley said.

"Please, may I see my brother?" Miss Darcy pleaded abruptly. Her haste sounded impolite, even rude, but the depth of her sorrow was obvious. Elizabeth's heart was touched; she gently released Jane's hand although she knew her sister was suffering too. But between the two kinds of sorrows, she chose to comfort the stranger's.

"Miss Darcy, I am Elizabeth Bennet. I shall take you to your brother." Miss Darcy's eyes moistened with tears and she hastily stepped forward.

"Thank you, Miss Elizabeth."

"I will join you," Dr. Cooper said. "Forgive me, but I must see the patient first. Any other conversation can be postponed."

The Bennets nodded, inviting the two to enter. Bingley hesitated a moment, looking from Georgiana to Jane; in the end, he remained with Mrs Annesley and followed the Bennets into the drawing room.

Jane was so devastated that she could barely walk, her restraint puzzling Bingley even more. Distressed, he sat near Mrs Annesley on the sofa, glancing at Jane from time to time while she stubbornly avoided his eyes.

The Bennets talked, asking and providing information about Darcy all together. Bingley asked for details and the entire story was narrated to him. He listened and wondered, astounded, repeating how good a rider Darcy was.

"He had looked unwell all week. I think he has had a bad cold since that day in the cottage," Bingley declared. "I strongly opposed him riding all the way to London! He planned to meet Stevens at an inn, but we asked there and we were told Darcy never arrived and Stevens returned to look for him."

Mr Bennet nodded.

"I feared something might happen and it did. I was shocked when I received your letter. I had just arrived home and I planned to meet my solicitor today and then such news...I immediately went to Georgiana...to Miss Darcy. She was devastated and almost fainted from fright. She was crying and wished to come here in the middle of the night. Alone, with only Mrs Annesley. Her closest relatives, the Matlocks, are at their property in Derbyshire until spring. She was waiting for her brother to spend Christmas together and instead she received such horrible news."

Mrs Annesley nodded silently in agreement, while Bingley continued to mumble with little coherence, combining questions with answers in a barely rational conversation with Mrs Bennet.

"Well, where are my manners? You must be tired and hungry; let me order some refreshments. I shall ring for Hill. No, I had better go and talk to her personally," Mrs Bennet suddenly said, leaving the drawing room before anyone had the chance to reply.

Silence fell upon the rest of the party, and Jane's obvious avoidance of Mr Bingley became even more pronounced.

"Miss Bennet, Mr Bennet, we thank you for your kindness towards Darcy," Bingley finally addressed Jane.

"We did nothing special, sir," Jane replied shyly. "If only he would improve soon."

"Will you return to London to complete your business?" Mr Bennet asked their guest.

"I am not sure yet. It depends on what Dr. Cooper suggests. My main concern is to support Miss Darcy during this difficult situation. I must be near Darcy until he fully recovers."

"That is truly admirable. I would imagine your business was important. To abandon it for your friend's comfort is proof of your character, Mr Bingley."

"Thank you, Mr Bennet, but I deserve no praise, I assure you. Darcy is like part of my family and he would have done the same for me."

The exchange, which impressed the others, hurt Jane so profoundly that she felt her heart bleeding. There was no doubt regarding the bond that tied Mr Bingley to the Darcys. Caroline Bingley had been right, for once. All her hopes—silly and groundless–vanished, replaced by painful despair. She was at least content that Mr Bingley had chosen someone better and more worthy than she.

"My brother Gardiner and his family will arrive in a few days, to spend Christmas at Longbourn! I hope you will be here to meet them. My brother has a very successful business and my sister is a truly fashionable lady," Mrs Bennet explained.

"I would very much like to meet them, but as I said, I am not sure of my plans yet. It all depends on Darcy," Mr Bingley admitted and Jane was sure she understood his meaning. As soon as Mr Darcy recovered, they would return to town together and likely never return again.

$\infty\infty\infty$

Elizabeth pushed the door open carefully, inviting Georgiana and the doctor in. Mr Jones, Peter, and Stevens jumped to their feet and Elizabeth began the introductions.

Miss Darcy gasped and, ignoring everyone, hastened to her brother's bed. She sat by his side and held his hands. She called his name repeatedly, sobbing and kissing his hands. The sight was heart-breaking and Elizabeth approached, her own eyes tearful, and gently put her hand on Georgiana's shoulder.

The girl turned her head to Elizabeth and whispered, "I have nobody in the world but him. He cannot leave me. He always takes care of me. We only have each other. What would I do without him? He cannot leave me…"

There was little to say in such an upsetting circumstance and Elizabeth could not find even a few proper words. Even if she had, the sudden lump in her throat trapped her in silence. She wished to assure Georgiana that her brother would be well. To convince herself that he would be well. But she did not dare share such delusions with any of them.

"We will take care of him, and give him the best of care," Elizabeth whispered to the grieving girl.

"Thank you, Miss Elizabeth. My brother wrote to me that you were the bravest lady he had ever met and that you can accomplish anything, if you decide to. I hope that is true," Miss Darcy murmured back, forcing a smile and stroking Darcy's hand tenderly.

Elizabeth's eyes and lips widened in astonishment and she glanced from one sibling to another. Did he write to his sister about her? When? And why would he do that?

With significantly more reason and less sensibility, the men discussed the important aspects regarding the patient. Upon learning the identity of the doctor, Mr Jones was so impressed and became so nervous that he needed a while to put his thoughts in order. Trying to provide useful information about Darcy's state, he repeated countless times that he had read Dr. Cooper's articles in the London medical magazines as regularly as he went to church.

"Miss Darcy, Miss Bennet–I must ask you to leave now, as I need to examine Mr Darcy," Dr. Cooper demanded.

Reluctantly, Georgiana rose from the bed and Elizabeth took her arm, leading her outside. From the doorway she gazed at her brother desperately, until finally the closed door took him from her sight.

They returned to the animation of the drawing room and were immediately overwhelmed with questions to which neither had any answers.

Bingley helped Georgiana to sit and she chose a place near Mrs Annesley. Elizabeth sat near Jane, wondering at her sister's increasing apparent distress.

"Miss Darcy, you must eat something. Here, let me prepare a plate for you. And some hot tea–Lizzy, prepare Miss Darcy a cup. Mr Bingley told us you travelled through the night; you should not have done that. It is too dangerous and you should have known that we would take care of your brother," Mrs Bennet chatted volubly.

"We did not doubt your care, Mrs Bennet. Quite the contrary. I told Miss Darcy that of all the places in the world outside his own family, Darcy could not find better care than here," Mr Bingley offered.

"Oh, my dear Mr Bingley, you are too generous with your praise. We were lucky that Lizzy found him. My second daughter is a little wild in her customs of wandering around the fields and taking long walks no matter the weather but that proved to be a fortunate practice yesterday, since she discovered Mr Darcy had fallen in the woods. She ran back home to inform us, and then she ran back to keep him company until help arrived with the carriage," Mrs Bennet continued her tale.

"Mama, please," Elizabeth tried unsuccessfully to end the long and embarrassing narration.

"But they are all good girls, I assure you, especially Jane, whose beauty and kindness are admired everywhere she goes," Mrs Bennet spoke further.

"Mama!" Jane interjected in a scolding, desperate voice, while the guests only looked at her and smiled politely.

"What did Dr. Cooper say?" Bingley enquired, with another disappointed glance at Jane, who still refused to look at him.

"Nothing, yet. He is examining Mr Darcy now," Elizabeth replied, while Georgiana took the cup of hot tea with trembling hands and gently refused to eat anything.

"Good. After that, we will write to your family to inform them of the situation," Bingley turned to Miss Darcy, who agreed silently.

"And to my sisters, since I left in such a hurry that I did not have a chance to speak to them," Bingley added. "Oh, I forgot. Mr Bennet, may we send someone with a note to Netherfield to prepare rooms? Or should we go and settle there and return later? It is only three miles away; we will be there in no time," Bingley looked at Georgiana and Mrs Annesley for approval.

"I am not going anywhere without William," Georgiana responded harshly. "I will stay with him until he recovers and talks to me."

She paused, aware of her demanding, improper tone, and

looked at Mr and Mrs Bennet. "I beg your forgiveness; I do not intend to be rude. If you would be so kind as to allow me to stay, I only need a chair near his bed. Nothing else. I will not trouble you in any way. But I cannot abandon him."

She pressed her lips and eyes together, fighting against threatening tears. The hot cup trembled in her hands and Elizabeth took it gently.

"Miss Darcy, you may stay as long as you want," Mr Bennet answered kindly. "You may have to eat to escape Mrs Bennet's insistence, but except for that, you may do as you please. We will try to accommodate this situation the best we can."

"Thank you. Thank you," Georgiana repeated, wiping her eyes.

"You are most welcome. Mr Bingley, I will send John to Netherfield right away."

"Thank you, Mr Bennet."

The waiting was hard and tormenting, and the conversation scarce, as everyone repeatedly glanced towards the door.

Mrs Bennet felt content and proud but slightly overwhelmed at the thought that Miss Georgiana Darcy–Mr Darcy's sister and the niece of an earl–was in her house and planned to remain there.

The young lady appeared to be shy, but polite and kind, despite her turmoil. She did not speak, nor did she eat anything, but she expressed her gratitude and thanked them for every little gesture.

Mr Bingley was near her all the time, but Mrs Bennet–frightened at the prospect of losing Mr Bingley as a potential suitor for Jane–found nothing to worry about in the gentleman's behaviour. He was attentive to her but in a brotherly way. Furthermore, his repeated glances at Jane and the silly grin on his face every time he looked at her, left little doubt about where his preference lay. Regarding Jane's cold manners toward Mr Bingley, Mrs Bennet was intrigued, vexed, and impatient to have a private word with her.

Finally, Dr. Cooper appeared, followed by Mr Jones and Peter. Everyone rose to their feet, surrounding him. He asked for a drink and chose a chair before he began to speak.

"Mr Darcy is still unconscious, and I cannot estimate how long it will take to see any improvement. He has a high fever which I believe is due to a bad cold. He also has a wound on his head and one on his leg, and I suspect he has several broken ribs. I cannot be sure since he did not even react to the pain."

"So, what should we do?" Georgiana asked, with trembling lips and hands.

"I will treat him the best I can, and you will wait. Patiently," Dr. Cooper joked tenderly, stroking Georgiana's hair. "He is young and strong, and I trust he is not easily defeated by a fall and a cold. He had worse injuries when he was a young boy."

Dr. Cooper sounded very much like Mr Bennet, jesting even in such upsetting conditions, and Elizabeth smiled at the revelation. In contrast to Mr Jones's anxiety, Dr. Cooper showed confidence that put them somehow at ease, despite his discouraging report.

"Can we move him to Netherfield?" Bingley asked.

"Move him? Absolutely not until he is fully conscious and I can evaluate more precisely the extent of his wounds," Dr. Cooper replied. "I will release Mr Jones from his duty; he may return home and I will ask for his assistance if needed. I will remain here as long as Darcy stays. If you would be so kind as to accommodate me, I would greatly appreciate it. Any chamber will suffice. And Stevens needs a place to sleep–a sofa will do. He will serve as my valet, too, since I did not bring my own."

Dr. Cooper was obviously accustomed to giving orders and being obeyed. There was a certain arrogance in his manners, born from his professional expertise or perhaps just a trait of his character. He was not being insolent, just expressing his needs, and he expected them to be fulfilled.

Mr Bennet exchanged a brief look with his wife, then he cleared his voice.

"Dr. Cooper, we will do the best we can to make everyone

comfortable, for Mr Darcy's benefit. We can certainly bring in a sofa for Stevens. As for the rooms, Mrs Bennet gave hers to Mr Darcy, so he did not need to be carried upstairs. We have a rather large guest room which is fortunately empty since my cousin Mr Collins left yesterday, but he could return at any time. Miss Darcy wishes to remain here too, and I suspect Mrs Annesley will join her. In my daughters' chambers, there is not enough room for another person. So I would appreciate it if you might discuss and decide the best way of solving this situation."

"Oh, I do not want to disturb you, nor to bother anyone! I will sleep on a chair. And Mrs Annesley can go to Netherfield," Miss Darcy responded.

"My dear, this is ridiculous and unwise," Dr. Cooper declared in a tone that proved his relationship with the Darcys was beyond that of just their doctor. "You cannot sleep on a chair, and you have no business being here all the time. Quite the contrary. There are some procedures I will perform that forbid the presence of a lady, sister or not, so you will be more of a bother to us than a help. I need to be here to heal him. Anyone else is of little use presently. Therefore, I will take the guest room evidently, and you will all go to Netherfield and return to visit your brother when you wish. It is as simple as that."

"Dr. Cooper, I am not leaving William," Georgiana responded with a severity that surprised the others.

"Well, then you may stay on the chair till morning and that surely will defeat your stubbornness," the doctor ended rather rudely. Elizabeth glanced at Jane, then she addressed Georgiana, trying to end the embarrassing dispute.

"Miss Darcy, you may stay with Jane and me for now. It is a small room, but you will still be able to rest. And we shall make further arrangements according to Mr Darcy's progress. If this is acceptable to you..."

"Thank you, Miss Elizabeth. It is very considerate and generous."

Bingley suddenly stepped forward, serious, solemn and obviously embarrassed.

"Mr Bennet, Mrs Bennet, I have a suggestion, and I pray that you will not take any offence at it. I truly believe it is the best way for everyone."

"What is your suggestion, Mr Bingley?" Mrs Bennet asked, intrigued.

"Due to your generosity, we have Longbourn full of people and Netherfield, which is three times larger, empty. Would you not consider that part of the family who need not be here all the time could move to Netherfield for a few days? And I would be happy to invite Mr and Mrs Gardiner when they arrive, as well as Mr Collins if he happens to return."

Bingley stared at them hopefully, while the Bennets remained silent in astonishment. Jane blushed, then turned pale, and Mrs Bennet seemed to struggle to breathe.

"We cannot ask your family to move to accommodate us," Miss Darcy replied, outraged by such a notion. "That would be an abuse of your kindness!"

"No, no indeed–that would be a wonderful solution," Mrs Bennet finally burst out. "The girls can move to Netherfield–all of them–with Mr Bennet, to chaperone them. My dear, you may stay in the library all the time. Jane, Lizzy, girls–go and pack! I will remain here to take care of everything!"

"Mama, we should discuss this and decide later," Elizabeth intervened and Jane desperately supported her sister.

"It is a generous proposal, but we need a little time to examine it," Mr Bennet answered, stopping his wife's effusions.

"Well, I need someone to show me to the guest room, so I can settle and return to Darcy," Dr. Cooper said, with little concern for the apparently distressing situation he was leaving behind.

"And I am going to stay with my brother," Miss Darcy added, addressing the Bennets. "Please think only of your family's comfort. You have already done so much for us, please do not trouble yourself even more."

She then excused herself and left, while Elizabeth hesitated, not knowing whether to follow her or to remain with her family.

"Mr Bingley, you and Mrs Annesley should go to Netherfield, arrange everything to your liking and return later for dinner. In the meantime, we will make a decision and let you know," Mr Bennet suggested.

"Very well, sir. Please take into consideration that you will have everything you need at Netherfield. You may consider yourself at home, just as if you were at Longbourn."

After Mr Bingley, Mrs Annesley, Mr Jones and Peter had departed, the Bennets remained in the drawing room, and the noisy disputes began.

In only a few hours, so many things occurred that it seemed a week had passed. The circumstances were thoroughly analysed, but an agreement was not easy to reach.

"I do not understand why we keep arguing in vain! The girls should go to Netherfield!" Mrs Bennet declared. "And you, Mr Bennet, should join them to avoid any gossip, since Jane and Mr Bingley are not married yet!"

"Mama, you keep talking about a marriage that might well never happen. Please stop, before we are all embarrassed and hurt," Jane pleaded.

"You are so silly and absurd, Jane! How can you not see that he has done everything for you?"

"No, he has not, Mama. He did it to create the best circumstances possible regarding his friend's situation."

"Well, say it as you like, you will go to Netherfield, Jane! And take your sisters with you!"

"Mama, I am not going," Elizabeth interjected severely. "We cannot leave Miss Darcy alone here, without anyone of her own age. I will take care of her since you have so many things to worry about! I am decided, so let us not discuss this further."

"I want to go! I have never lived in such a large house!" Lydia said.

"I want to go too," Kitty supported her.

"I would love a chance to explore the library," Mary declared.

"Very well. Lizzy and your mother will stay at home, and the rest of us will move to Netherfield for a few days," Mr Bennet decided.

"Mama, if they leave, there will be plenty of rooms available. I want to stay too. Please do not force me to go; it would deeply pain me. I would feel ridiculous, like I am chasing Mr Bingley. Please do not embarrass me in this way!" Jane pleaded, now tearful.

The argument began again, even more heated, and not even Mr Bennet was able to reach a truce between the ladies.

So caught up were they in the dispute, that neither noticed Miss Darcy standing in the doorway, watching them.

"Please do not force Miss Bennet to do anything against her will. And I beg you, do not argue because of me," Georgiana whispered, stepping forward.

Silence fell upon the room, and the Bennets looked at each other, under Georgiana's tormented blue gaze, mortified at being caught in such an awkward conversation.

Finally taking his role as the master of the house seriously, Mr Bennet took charge of the situation decidedly.

"You are right, Jane. There will be plenty of rooms if we leave. Girls, this is the first time you will go somewhere with only your father," Mr Bennet addressed his youngest three daughters, with a smile. "Gather your things but only the useful ones. Mrs Bennet, please make sure we have a healthy dinner tonight, as we are all tired and hungry. And now excuse me, I will be in my library for a few hours."

Chapter 15

A glimpse of light cut through the darkness and Darcy wondered if the dawn had come. He did not know how long the night had lasted, but it seemed longer than usual. He was lying down somewhere, but he did not recognise his whereabouts. Nor could he see much around him. Some voices sounded familiar at times, but then faded and disappeared. And, like a prize he could not reach–her scent, her voice, her nearness, her touch. And another presence, equally familiar. Who could it be? He had to see, or at least to ask, but speaking was as hard as seeing. His lips disobeyed him as much as his eyes and his hands. Was he imprisoned somewhere? Was he being kept against his will? The sharp pain in his head blurred his thoughts, and then darkness again... Where had that light gone?

∞∞∞

The rest of the afternoon passed somewhat more calmly, though not more comfortably. The worry about Mr Darcy's state remained equally strong, but the uproar in the house diminished as everyone returned to their chambers.

Miss Darcy, exhausted and sorrowful, refused any food or rest and preferred to remain at her brother's side. A sofa was added to Darcy's chamber–not comfortable enough to sleep on, but able to provide a small amount of comfort to those who were watching the patient.

In their room, Elizabeth and Jane shared a pot of tea and the former tried to calm her eldest sister.

"I hope Dr. Cooper will heal Mr Darcy. Mr Jones said he is

one of the best doctors in England."

"I hope so too, Lizzy. But he seems to be a severe man. And he spoke almost rudely to Miss Darcy, did you notice?"

"I understand he has been their doctor for many years, so he knows how he is allowed to behave. I think he tried to convince her to go to Netherfield and to accommodate herself properly. That entire discussion about the rooms became rather troublesome for everyone."

"We made a spectacle of ourselves in front of Miss Darcy, Lizzy, and it was all my fault."

"Yes, we did. I will not argue that. But the fault was shared among us."

"Lizzy, I cannot possibly go to Netherfield. I simply cannot."

"I understand, Jane. I have my doubts regarding your reasoning, but I will respect your choice."

"Surely you noticed how close Mr Bingley and Miss Darcy were to each other."

"I did notice, Jane. But to me, his behaviour towards her seemed completely different from his manners towards you. It was still very gentle and kind, but different."

"I know, Lizzy. Because he was only being friendly to me, and I foolishly assumed more than I should have. To her, he has no reason to restrain or conceal his affection."

"He was rather open in showing his affection to you, too, Jane. Nobody who saw you together doubted that."

"I do not blame him, Lizzy. Not at all. And I do not blame Miss Darcy either."

"If someone is to blame, it surely would be Mr Bingley. Miss Darcy has no fault. In truth, you both could be victims of Mr Bingley's reckless behaviour in showing admiration for a young woman, while he was already bound to another."

"Mr Bingley is amiable and friendly to everyone, Lizzy. We should not criticise those qualities that we once admired in him."

"Very well. So you suffer, but he is faultless," Elizabeth

concluded, rolling her eyes. "I do blame him, Jane, both for your pain and for Miss Darcy's. Thank God she gives no consequence to anything around her, as she is too preoccupied with her brother's health. If she truly has some understanding with him, just imagine how she would feel adding more turmoil to her suffering."

"I pity her, Lizzy. That is why I try to behave as properly as I can. I do not want her to suspect any of my thoughts. She looks so frightened that she might lose her brother. She does not seem proud and arrogant at all."

"No. I believe she is rather shy and restrained. Quite different from Mr Darcy and from what I expected of her. I wonder how Mr Wickham could have misjudged her so completely since he has known her for so many years."

"Perhaps Mr Wickham is not a good judge of character."

"He must be one of the worst, Jane."

A few minutes and a few sips of tea later, Jane spoke again.

"My presence at Netherfield would have been so awkward and distressing for Mr Bingley, for Miss Darcy, and for me. I know Mr Bingley tried to be polite and helpful, but his invitation was not appropriate. Not for me."

"Jane, I am still far from being sure of Mr Bingley's intentions. And I am too tired to consider it thoroughly. But why would he host a ball for you? Why would he call on us so often? Why would he dance with you and show his preference for you so openly?"

"Perhaps he did not believe he was doing anything wrong, Lizzy."

"But why would Mr Darcy allow him to misbehave so utterly if he had a special connection to his sister? At first I thought Mr Darcy disapproved of Mr Bingley's admiration for you, but lately, my impression has changed. He has said many small things that show his change of mind. He would never allow his friend to trifle with you."

"I do not know, Lizzy. I truly do not know," Jane said, wiping her tears.

"Dear Jane, if I were not so exhausted worrying about Mr Darcy's health I would really hate Mr Bingley for all the distress he is causing you. This situation must be resolved soon."

"Oh, Lizzy, promise me you will not do anything," Jane begged in panic.

Elizabeth embraced her. "As I said, I am too exhausted and so are you. I promise I will not stir the waters–at least for now."

That evening, Mr Bingley came to dinner, but Mrs Annesley preferred to remain at Netherfield to rest. He visited Darcy briefly as he did not do so before and returned grieved and helpless, spending a few minutes in private conversation with Georgiana.

Miss Darcy and Dr. Cooper ate briefly and returned to watch Darcy.

Stevens still did not leave his master's side.

There was not much conversation between the courses, nor any entertainment.

Rather early, Mr Bingley returned to Netherfield with Mr Bennet and his youngest daughters, disconcerted and tormented both for his friend and at Jane's restrained behaviour. Behind him, the eldest Miss Bennet stared at the carriage from the window, heartbroken.

Mrs Bennet scolded Jane for a good few minutes, reproaching her ridiculous refusal to go to Netherfield. In the end, both retired to their chambers, allowing Elizabeth some peace and quiet.

Elizabeth took charge and brought Hill and John to change the sheets and to prepare the now available rooms–one for Miss Darcy and the other for any future guests. The last two days had been so full, so tormenting, so tiresome that her mind barely noticed what her body was doing. She walked up and down the stairs, wondering if her feet were still moving. Eventually, when everything was settled, she attempted to convince Miss Darcy to sleep for a little while. She met with no success, and she abandoned the fight. She was too exhausted, and the entire situation was too nerve-wracking to start a battle she could not control. So she returned to Jane, avoiding any further conversation. When she fell asleep. It was almost midnight.

∞∞∞

Darcy had hoped for so long for the coldness to go and now, it had happened. But the heat that enveloped him was even more insupportable. His right arm was burning the most, and something was slowly licking the life itself from his body. He knew he needed to do something, but he still could not move. He shouted, but nobody responded to his calls. Where was she? If she was there, she would have helped him. She was ready to walk with him through the storm when they were trapped in the cottage, and she freed him from the horse's reins when he had fallen. She put her coat under his head, then she placed his head in her lap, and she held his hand. She would help him, but where was she? If he could only shout to her! He screamed, but not even he could hear his words. He tried again and again, but he was still alone in the dark. She did not come.

∞∞∞

Elizabeth startled awake, trembling, her body shivering with countless chills, while her forehead was covered in sweat. A deep fear overwhelmed her, and she glanced around, wholly lost. She sensed she had to do something, something of great importance, and she had missed it.

With a sense of fright that something horrible had occurred, she tied her robe, quickly brushed her hair, and in moments she was knocking on Darcy's door.

She found Miss Darcy, Stevens and Dr. Cooper all around Darcy. It appeared the doctor had released some of his bad blood, and his arm was lying at his side, bandaged, still bleeding.

The three were all so pale and obviously tired that they

looked as ill as the patient. Miss Darcy especially looked so exhausted that Elizabeth wondered how she was still standing.

"He spoke!" Georgiana told her, tearfully.

"Did he? That is wonderful!" Elizabeth replied whole-heartedly, a huge burden removed from her shoulders.

"We did not understand what he said, but he spoke and he moved!" the young lady added.

Elizabeth ignored the impropriety of her gesture and touched Darcy's hand, then his forehead again.

"He still has a high fever," she addressed Dr. Cooper.

"He does. Stevens and I were about to chill his body with some cold water."

"May I help?" Elizabeth asked genuinely.

"No, but we appreciate your concern. Miss Bennet, forgive my forwardness, but neither you nor Miss Darcy should be in Darcy's room much while he is unconscious. He is a proud man and would not approve of being seen in such a helpless situation and so improperly attired. I cannot persuade Miss Darcy to see reason, but I hope you will not be equally stubborn."

Elizabeth looked at Miss Darcy, then at the doctor.

"I am very sorry to disappoint you, sir. I would do anything you ask to help Mr Darcy's condition improve, but staying away from this room is not one of them. I am afraid I will come to enquire after him quite often, and I assure you his attire is the last thing that impresses me. I look forward to his recovery so he can personally condemn my behaviour."

Dr. Cooper was taken aback. "Upon my word, you express your opinion quite decidedly for someone so young. You found him, am I right? I understand you showed remarkable bravery in saving him. You must have a particular interest in his well-being."

"No bravery at all, I assure you. I just ran back and forth to bring help. My best quality is that I am a good walker and my only interest is in protecting a friend. Mr Darcy showed great courage in saving me, my mother, and sisters from a tragic accident that could have cost our lives only a week ago. It is our turn to show our gratitude."

"Oh, I see. That explains your family's anxiety around him."

"Not quite, Dr. Cooper. We would take care of anyone who suffered an accident near our house, even if that person had not saved us at another time," Elizabeth replied with half mockery.

Dr. Cooper might have been a brilliant doctor, but his tone was too superior and arrogant for her taste and for her state of distress. To her surprise, he laughed.

"Yes, I imagine as much. Well, I shall tell Darcy that you forced your presence in his chamber against my will."

Elizabeth's tone softened from harsh to teasing. "As I said, I eagerly wait to argue with Mr Darcy. It has been our habit since we first met."

"So it would be my duty to ensure the circumstances to carry on your habit, it appears," Dr. Cooper concluded with a trace of amusement in his voice. "Now, would you two ladies leave before we undress the patient?"

Elizabeth blushed, glancing at Georgiana.

"Immediately, sir. First, I want to convince all three of you to save your strength, to Mr Darcy's benefit. I see no reason to exhaust yourselves all at the same time. You should take turns so you can rest from time to time and enjoy a proper meal. I am willing to keep Miss Darcy company while you and Stevens sleep or eat, and then I will make sure she does the same while you take care of him. Please be wise and accept my suggestion, since I have no intention of accepting your refusal and we may stay here arguing all night."

"I do not wish to leave my brother," Georgiana whispered.

"I fully agree with Miss Bennet," Dr. Cooper said. "And we should start by you going and resting, Miss Darcy. Just imagine what Darcy would say if he were to wake up now and see you in such a state. He would be rightfully upset with us all."

"Come Miss Darcy, we should rest until morning, then we will come to sit with Mr Darcy while Dr. Cooper and Stevens find some sleep," Elizabeth insisted.

"Will you call me if anything changes?" the girl pleaded with Dr. Cooper.

"Of course I will, my dear."

The girls walked to the door, arm in arm, when suddenly a weak voice broke the silence and made them run back to the bed.

∞∞∞

She was there, he knew she was; he could not mistake her voice, her scent, not even her steps. He felt her presence, although his eyes would not open enough to see her. She spoke to someone, but whose voices were those that sounded so familiar to him? Could it be Georgiana? Were they at Pemberley? Or else, how could Elizabeth be with his sister? Or was it only another of his disturbing dreams? Was she truly there, or had she entered so profoundly into his being that he could sense her even when she was away from him?

"Elizabeth..."

∞∞∞

"William? Can you hear me? Please look at me!" Georgiana begged, taking his hand. "Dr. Cooper, why is he not answering?"

"He is not conscious yet, but he can speak. This is a good sign. He is a strong man. I trust he will recover soon," the doctor responded.

"But what did he say?" Georgiana asked.

"I believe he said *'Elizabeth',*" the doctor replied, looking at the lady in question. She felt her cheeks burning, as she had heard the same and was even more puzzled than the others. Why would he call her name, of all people, when he was in such a condition?

"He must remember that I was the one who found him. Or perhaps, he already wishes to scold me for being in his room without his permission," she finally found the strength to jest.

"Come, Miss Darcy, let us leave and allow Dr. Cooper to do what he knows best. We want you to look your best when your brother recovers."

Hesitantly, Georgiana eventually agreed.

Although she tried to keep her countenance, Elizabeth was increasingly distressed as she led Miss Darcy to her chamber. Mr Darcy did not say *"Miss Bennet,"* nor *"Miss Elizabeth,"* but *"Elizabeth"*. Simple and so familiar. Her name sounded so strange and different on his lips, even from the depths of his unconsciousness.

"Miss Darcy, I hope you will feel comfortable here. The rooms are neither as large nor as elegant as those at Netherfield," Elizabeth said when they entered the chamber.

"It is lovely and just perfect" the girl replied with a faint little smile. "I apologise again for causing you and your family so much trouble."

"Please do not mention it. We help each other in times of need."

"I have rarely met a family as generous as yours. I am even sorrier that I distressed Miss Bennet with the move from one house to another."

"It is not your fault, I assure you," Elizabeth tried to calm her. "But perhaps you would have been more comfortable at Netherfield. You would have been better attended to, as there are many servants, and there is Mrs Annesley and especially Mr Bingley. I am sure you would prefer to be closer to him in these difficult circumstances."

"To Charles? Oh no, I want to be closer to my brother. Please do not believe me to be a spoiled young heiress who only cares to be better attended to. I care about nothing else but my brother's health. He is the only one who matters to me."

Tears moistened the girl's eyes again, and Elizabeth took her to sit on the bed, holding her hands.

"I most certainly do not consider you such. I applaud your loyalty and affection for your brother. I have heard him praise you many times, and now I see he had more reasons than just his brotherly regard."

"He is the best brother one could hope to have! He has been almost like a father to me. I cannot imagine my life without him," Georgiana said.

"I envy you a little," Elizabeth smiled. "Growing up with four sisters, I often wonder how it would be to have a brother."

"I would love to have a sister, too," Georgiana replied with a warmth that touched Elizabeth.

"Come now, you must sleep a little. Let me help you with your gown and your hair. I am afraid we do not have a maid for this specific task but being five girls, we help each other," Elizabeth smiled.

"Miss Bennet?" Georgiana said as Elizabeth removed the pins from her hair.

"Yes?"

"My brother wrote to me about you last week. He said I would like you very much if we met. He was right. But then again, my brother is always right."

Elizabeth's cheeks burned from an embarrassing delight as such a statement implied more than she dared consider.

"I thank you, Miss Darcy; you are very kind. I hope that the unfortunate circumstances that brought us together will change for the better soon. As for Mr Darcy, I am not certain if I should be pleased or worried that he wrote to you," she tried to conceal her nervousness behind her humour.

"Why would you worry?"

"Well, Mr Darcy and I had a rather challenging start to our acquaintance. Our mutual opinion of each other was rather poor. So I wonder what he could write about me."

Georgiana was genuinely concerned. "My brother would never write unkind things about anyone. And his opinion of you did not sound ill at all."

"I am glad to hear that."

"But...Miss Bennet, forgive me, why would you think ill of my brother? He is truly the best of men and everyone who knows him appreciates his generous nature and his noble character."

Elizabeth smiled at such sincerity and devotion.

"We heartily admired Mr Darcy's character, once we had the chance to discover it. For a while, his true nature was deeply hidden behind his rather distant manners. This can be misleading for those who are barely acquainted with him."

"Oh...I understand," Georgiana replied in shy agreement.

"But, Miss Darcy, your brother is truly an exceptional man; now I can testify to that. He saved our lives, jumping on galloping horses, in the middle of a storm. Without him, our carriage would have been crushed, and all of us hurt, if not worse. Did he tell you that?"

Georgiana shook her head. "No. He wrote to me that your family had suffered an accident and you were all trapped in a cottage for a few hours. He mentioned that you were fearless and kept everyone safe and even intended to walk through the storm to bring help."

Elizabeth stared at her in disbelief. "I did not do such things! I mean, I did, but they meant little compared with what he did. I do not deserve such praise."

It was Miss Darcy's turn to force a smile.

"It seems both you and my brother did things that are worthy of mentioning only by others, not by yourselves. Quite a similar disposition you have."

Elizabeth blushed even more, and her fingers dropped the pins to the floor from distress she hardly dared to admit.

"Well, enough conversation for tonight. You have some water here and some biscuits if you are hungry. My room is the third on the right if you need me. I will leave you to rest."

"Thank you, Miss Bennet!"

"You are most welcome. I am going now before Jane starts to worry about me."

"Please apologise to her from me one more time. I hope I did not upset her with my presence."

"There is no need to apologise, Miss Darcy. My sister is the kindest and most understanding person. She is often kinder to others than to herself."

"And she is lovely too. Just as Charles described her. I hope they will be very happy together, they are truly a perfect match."

Elizabeth stopped breathing. She pressed her hand to her chest and stepped back, closer to Georgiana.

"Excuse me?"

The girl turned pale and put her palm over her mouth.

"Oh dear Lord, please forgive me! I did not mean to intrude! I am such a fool! I did not know it was a secret."

Elizabeth sat down next to her again.

"No, no, please do not worry. It is just...I was not aware that Mr Bingley had told you of such intentions. I thought..."

"He called on me as soon as he arrived in town to inform me about my brother's delay. We had a cup of tea while he told me about his business and his desire to return to Netherfield as soon as he could. He mentioned his admiration for Miss Bennet quite a few times. Then the following night the tragic news about William came and...I hope I did not betray his trust. He is such a wonderful friend and almost like a brother to me."

With little consideration for propriety, Elizabeth spontaneously embraced Georgiana and took her hands for another moment.

"You did not betray anything, quite the contrary! If you could know how helpful our little talk has been! Please rest a little, then we will go back to watch your brother. Good night."

"Good night, Miss Bennet," Georgiana said, surprised and puzzled by the embrace and by Elizabeth's sudden change of disposition.

She leaned against the pillows, but she had no time to think of anything else, as exhaustion defeated her in moments.

∞ ∞ ∞

Once in her room, Elizabeth climbed onto the bed, embracing Jane, who was lost in restless dreams. Happy news was waiting as soon as she should awaken and at least her sister would be as happy as she deserved.

Elizabeth closed her eyes, cuddling the pillow. What about herself? Could she allow herself to think of her own happiness? Could she dare think of him in a way that she had never ventured to think of a man before?

He wrote to his sister about her, and he danced with her alone at the ball, then wished to talk to her privately, then called out for her during his ordeal, when his mind was blurred. He did not call for his beloved sister, nor his close friend. Only her. When his thoughts were clouded, he thought of her. There could be only one reason for such an occurrence. Could she have miscomprehended the meaning of all this?

Mr Darcy, of all people, held tender feelings for her? And if so, what did he intend to do about it? Could he pursue any plans that would involve them both? Could he intend to bind his future to hers, despite the difference in their situations and his harsh disapproval of her family? Or was he only betrayed by his fever and suffering, that disclosed intimate feelings he never wished to expose?

Were those feelings real, or was she assuming too much? She had already allowed herself to be deceived by Caroline Bingley's manipulation. Could she trust her judgement on such a delicate matter?

Elizabeth tried to fall asleep but with little success; she was so tired that her head was hurting. Until dawn, she could still not decide if she felt thrilled by all the extraordinary information she had unexpectedly discovered, or if it had only increased her turmoil.

Either way, she could only think of Darcy, so profoundly and so powerfully that sleep entirely evaded her.

Chapter 16

*E*lizabeth jumped up from her bed when the wind rattled the windows and sunshine pierced through the closed curtains. She was alone in the chamber and the late hour alarmed her. She dressed carelessly and hurried downstairs but nobody was there. Eventually, she discovered Mrs Bennet and Jane in the kitchen, talking to Hill.

"Good morning. I am afraid I overslept. How is everyone?"

"Do not worry, Lizzy, everything is fine. Dr. Cooper and Stevens are sleeping. Miss Darcy woke up an hour ago and she is with her brother. I am taking her something to eat," Jane said.

"How is Mr Darcy?" Elizabeth asked.

"Dr. Cooper said he is the same, but is content that his state did not worsen in the night. Mr Jones came to enquire about him earlier," Mrs Bennet replied. "Oh dear, I have never had such disruption at Longbourn. I hope everything is resolved soon. It is time for some relief."

"I hope Papa and the girls had a pleasant night at Netherfield," Jane said.

"Why would they not have? You would have had the same, if you were not too stubborn to go. Upon my word, Jane, sometimes you are more obstinate than Lizzy."

"I am more useful here, Mama. I am sure you and Lizzy need my help."

"We do not, I assure you. I would be most satisfied to know you are with Mr Bingley and that he has the chance to speak privately with you, if he chooses to do so."

"I am sure Mr Bingley will find a way to speak privately

to Jane, if he wishes to. Miss Darcy confessed to me last night that she believes Mr Bingley and Jane would be a perfect match. Apparently, she and Mr Bingley are good friends, and she is preoccupied with his future felicity in marriage," Elizabeth declared, looking at her sister with a meaningful stare.

Jane paled, then coloured and her eyes widened in disbelief. Elizabeth smiled reassuringly.

"Did she say that?" Mrs Bennet cried. "Oh, what excellent character and superior education this young girl possesses! She is one of the most accomplished young ladies I have seen, I can tell you that. And so kindhearted! So wise, to know what is best for her friend! She takes after her brother in wisdom, of this I am certain. Except she is less proud and unpleasant. Oh, I am sure she will befriend you in the future, Jane! How fortunate that she came to Longbourn with Mr Bingley!"

"Mama, let us calm ourselves before Miss Darcy hears us again. Her visit to Longbourn is not quite so fortunate since her brother is so very ill," Elizabeth tried to temper her mother, regretting her thoughtless lack of secrecy. She should have known better and waited until she could tell Jane alone. Now, the damage was done, and Mrs Bennet needed another powerful inducement to be stopped.

"I know that. But I am sure Mr Darcy will recover–he cannot possibly die from a trifling cold. Thank God Dr. Cooper was fetched. Poor Mr Jones looked so lost, so frightened at the notion of treating Mr Darcy! It was almost laughable! It was like he had never seen a cold before!"

"Mr Jones did his best! But yes, it is a great relief that Dr. Cooper is here," Elizabeth admitted.

"It is so remarkable how many people are loyal to Mr Darcy, is it not? Mr Bingley, his sister, Dr. Cooper...and Stevens has barely left his side," Jane spoke, slowly regaining her strength and her spirits. Her face was suddenly brighter and her eyes were gleaming with joy and happy tears.

"All of them speak highly of him," Elizabeth agreed, blushing at her own feelings regarding the subject of the conversation.

"Well, I like him much better now than when we first met," Mrs Bennet approved.

The conversation lasted for a little while, until Hill came in with a tray for Miss Darcy.

Elizabeth took it and Jane readily followed her. As soon as they were alone, Jane expressed her incredulous excitement.

"Dearest Lizzy, are you certain of what you said earlier?"

"Yes; more than certain. And now I wonder how it happened that we were both so silly as to give credit to Caroline Bingley and to doubt Mr Bingley's honour."

"We did no such thing!" Jane whispered. "I never doubted Mr Bingley's character!"

"Yes you did, since you assumed he was trifling with you while he was promised to another. But all is well now; I hope you will learn your lesson from this and treat Caroline as she deserves."

They knocked on the door and slowly entered. Miss Darcy was alone, sitting on the bed, holding her brother's hand. He was resting on his back with several pillows propped behind him so he was almost sitting.

Georgiana smiled shyly at them; Elizabeth put the tray on the small table and sat on the other side.

"How is he?"

"Nothing has changed," Georgiana answered. "I tried to give him a little of this medicine, but I mostly spilt it on myself," she murmured, showing her wet, soiled dress.

"Let me help you to try again," Elizabeth offered.

She took the teaspoon and the cup with the medicine, poured a bit and tried to place it between Darcy's lips. They were tight together and, after a moment of hesitation, Elizabeth gently parted them with her fingers, carefully placing the tip of the teaspoon inside, allowing the medicine to slip into his mouth. He gulped and they looked at each other with contentment. Elizabeth repeated the gesture, then she brushed a drop of medicine from the corner of his mouth with her thumb.

Darcy moved his head and moaned; the three girls gasped and gathered closer, calling his name.

∞∞∞

The dark hole that had kept him prisoner became larger and at times he felt he could escape. Glimpses of light broke inside more often and the sounds around him were a regular companion. He forced himself to stay alert to catch any sign that Elizabeth was nearby and his endeavour was rewarded again. This time, as if in answer to his hopes, she was so close that he sensed her body touching his. She asked him something and he would readily obey, but could not hear her request clearly. But then, a shiver shook him when her fingers pressed against his lips. Every fibre of his body stirred under her touch and his lips parted at her gentle demand. If only he could raise his hand enough to touch her too. Or to gently pull her closer to him and taste her lips with his own. He was thirsty, but he knew her flavour would be enough to satiate him. If only he could move... he struggled, but to no avail. He tried to speak, but his dry lips betrayed him again. He heard her calling him and had at least the comfort of knowing she had not left him alone in the darkness.

∞∞∞

"He is still not answering...I wonder if he can hear us," Miss Darcy said, disappointed and tearful.

"I am sure he will answer soon," Jane attempted to comfort Georgiana.

"I am sure too," Elizabeth smiled warmly. "Miss Darcy, perhaps we should change your gown now that we have succeeded with the medicine?"

"My gown? Oh, yes," the girl replied, absently.

"I will be happy to assist you," Jane offered and Georgiana reluctantly accepted.

When the door closed behind them, Elizabeth realised she should not be alone with Darcy. But she heartily enjoyed the moment of solitude.

With increasing curiosity, she looked at him; his face was slightly coloured, which she found to be a significant improvement. As his body was elevated slightly with pillows, he appeared to be sitting up, ready to talk to her.

She noticed the lock of hair on his forehead and temples, the sideburns, the long lashes, the lips pressed together... she did not allow her eyes to leave his face. She took the liberty of admiring his fine features, wondering about this complicated man's true nature. Such a mix of arrogance and kindness, rudeness and gentleness, disdain and generosity, indifference and courage, all in one handsome package so hard to unwrap.

So much had changed in only a fortnight, and it was all related to him. He was so deeply connected to their lives now that Elizabeth dreaded to consider what might happen if he should leave.

The revelation about his interest in her was still overwhelming; what his thoughts and intentions might be, she still did not dare consider thoroughly. She was fearful and desirous at the same time of discovering more about him. But for the moment, she only wished him to be healthy again.

His fever seemed lower and that had to be a good sign. Elizabeth put another log on the fire and pulled the curtain open wider. Perhaps more light would benefit him. She returned to sit on the side of the bed and took his hand. It felt cool enough. She touched his forehead and it was rather cold too.

Blushing, she made a wild decision and slowly leaned towards him, pressing her lips to his temple, just as her mother had demonstrated. It felt normal, and she breathed in relief: at least the danger of fever seemed gone. She smiled at him and brushed a lock of hair from his forehead. And only then did she notice Miss Darcy standing in the doorway, gazing at her in surprise.

Elizabeth almost jumped to her feet, brushing her gown

hastily.

"His fever is gone," she said, abashed and nervous. "My mother taught me to check for fever by touching the temple with the lips. She said it is the most accurate observation."

She kept blushing, averting her eyes, pacing around, undecided if she should stay or leave.

"This is happy news indeed," Georgiana said lightly, with a puzzled expression that Elizabeth did not miss.

"Did he say anything else?" Georgiana asked.

"No."

"I hope he will soon. Mr Bingley has arrived with your father and sisters. Mrs Bennet said breakfast will be ready soon," Georgiana continued in a light voice.

Slowly, Elizabeth gained some composure. "Oh, have they? I will go and greet them. May I bring you anything?"

"No, thank you. Charles told me he wrote to my aunt, Lady Matlock, yesterday and to my cousin, Colonel Fitzwilliam."

"Good," Elizabeth replied, fearful at what the girl might think of her.

"Miss Bennet?"

"Yes, Miss Darcy?"

"I am glad your opinion of my brother has improved since the beginning of your acquaintance."

Elizabeth stared at her, dumbfounded, meeting the girl's shy, blue eyes and her small smile.

"Anyone who knows Mr Darcy holds him in high regard– you said that yourself. I only had to pay more attention and overcome my false first impression," Elizabeth replied. "Now, if you will excuse me, I will leave you for a short time."

In the hall, Elizabeth leaned against the wall, and caught her breath, struggling to dissipate the torment in her mind.

Afterwards, she joined the others in the drawing room, where Jane was closely engaged in conversation with Mr Bingley, both smiling at each other, blushing and beaming with happiness. All was well in that regard.

∞ ∞ ∞

Around noon, Mr Bingley left to meet some officers in Meryton, and Mr Bennet joined him. Stevens and Dr. Cooper were with Darcy, while Miss Darcy finally spent some time with the Bennet ladies.

Georgiana was still restrained, finding some shelter between Elizabeth and Jane, while Mrs Bennet, Lydia and Kitty talked loudly about various subjects.

To their surprise, callers were announced, and Lieutenant Denny, Lieutenant Reeves and Mr Wickham all entered, bowing to the ladies charmingly.

Their surprising visit was received with cheers from the youngest girls, with joy by Mrs Bennet, and with reluctance from Elizabeth. What were they doing there, since they must have known Mr Bennet was not at home?

Elizabeth looked at Georgiana to make the introductions, realising that the girl was already acquainted with Wickham. She startled as she saw Miss Darcy pale, then frown, her face changed by a deep and apparent turmoil. She seemed unsteady on her feet as if she was in danger of fainting, her eyes and lips widened in disbelief.

Wickham stepped towards her with a broad smile, bowed to her and took her hand in his, ceremoniously bringing it to his lips.

"My dear Miss Darcy, I am so happy to meet you again here. Truly happy. I can hardly believe my good luck," he said.

"Mr Wickham..." she responded barely audibly, withdrawing her hand. "It is not good luck for anybody since my brother is ill."

"Oh, yes, yes. Of course. How is Darcy? We were wondering about him," Wickham continued.

"He is improving," Elizabeth answered. "Gentlemen, please sit down," she indicated the opposite sofa, while she sat next to Georgiana.

Mrs Bennet ordered tea and the officers quickly became engaged in conversation with the younger ladies.

Jane spoke little, Georgiana not at all.

Elizabeth turned to the girl and whispered.

"Miss Darcy, are you unwell? May I help you in any way?"

"No...Thank you. I will soon go to my brother."

"I forgot to mention Mr Wickham, please forgive me. I did not expect to see him here, as I know he and your brother are not on friendly terms."

"I did not expect to see him either..."

"Are you troubled by his presence? We may leave if you prefer."

"I would like to return to my brother soon, if possible..." Georgiana confessed. Her hands trembled so violently that the girl dropped the cup of hot tea, right into Elizabeth's lap. They both gasped, the gentlemen rose to help, and Elizabeth found herself uncomfortably wet.

"Are you hurt?" Georgiana asked, her voice trembling with worry.

"No, I am fine. Just a little wet," Elizabeth smiled. "I will go to my room to change; please wait for me only a moment. Jane will take care of you."

Georgiana nodded, and Elizabeth hurried out, glancing at the girl from the doorway. She was talking to Jane privately, keeping her eyes to the floor.

With a grip in her chest and a sense of danger troubling her, Elizabeth went to her room and changed. She returned several minutes later, wearing a new gown and concerned gaze, looking for Georgiana.

Jane was talking to her sisters and the two officers, her mother was on the other side of the room speaking privately with Hill, and Miss Darcy was alone in a corner, staring out of the window in a way that reminded Elizabeth of her brother.

With disbelief and anger, Elizabeth noticed Wickham moving nearer to Georgiana. The girl startled, but he stepped closer, saying something that obviously upset her. Elizabeth hurried towards them, careful not to make a scene, catching a most disturbing exchange.

"Georgiana, dearest, you look lovelier than ever."

"Please do not call me by my name, Mr Wickham."

"Come, dearest, I thought we had long stepped over this line. We share the same name and furthermore, if not for your horrible brother, we would be married by now. You would be mine."

"You have no right to speak to me like that, nor to offend my brother. I will talk to Mr Bingley straight away."

"Really? And tell him what? Come, my dear, surely you have missed me, you cannot deny it," said Wickham.

Elizabeth was shocked by the words, by Georgiana's troubled countenance and Wickham's grin. They had not observed her, and she was uncertain how to intervene in such an intimate conversation without causing a scandal in front of the others.

To her surprise and panic, she noticed her mother approaching from the other side of the couple. Mrs Bennet was not close enough to hear the two yet, but her expression spoke much of her displeasure with the scene.

The couple was so engaged in their conversation that they seemed oblivious to everything else around them.

Miss Darcy continued in a low and troubled voice. "Mr Wickham, I would ask you to leave me alone. I am waiting for my brother to recover; I am in no need of company. If he knew you were here, talking to me, he would take measures."

"We should take advantage of the fact that he is unconscious. I am sure everybody is happy that he is ill. You must know he is the most despised man in the area, although he has been here for less than two months. His arrogance, his disdainful behaviour, his pretensions of superiority have appalled everybody. If he passes away, you will inherit Pemberley, will you not?"

Georgiana was tearful.

"You are just as mean and cruel as I was told. My father would be so disappointed to see you. I cannot spend a single moment in your presence. If you do not leave, I shall."

"Leave where Miss Darcy? What is happening here? Why would you want to leave, Miss Darcy?" a voice called out, breaking up the discussion, disconcerting the entire party. All eyes turned to the couple, dumbfounded.

Miss Darcy mumbled something, pale and alarmed, while Elizabeth readily took her arm.

"It is nothing...I apologise, Mrs Bennet. My manners are rather improper. I am just in no need of company...Forgive me," Georgiana whispered.

Wickham grinned with a self-satisfaction that disturbed Elizabeth.

"Do not worry, Mrs Bennet, I will convince her otherwise. We are good friends, and I know what arguments are convincing to her."

Mrs Bennet raised her eyebrow, her face colouring from ire.

"Do you? It appears to me Miss Darcy is not desirous of your company so I would suggest you remove yourself from her proximity and tell me at once what is happening."

"Mrs Bennet, with all due respect, this is my private business with Miss Darcy, and I would like to keep it this way, without anybody interfering. I am having an intimate conversation with an old friend."

Such impertinence astonished Elizabeth and made Georgiana almost faint again. The girl searched for support from Elizabeth, while Mrs Bennet stared at Wickham with her mouth open in disbelief, gulping repeatedly.

Fury kept Mrs Bennet silent for a moment, then suddenly her words burst out with such power that Wickham took a step back.

With her hands on her hips, the lady took a step forward, to be closer to Wickham, her eyes narrowed, sending sharp arrows at him.

"Excuse me? Your business? No interference? Intimate conversation? What due respect? Surely you are joking, sir. You are in my house, talking to a young lady who is my guest. She asked you to leave her alone, yet you insisted on upsetting her further. And you demand that I not interfere? Who do you think you are?"

"Mrs Bennet!" Wickham's countenance was still insolent, and Mrs Bennet did not miss it.

"Mr Wickham! Maybe my daughters' preference for you makes you believe you possess more rights than you truly do and that you are entitled to some special favour, which is far from reality. I do not know of your past dealings with Mr Darcy and I trust he knows how to deal with you, but to upset a young lady in my house, under my nose! How dare you? You have overstayed your welcome, sir!"

"I did not do anything to upset Miss Darcy," Wickham claimed serenely.

Mrs Bennet grew angrier.

"You did not? What can you mean? If a young lady is bothered that you simply breathe near her, a gentleman should understand and leave. What on earth are they teaching you in the militia lately? You cannot handle a scared horse, you cannot start a fire, you do not behave properly in the company of ladies, you reply impolitely to the mistress of the house! You lack many skills, sir! Officers are not what they used to be!"

"Mama, let us calm ourselves," Elizabeth whispered.

"Do not shush me, Lizzy! Mr Wickham, if you behave, we are pleased to have you. Go and sit over there near Lydia and Kitty—they will surely not be bothered by your company. Or near Lizzy—she can handle impertinent men. I recollect her slapping the youngest son of a duke several years ago, and she was only seventeen."

"Mama, please!" Elizabeth interjected, red from embarrassment, holding Georgiana's arm.

"I would rather leave, ma'am," Wickham said with apparent vexation. "I already have some fixed engagements that will suffer no further delay. I only wished to greet you and Miss Darcy. I apologise for intruding. I will not stay where I am not welcome."

"When one's manners are proper, there is no intrusion. We are sorry that you must leave, as you are usually pleasant company. But be it as you wish."

"Mama..." Jane begged, trying to make her mother sit after Mr Wickham exited the room.

"No mama, Jane! I am so angry that I can barely breathe! What is wrong with young men nowadays? I truly hope you have better manners with the ladies," she addressed the other two officers, who watched her with embarrassment, unsure of what their mistake was.

"Mrs Bennet, I assure you it must be a huge mistake. We had no intention of upsetting anyone. Wickham suggested we come and enquire after Mr Darcy, that was all," Lieutenant Denny struggled to explain.

"I am glad you came, sir! And please do so anytime you want–your presence is always agreeable to us. But as a mother of five daughters, I cannot bear to see a young woman displeased with a man's behaviour and his reluctance to remedy his error!"

"Mama, why are you upset? What happened?" Lydia cried.

"Nothing of consequence happened. It was all my fault. I truly apologise. Please forgive me," Miss Darcy whispered, then excused herself and hurried to her brother's room.

Elizabeth followed her, while Mrs Bennet shrugged and continued to comment about some young men's poor manners.

Chapter 17

*S*oon after Wickham left, the other two officers departed too. Their visit had broken the rare tranquillity at Longbourn and more questions remained unanswered.

Elizabeth was the only one who had caught a few words from the heated, yet private conversation and she was deeply shaken by the revelation. Mr Wickham and Miss Darcy appeared to have been entangled in a relationship that could have resulted in a marriage which Mr Darcy opposed.

It would not be the first or the last story she had heard involving a young heiress in love with someone below her position, who her family opposed.

There could be many reasons for Mr Darcy to reject such a union, even if Wickham was his father's godson. His disapproval was plausible, just as Mr Wickham's grudge against him was understandable. But Miss Darcy's reaction to seeing him showed no affection, no tenderness, no regret, but only distress and even fear. And his behaviour was impertinent, cold, intimidating, far from how a man should act if he planned to pursue a lady and convince her brother he was worthy of her.

Elizabeth was now lost as to how to proceed further. She could not speak to Miss Darcy of what she had overheard, nor could she reveal the secret to anyone. She could only protect the girl against further distress and wait and pray for Mr Darcy to recover.

About Wickham she did not worry too much. He had upset Mrs Bennet so profoundly that he was unlikely to appear at Longbourn anytime soon. And even if he did, he meant nothing to them.

For a moment, she wondered how much Mr Bingley knew of Wickham, if anything. Perhaps he, as the closest friend of the Darcys, should be informed about a possible conflict between Wickham and Georgiana. But how to approach him on such a delicate subject was still a challenge to Elizabeth.

Miss Darcy remained at her brother's side for the rest of the morning and nobody could take her away from there, as though it was the only place where she felt safe. Elizabeth and Dr. Cooper insisted on her leaving the room and resting, but they met with no success so eventually they abandoned any further attempts.

In the afternoon, Mr Bingley and Mr Bennet returned. All Elizabeth's reluctance proved useless, as the moment they entered, Mrs Bennet told the gentlemen how Mr Wickham had upset Miss Darcy.

As expected, Mr Bingley became angry and wished to confront the man immediately, but Mr Bennet and Jane managed to calm him enough to discuss the situation rationally.

"We are not certain about the nature of the conflict between them, so we should not expose them to any rumours or speculations," Elizabeth said. "Let us make sure Miss Darcy is not bothered again, and wait for Mr Darcy to recover and decide if and how he intends to solve the situation."

"I second Lizzy in that reasonable suggestion," Mr Bennet approved. "I am sure it is only a minor family conflict that does not need any intervention from strangers. Let us not make more of it than is necessary."

"But Wickham needs to hear a piece of my mind," Bingley said indignantly.

"Oh, you should not worry about that. He did hear a piece of my mother's mind and I doubt he has ever been rebuked so severely," Elizabeth replied lightly.

The gentlemen looked at Mrs Bennet, who arranged her dress with apparent contentment.

"Well, young men should be properly scolded and

even punished whenever needed, to avoid becoming arrogant rascals," the lady declared with self-confidence.

"If Mrs Bennet is displeased, you may be certain that everyone knows it. And you should steer well clear of her," Mr Bennet concluded mockingly.

"When someone is under my protection, I feel entirely responsible for them. Everyone who knows me is aware of that," Mrs Bennet concluded decidedly. "Now let me ring for tea; I am still distressed and I need something to calm my nerves."

∞∞∞

As the hours passed, life became calmer at Longbourn. Mr Bingley returned to Netherfield but promised to return for dinner again, together with Mrs Annesley.

It was the third day of Mr Darcy's ordeal and the second day since Miss Darcy had arrived, but with the many changes that had occurred, it felt as long as a month.

After the incident with Wickham, the newly-forged friendship between Elizabeth and Georgiana seemed to suffer. The girl returned to her usual shyness; she barely spoke at all and insisted on remaining by her brother's bed, refusing to eat or drink anything.

At dinner, Georgiana quietly greeted the family, talked with Mrs Annesley briefly, then returned to Darcy, allowing Dr. Cooper to benefit from a proper meal.

After the first course, Elizabeth excused herself and hurried to Georgiana; she could not remain indifferent to the girl's distress and, although they barely knew each other, she felt connected to her in a way she rarely felt for any stranger. Whether from the disappointment of Charlotte's engagement, or because of Miss Darcy's generous support of Jane and Bingley, or just because she was Mr Darcy's sister, Elizabeth enjoyed the girl's company and valued their new acquaintance.

As she expected, Elizabeth found Georgiana sitting on

the bed, holding Darcy's hand and speaking to him. In the candlelight, she seemed even paler and her suffering and tiredness appeared more evident.

"May I sit?" Elizabeth asked.

"Of course."

"How is he?"

"Dr. Cooper said he moved a little and spoke a few words. But he is not coherent yet."

Elizabeth briefly touched his forehead and blushed, remembering the last time she had done that with her lips.

"His fever is gone."

"Yes. Dr. Cooper said it is remarkable how quickly he recovered after such a bad cold."

"He is a strong man. And I am sure he is eager to recover, to spare your concern," Elizabeth smiled at Georgiana. "He is such a good brother that I am sure he would do that."

Georgiana returned a little smile. "I am sure he would."

"Miss Darcy, how are you feeling?" Elizabeth insisted. "I do not want to intrude, but I can see you are unwell. I only wish to know if I may help you in any way."

"I thank you for your care, Miss Bennet. Please do not worry for me, I am fine. I am just embarrassed for making a spectacle of myself."

"You did no such thing! It was my mother who interfered a little too...forcefully. She has a tendency to do so, but please be sure that she meant well."

"I know she did. I am truly grateful to Mrs Bennet and to all of you."

"Miss Darcy, is there anything you want us to do regarding Mr Wickham?"

Georgiana declined, shaking her head.

"Miss Bennet, did you hear what he said to me?"

Elizabeth hesitated a moment.

"I confess I did. I apologise; I did not mean to be tactless, but I noticed you were displeased with the conversation and I decided to intervene."

The girl looked at her for a moment, then abandoned all struggle and allowed tears to fall down her cheeks. She seemed to have lost her strength and her will; her sobbing revealed long-concealed suffering and her words came out unguarded.

"I have never spoken to anyone about that, except for my brother and my cousin. I made such a terrible mistake, and I hurt William. I have been a complete simpleton. I have known George all my life and I grew up with him as a most important part of my life. He was always around and always so friendly to me. Then last summer, when I was in Ramsgate, he came to visit me and he confessed he had been in love with me for a long while. And that my father often said he would like for George to become his true son."

She paused and Elizabeth waited in silence until she wiped her eyes.

"I knew I cared deeply for George. So I agreed to marry...To elope. He insisted we should keep our plans secret, and I allowed myself to be convinced not to tell William. But my brother sensed something from my letters so he came to visit me only days before the elopement. And then I could not deceive him anymore. I told him...I expected him to be angry but he was so sad, so disappointed that it broke my heart."

Georgiana paused and again a heavy silence fell in the room.

"William told me that George was not an honest man. That he had tried to take advantage of my father and my brother for years for pecuniary gain. And that I would be miserable if I married him. William did not tell me as much, but I understood that George wished to elope with me only for my dowry. And I had been such a fool to agree to such a horrid act. I thought he truly loved me and I cared for him so much! He had been my friend my whole life. But he simply deceived me. If William had not happened to visit me, I would have hurt him and my entire family forever, and for nothing."

"I am sure your brother was more concerned about the harm you would do to yourself than to him," Elizabeth finally said, her heart aching for the girl.

Everything that had occurred since Wickham arrived in Meryton made perfect sense now. Although there were reasons to presume that Darcy acted for selfish reasons rather than from generosity, Elizabeth did not doubt his motives for a single moment.

The notion that a man would convince a girl of fifteen to deceive her brother to elope with him was nothing honourable and had no excuse. And Wickham's impertinent manners towards Darcy were now easier to understand: he likely assumed that Darcy would never allow a scandal to arise, out of fear that it could harm his sister's reputation.

"He talked to George privately and George simply disappeared. William was upset and sad for a long while. He came with Mr Bingley to look for an estate, but I know he was trying to stay away from me. He was kind enough to write to me regularly and he promised he would spend Christmas with me. But I know he is still disappointed in me and rightfully so."

Other thoughts troubled Elizabeth's mind now, as she imagined Darcy's turmoil when he arrived at Netherfield. With such a painful, recent event fresh in his mind, it was easy to understand and to excuse his reluctance to dance or to entertain people, and his reservation about Bingley marrying a woman who could have more interest in his fortune than genuine affection for him made sense.

Elizabeth gently caressed Georgiana's hand that was holding Darcy's, in an attempt to comfort both of them.

"Miss Darcy, every time I heard your brother talking about you, I was impressed by his obvious affection and his genuine pride in your accomplishments. I am sure he was pained and suffered for you, but I doubt he is upset or disappointed in you."

"You are too kind, Miss Bennet. Thank you for listening to my silly story. I have never shared it with anyone, not even my closest relatives. My cousin knows, because he is my second guardian."

"Thank you for trusting me. I will never betray your secret

to anyone, not even to Jane."

"I have no concerns about your secrecy, Miss Bennet." Georgiana smiled shyly. "I wonder how George found his way into a militia regiment and how poor William could have handled his presence here. I would have imagined my brother would have left Hertfordshire immediately, only to be away from him."

Elizabeth wondered the same and blushed, reluctant to assume a purpose that would give her unreasonable hopes.

As though wishing to answer their questions and worries, the patient moved and moaned several times, gripping Georgiana's hand and pushing the sheets with his feet. Both girls startled, rose from the bed and leaned towards him.

Darcy heard voices around him—beloved voices that made his heart race. He felt their sadness and in some whispers, gentleness, and compassion in others. And he sensed a danger that he knew he had to fight against. Both of his hands were now trapped, then released, then held again. He felt cold and suddenly realised he was wearing no clothes. He felt the sheets around him but shivered from chills. The voices became clearer, and a trace of light pierced the darkness. Slowly, the light became so powerful that it hurt his eyes. He squeezed them shut, then breathed deeply; breathing was now more comfortable, as if the cage that had pressed into his chest for so long had suddenly opened. He knew it was time to move—now, while he felt stronger and freer. But he still could not and asked for help again. Could no one hear him and help him? Was Elizabeth still there? He called her name until he finally heard an answer and felt soft, delicate fingers gripping his arms.

"William? Oh, William! You are awake! How are you feeling?"

"Mr Darcy! Please open your eyes."

His confused mind did not trust his comprehension; Elizabeth and Georgiana? Together? Was he still dreaming?

"I am fine...I think." He blinked and attempted to look around, confused and troubled by a blinding headache. "Where am I?"

"You are at Longbourn! Do you remember what happened? You fell from your horse, and Miss Bennet found you!" Miss Darcy explained.

"At Longbourn? And what are you doing here, Georgiana?"

"I came to be with you."

"At Longbourn? Am I hurt? I do not remember what happened. But I do remember Miss Bennet finding me." He turned to her and his aching eyes met her tearful gaze.

"Good day, Miss Bennet. Or it is night?"

Elizabeth released a peal of nervous laughter.

"I am glad to see you conscious, Mr Darcy. It is evening, actually. Dinnertime. I am going to fetch Dr. Cooper."

"Dr. Cooper? Is he here?"

"Oh yes. You were very ill. Very, very ill. Mr Bennet wrote to Charles and to me and we came immediately," Georgiana explained.

"Dear Lord, how many problems I have created. I fell from my horse? How did that happen?"

"It does not matter now. I am so happy that you are awake!" Georgiana said, kissing his hand. He kissed her hands back.

"Please do not cry, dearest. I am fine. How long have I been unconscious?"

"Three days."

"Three days? Dear Lord, my head hurts. And my leg. So I fell from my horse?"

239

"I am going to fetch Dr. Cooper," Elizabeth repeated and almost ran through the door.

Her heart was pounding and she felt so relieved, so light that she could fly. He was not just awake, but conscious enough to talk to them. And again, he had called her name in his sleep. Her name only.

∞∞∞

The extraordinary event of Mr Darcy awakening turned dinner into a celebration. Dr. Cooper, Stevens and Mr Bingley remained with him for more than an hour, helping him to wash and change into clean nightclothes. He could not eat or drink much and did not recollect any details of the accident but he spoke coherently, his fever had gone and his wounds had started to heal. His ribs were still swollen, he could hardly move and standing was impossible yet. But he was back.

Miss Darcy reluctantly agreed to join the family for the rest of the evening, as she was banished from her brother's chamber. Her happiness, mixed with tears, was heartwarming and the Bennet girls tried to cheer her.

A while later, Bingley returned to the dining room.

"He is all set for the night. Darcy, I mean. Dr. Cooper and Stevens will remain with him overnight. Dr. Cooper demanded that we do not disturb him until morning.

Georgiana attempted to protest but Bingley glanced at her. "Not until morning," he repeated, much to Georgiana's disappointment.

Although the demand was not addressed to her, Elizabeth blushed, feeling the same regret as she too had hoped to be able to exchange a few more words with him. But that was a silly feeling, she knew that. She would have all the time in the world to talk to him–if he wished to.

"Georgiana, Darcy would like to hear you play, if you do not mind. At the pianoforte. Would you?" Bingley requested.

Georgiana looked around with palpable panic; glancing from one to another, she blushed and hesitated to reply. Her eyes remained on Elizabeth, who smiled at her.

"I could turn the pages for you," she offered.

"I would not want to disturb you," Georgiana said, looking at the family.

"Oh, we would love to hear you play! Can you imagine? Mr Darcy's sister playing for us! Just wait until I tell Mrs Long and Mrs Phillips. That will surely outdo Lady Lucas's boasting about her daughter's marriage to that clergyman!"

"Mama, please!" Jane begged, but Georgiana laughed.

"I would be glad to please you, Mrs Bennet," the girl agreed.

They moved to the drawing room where the pianoforte was and chose their seats: Elizabeth next to Georgiana, Jane next to Bingley, Mr Bennet on a chair, Mrs Bennet and Mrs Annesley on a sofa, and the youngest girls together.

When Miss Darcy's hands touched the keyboard, a chill ran through each of her companions. The magic in her fingers soon struck them and they listened unmoving, speechless, spellbound.

Dr. Cooper appeared in the doorway, smiling approvingly, then returned to the patient. The door remained wide open and Elizabeth spotted the servants in the hall peeking in with astonishment, lost in admiration.

The bewitching performance continued for three more songs and was rewarded with emotional applause and cheering.

Miss Darcy appeared exhausted, but a timid smile glowed on her face. "My dear Miss Darcy, that is just outstanding. I have never heard anything so beautiful! My daughter Mary studies the pianoforte and Lizzy plays a little. But you, you... This is just wonderful!"

"Miss Darcy is not only exceptionally talented but she practises diligently too," Mrs Annesley interjected. "She studies all the time, not just music but also science, geography, and languages. She continuously improves her mind and her spirit. She is a pleasure to be around."

"Thank you; I am sure I do not deserve such praise," Georgiana blushed. "But I confess I am very fond of music. The rest is to my brother's credit."

"Why is that?" Mr Bennet asked.

"William has encouraged me to play and to read since I was very young. And he always took me to the opera and theatre, and anywhere I could learn something new. He taught me so many things."

"He did an excellent job, there is no doubt about that," Mr Bennet replied.

"Thank you," the girl repeated.

"Now, I believe we should retire for the night. We still have to return to Netherfield, and it is very late for me. But I dare say this day was truly worthy of any exhaustion," Mr Bennet concluded.

∞ ∞ ∞

The enchanting music enveloped Darcy like a wave of pure bliss, easing his pain and clearing his mind. There were many things he needed to think of, to settle, to solve, but it was too soon. He would start tomorrow.

For that night, it was enough for him to know that Elizabeth and Georgiana were together and seemed to be on friendly terms. It had happened naturally, without his intervention. Dr. Cooper told him they had both stayed at his side most of the time. The doctor praised their devotion and expressed his admiration for Elizabeth. She showed remarkable concern and preoccupation for him, the doctor said.

Could he dare assume the reason behind her dedication? Was it a mere expression of her generous nature? Clear proof of friendship? Could he trust his memories of her holding his hand, touching his lips, and even kissing him? Or was it all a dream?

But her staying near and worrying for him day and night was a reality. The others had confirmed it. Just as her care of his sister was genuine.

Now, she was assisting Georgiana as she played. That was the picture he had been imagining for several weeks, the one he hoped to draw one day.

And with it filling his thoughts and his soul, Darcy eventually fell into a deep, restful sleep.

Chapter 18

*A*fter the previous night's anguish, the excitement of seeing Darcy on the road to recovery kept Elizabeth, Jane and Georgiana awake long after the rest of the family had retired to Netherfield.

Miss Darcy visited her brother briefly, but Dr. Cooper did not allow her to spend more than a moment near his bed, declaring all of them needed peace, quiet and sleep. Elizabeth was anxious to see him too, but she did not dare take such a liberty. Visiting a patient was one thing; entering the chamber of a sleeping man in the middle of the night was something completely different.

However, a few hours of rest allowed her to wake up early, restless and in high spirits. She struggled to keep her hopes under good regulation and barely permitted herself to consider the reason for her excitement.

Never being in love before, nor even favouring one man over others, the novelty and the power of the new feeling excited her. Only a month ago, Mr Darcy was the last man in the world who she could think of in a tender way. That they would grow from enemies into friends was hard to imagine; but to consider they could be bound by mutual admiration and affection was truly unbelievable, even laughable. She and Mr Darcy, two people who disliked each other so utterly? Could it be real? How did such a change occur? When?

Her mind told her heart to be prudent, to search her own wishes carefully and not to presume his feelings without solid proof.

But her heart responded that she thought of him as she had no other man before, that touching his hand gave her shivers, that his illness was a time of great sorrow for her. That her heart was broken when she found him fallen from his horse and that she ran through the rain for him without a second thought. And that he had called her name during his suffering. Her name only.

Torn between so many reasons for distress, Elizabeth chose a dress that she knew would become her and arranged her hair with much care. She blushed as she admitted to herself that she wanted to look pretty–for him.

As Jane was still asleep, she knocked at Georgiana's door then entered. The room was empty and Elizabeth had no doubts about the girl's whereabouts. She went downstairs but in the hall she stopped, suddenly reluctant to enter the chamber where she had been countless times lately. Should she dare? Inside, there was certainly a conversation between brother and sister going on. Had she any right to interfere? Was she welcome in their proximity, now that the danger was gone?

Eventually, she knocked and entered only after she heard the invitation.

Georgiana was sitting on the bed and Darcy was sitting up, supported by the pillows. Both met her with a genuine smile.

"Forgive me for interrupting you; I came to see how you both are this morning."

"We are fine, thank you. And you?" Georgiana asked, her face finally free from the shadow of sadness.

"Miss Bennet, please come closer. Would you like to join us for a little while?" Darcy enquired, inviting her with a gesture.

Elizabeth smiled in agreement, looked around, then took a chair and placed it near Georgiana. Sitting on the bed, next to Darcy, was completely unacceptable under the present circumstances.

"You do look well, both of you," she said lightly.

"And we owe it to you…and to your family, of course. But

we know that without you, things would be tragically different now," Darcy declared.

Elizabeth blushed. "Please do not be so solemn, sir. I did far less than you did for us. So let us call it a truce. Or even," she offered. "And let us be content that we are all safe and sound."

"You are right, of course," Darcy admitted. "But I must be allowed to express my gratitude as soon as I escape from this bed."

Elizabeth's cheeks and neck were burning. "You should not even dare to consider leaving the bed until Dr. Cooper allows it. I barely know him, but I can see he is not a man to trifle with," she teased him.

Darcy laughed. "I have known him all my life and I still do not dare upset him."

"He almost threw me out of your room," Georgiana complained in jest.

"But he told me that Miss Bennet opposed him quite decidedly. He was impressed with your determination, Miss Bennet. And he is rarely impressed. But then again, I am not surprised to hear that," Darcy uttered, his eyes holding hers.

Elizabeth laughed sheepishly. "We had a little disagreement in the beginning. But we soon reached an understanding. We are grateful that he is such a remarkable doctor. That is all that matters."

"True," Darcy approved, still looking at her with a meaningful gaze that made her quiver. "I am afraid he insisted I should stay still for a few more days. My ribs might be broken and he is concerned that any movement could be harmful. So I fear you will have to endure my presence a little longer."

"Oh, I am sure we can manage it," Elizabeth replied lightly. "Although, I am not sure you will be able to endure our company, now that you are awake and alert."

"I am sure I will enjoy it very much," Darcy declared. "And spending more time together, perhaps I will find a way to show my gratitude at least to your family, since you are determined to reject it."

"Be careful what you wish for, sir," Elizabeth laughed.

"I heard that your mother gave up her room for me. That is truly impressive," Darcy spoke in earnest. "I was touched by such generosity and I am ashamed to admit I did not expect it."

"My mother was genuinely worried for you, sir. You should not be surprised. She might not behave properly all the time, but she is goodhearted and caring by nature."

"I noticed that the first moment I met Mrs Bennet," Georgiana confessed. "She might be intimidating, though in a different way from Dr. Cooper, but her caring and considerate disposition are apparent."

"Unfortunately, I was too busy acting proudly and thoughtlessly to notice the good traits of the people around me," Darcy admitted. "I hope I will have the chance to talk to Mrs Bennet and thank her personally later today."

"Mama will be pleased to talk to you, I am sure. And let us agree that we all were unable to notice the good traits in people when we first met," Elizabeth suggested. "None of us were flawless."

"Let it be as you wish but I am aware the biggest share of the fault is mine. Miss Bennet, may I ask you something delicate?" he enquired and she startled. What could it be? And in the presence of his sister?

She nodded in approval and he continued with a large smile.

"Did I dream this or did Mrs Bennet kiss me while I was asleep?"

Elizabeth stared at him, mortified, dumbfounded, unsure what to say. If he remembered that moment, did he recollect everything else?

"You did not dream it, sir. But she did not kiss you either. She checked your fever by pressing her lips to your temples. Mr Jones testified it is a proper method," she answered, trying to provide enough details to explain her own gesture.

"I see. Nevertheless, I was moved by such warm care," Darcy said, with a sudden change in tone. Elizabeth suspected he referred to her, and became nervous again.

"Miss Bennet, I spoke to my brother about the encounter with Mr Wickham. And about our conversation regarding my past dealings with him," Georgiana whispered with her usual shyness. She seemed troubled by the subject, but she wore a little smile.

"Oh..." Elizabeth looked from one sibling to another, waiting. How should she respond?

"My sister told me how protected and safe she felt thanks to you and Mrs Bennet. For that, I am even more grateful," Darcy added, bowing his head slightly.

"On this matter, I truly did not do anything, I assure you. I should have warned Miss Darcy about Wickham. But I never imagined his presence mattered so much. Had I known..."

"How could you have known?" Darcy replied warmly. "You protected her as much as was possible."

"Mostly my mother did," Elizabeth concealed her anxiety behind her laughter. "I doubt Mr Wickham has ever been scolded so harshly."

"I heard that. I would say Mrs Bennet was more severe to Wickham than I would have ever been in public," Darcy declared with half mockery. "But now it is my duty to settle this situation properly. I should have done it long ago," he added in a low and grave tone.

"What do you mean, brother?"

"Nothing to worry you, dearest. All is well. I would kindly ask you to leave now–I need to rest. Please send Stevens," he asked gently.

"Very well," the girl tentatively accepted. She seemed keen to enquire more but did not dare, so she rose to obey his request and Elizabeth followed her silently. She sensed a heavy tension in the chamber, but could not interfere between the siblings.

She startled at the sound of his voice calling her.

"Miss Bennet..." She turned to look at him. He was gazing at her intensely, quietly. She hesitated to move, gazing back at him, waiting.

"I am sorry we did not have the chance to meet as we planned. The subject I wanted to discuss is of no importance now, considering how things have progressed. But I still regret the lost opportunity."

"More opportunities will arise soon, I am sure," she responded.

"Yes, they will–hopefully soon enough. And...Miss Bennet?"

"Yes?"

"That medicine you gave me the other night...the taste was horrible, but I did enjoy it very much. It served me well, it seems."

Her eyes remained locked with his while she held her breath. His words sounded light and proper but their hidden meaning made her dizzy. He wished to tell her he remembered the moment when she touched and parted his lips.

Unconsciously, she licked her own lips and her eyes left his, as their dark intensity was almost unbearable.

Her glance lowered onto his face that she had touched several times, then for the first time moved to his shoulders and his torso.

Darcy was now fully dressed in a nightgown, but the closure was untied, revealing his neck, nothing more. Chills ran down her spine and, with a sudden lump in her throat, she gulped.

"I am glad to hear that," she replied, in a voice that sounded strange even to herself.

He bowed his head to her again, she sent him a brief smile and exited. She barely breathed again, and her heart pounded in her ears.

∞∞∞

The brief exchange with Darcy strengthened Elizabeth's trust and aroused her hopes regarding his feelings, so she finally dared to let hers fly freely.

Those few words, so plain, yet with so much intimate meaning to them, coupled with his eloquent glances in the presence of his sister, were proof enough even for her doubtfulness.

She yearned for the opportunity to speak to him more. To clarify all the remaining misunderstandings. To ask him what had happened in the grove. But he was not well enough, nor did she have the right to force a private encounter. She had to wait for the proper opportunity. To have patience.

The Netherfield residents arrived for breakfast, and a joyous gathering sat around the table.

Special courses were sent to Darcy's room and, while Stevens attended his master's needs, Dr. Cooper joined the family.

Once the concern for his patient was relieved, the good doctor proved to be pleasant company, with a great inclination towards teasing and making sport of others–a perfect companion to Mr Bennet.

After a proper meal, Mr Bingley proposed an impromptu stroll in the garden for a little beneficial exercise. Jane readily accepted, as did Mrs Annesley and Miss Darcy.

For the first time in a long while, Elizabeth declined and excused herself, preferring to retire to her room. She felt a bit tired, but mostly exhausted by her own emotions and needed a little restful and quiet private time. Even the company of those so dear to her became slightly overwhelming, and she took the opportunity to be alone finally.

Yes, taking the right opportunity made all the difference. Just as Darcy said.

However, only several minutes of solitude passed until a knock on the door disturbed her.

At her invitation, Darcy's valet entered, stepping inside hesitantly, looking at her with apparent embarrassment.

She frowned with worry. "Stevens, what has happened? Is Mr Darcy unwell?"

"No, ma'am. Forgive me for disturbing you, Miss Bennet. The master asked me to deliver this," Stevens said, handing her a letter. Then the valet bowed again and departed in a hurry, while Elizabeth gazed after him, dumbfounded.

She looked at the paper, holding it tight; it felt like it was burning her hand, and she struggled to catch her breath before opening it. A letter from Darcy?

Elizabeth paced the room for a few moments, then sat on the bed, then moved to the window and returned to the bed again. Finally, she unfolded the letter with trembling fingers and read with excitement and distress.

"Miss Bennet,

I beg you to forgive both the appearance and the content of this letter; I know neither is proper, as both my thoughts and my hand are struggling to write down what my heart feels.

I would rather talk to you personally, but I doubt the opportunity I mentioned earlier will arise anytime soon. And I feel I owe you complete honesty before I take any other steps; I only hope for equal frankness in return.

The subject I wished to discuss with you on the morning of my accident referred to Wickham. I wanted to warn you of his true character, and afterwards, I intended to talk to Colonel Forster too. You may wonder why I did not choose a more suitable location to do so, perhaps even at Longbourn. I trust your father would have gladly allowed us the chance to talk. But I confess now that I had other subjects—barely declared even to myself—that induced me to prefer a private conversation.

Regarding Wickham, I trust things are now clear to you. If you need other details, please feel free to ask me directly. I am deeply thankful to you for the affection and support that you so generously offered to my sister during these days of her painful torment. She was hurt so deeply by that scoundrel's betrayal that I feared she would not recover. And yet, you encouraged her to open her heart and confide in you, releasing the anguish that so undeservingly weighed on her pure soul. None but you could have done that. You must have a spell that has touched the Darcys most profoundly.

And with that, I will hesitantly move toward the other subjects that I mentioned above, but I am not sure if I should dare to approach them or if you would welcome such a discussion.

Therefore, I will ask before taking any other step and will only do as you please.

I remember you ran through the storm to bring help for me, while you put your coat under my head. I know you held my hand in the grove, and then several times here, in my chamber, while I fought the fever. I know you stayed by my side every time you were allowed. Even in my sleep, I was always aware of your presence, of your gestures, of your nearness. I am fighting with my reason, not to understand more than I should, but my mind is not clear enough. Even worse, it was not clear enough regarding you even before the accident. Therefore, I enquire, and I am counting on your genuine answer. Were all these efforts only a proof of kindness? Would you have done the same for any other person in need? If so, I will accept that I have made a fool of myself and I will remain silent on this matter.

Stevens just told me Bingley is taking a stroll in the garden with Miss Bennet. At least in this regard, I am sure there will be happiness.

I will end this now with one more confession. At the ball, Mr Collins informed me that he intended to propose to you. I convinced him that, while you are a remarkable young lady, you are entirely unsuited to the position of his wife and that Lady Catherine would be displeased with his choice. In both respects, I was sincere, but I apologise if I made a mistake.

Thankfully yours,
F. Darcy"

If the letter took her by surprise, its content threw Elizabeth into a tumult of feelings, all so strong that she cried and laughed at the same time.

He had written so little and yet so much, and she melted with joy as she read every word again and again.

Then she realised he was waiting–with distress and anxiety. So hurriedly she took a pen and paper and wrote hastily,

Mr Darcy,

I would have readily taken care of any person in need, but my feelings while doing so would have been utterly different.

I beg you not to remain silent–I eagerly await the first chance of talking more on the subjects of which I am no more certain than you are. And please rest assured that my mind is not clear on this matter either.

I doubt I possess any spell, but I am sure a real understanding is better than any charm.

I would rather say that you are a true magician since you prevented a most unpleasant confrontation and induced Mr Collins to make a more appropriate selection for his life partner.

As for Mr Bingley and Jane–yes, there is happiness!

Sincerely,

E. Bennet.

She folded the paper and a moment later she knocked on Darcy's door. Stevens appeared and she handed him the note, then returned to her chamber and locked the door.

She took Darcy's letter and read it again and again, at leisure, mixing smiles with tears, wondering how a piece of paper could bring so much joy. She did not sleep, but her mind and her heart finally got a well-deserved rest.

Later on, she was brought back from her reverie by many loud voices speaking at the same time. Reluctantly, she opened the door and took a few steps, until she could clearly hear her mother's rapturous cries indicating that Mr Bingley had finally proposed.

In his chamber, resting upon the pillows, still slightly weak and feverish, holding Elizabeth's letter as a most valuable treasure, Darcy listened to the expressions of celebration that sounded all over the house. Mrs Bennet knew how to make her feelings known, for sure. He smiled with contentment, then allowed himself to fall into a deep sleep.

∞∞∞

The news of Jane's engagement to Mr Bingley reached Meryton almost as quickly as Hill received it in the kitchen at Longbourn.

Before dinner, Mrs Long and Mrs Phillips had already sent their best wishes to Mrs Bennet, whose happiness was a great challenge to her nerves.

Mr Bennet and Dr. Cooper found shelter in the library, far from the din, while the ladies amused themselves in the drawing room.

Darcy heartily congratulated his friend and spent half an hour with him, making wedding plans and deciding who should be informed and invited to attend the ceremony.

To Elizabeth, the day was beyond any dream of happiness that had tantalised her youth. She witnessed her sister's pure felicity and was granted the promise of a blissful future for herself in a short letter from the only man in the world who had conquered her heart.

She did not need to see Darcy or to speak to him directly. She knew he was there–near her, waiting for the proper moment to talk.

"Lizzy, come with me," Mr Bennet asked his favourite daughter, taking her away from the loud party to the silence of his library.

"What is it, Papa?" Elizabeth asked with concern at such secrecy.

"There is something I wish to tell you; both Mr Darcy and I are counting on your secrecy."

"Of course, Papa."

"Mr Darcy confessed to me that he has recollected how the accident occurred. It seems he was on his way to meet you and he happened upon Mr Wickham. They had a brief argument, and

Wickham rode his horse past him and cut Darcy and his stallion with his sword. Darcy himself was dizzy from the illness he had been dealing with for days, so he did not observe whether Wickham's gesture was intentional or just an accident. So he is not accusing Wickham directly."

Elizabeth listened with astonishment, frowning in disbelief.

"But if it was an accident, why did Mr Wickham leave him there on the ground, in the rain?"

She had never even considered such a scenario and was taken aback to discover such cowardice.

"It seems this is Wickham's dishonourable character! The horse was scared from the pain and, since Darcy himself was already ill from a cold, easily threw him from the saddle. And Wickham abandoned them there, in danger of death. His godfather's son! Lovely man, Wickham is!"

"So…what should we do now?" Elizabeth asked angrily. "This cannot go unpunished!"

"Darcy plans to speak to Colonel Forster. He also asked Bingley to make some enquiries among the regiment and in Meryton, as he suspects Wickham has some gambling debts. This is what Darcy has told us so far. And he mentioned that I should inform you too–but only you. He fears such horrid details would be too distressing for the other ladies, especially for his sister."

"But Papa, they will find out–eventually!"

Eventually. For the time being, let them enjoy the news of Darcy's recovery and Jane's engagement. We have had enough excitement for one week."

"Very well. What a horrible man Wickham is! And what a lovely, pleasant appearance he has. And his friendly manners… Horrible, deceiving man."

"Yes. Wickham must be exposed before he misleads other honest people. Lizzy, how are you, my dear? We have not spoken much these last few days and I know you have had a trying time."

"I am fine, Papa. More than fine," she answered, kissing her father's cheek.

"I am glad to hear that. Now let me read a little before someone comes to disturb me again. Upon my word, moving to Netherfield permanently might not be a bad idea. That library is spectacular and nobody ever enters it!"

∞∞∞

The following two days brought additional joy and good humour to Longbourn. With her eldest daughter now engaged, and with Mr Darcy out of danger, Mrs Bennet was already planning the wedding.

Mr Bingley had already written to his sisters to invite them to Netherfield, and the Gardiners were expected to arrive, to mark the most wonderful Christmas that the Bennets had ever celebrated.

Elizabeth visited Darcy a couple of times during the day, with Georgiana and even with Mrs Bennet, who was happy to receive the gentleman's warm gratitude and an astonishing invitation to Pemberley for the entire family.

Mrs Bennet doubted that she would travel to Derbyshire for a mere visit, but the invitation was so gratifying and flattering, that it was shared with Mrs Long, Mrs Phillips and Lady Lucas in a short note, sent through Lydia, Mary and Kitty. Mrs Bennet was certain that Jane would often visit Pemberley in the future, so that was enough satisfaction for her.

Elizabeth and Darcy exchanged only several words, and a few polite glances and smiles. Those were enough to settle their tentative understanding and to help them feel confident about each other.

While Darcy's health improved, Georgiana's shyness slowly faded away. Miss Darcy grew friendlier not only with Elizabeth and Jane, but also with the younger girls.

Dr. Cooper gave them hope that Mr Darcy could be moved

to Netherfield in a fortnight, but he forbade any longer journeys for at least a month. It was clear then that the Darcys were to spend Christmas in Hertfordshire, a piece of news that pleased the entire party.

A week after Mr Darcy's accident, late in the afternoon, Bingley and Jane were walking in the garden, the younger girls and Miss Darcy, together with Mrs Annesley, entertained each other at the pianoforte, Mr Bennet and Dr. Cooper were in the library, while Mrs Bennet was asking Elizabeth's opinion about having fish for dinner.

Elizabeth spotted a large carriage stopping in front of the gate and for a moment she believed that the Gardiners had arrived earlier than expected.

She was irritated and disappointed to see Mr Collins jump out of the carriage and help down a lady of impressive stature.

The lady's proud and severe figure and her intimidating air, as well as Mr Collins' bending in front of her left no doubts that after hosting Mr and Miss Darcy, Longbourn was now favoured with the extraordinary presence of Lady Catherine de Bourgh.

Elizabeth rolled her eyes in exasperation, informing her mother about the visit. She intended to tell her father and Miss Darcy too but had no time, as the guests entered and a voice thundered from the hall.

"Where is my nephew? Where is Darcy? Where are you keeping him?" Elizabeth and Mrs Bennet stepped forward.

"Lady Catherine, welcome to Longbourn," Elizabeth curtseyed politely.

"Thank you. What a small, uncomfortable room you have here. Mr Collins, remind me to suggest some changes when you inherit this place. But for now, I wish to see my nephew right away!"

"Please sit down and allow me to inform Dr. Cooper of your presence, madam. We hardly do anything regarding Mr Darcy without his consent."

"I need nobody's consent. Who might you be, young lady?"

"Lady Catherine, allow me to..." Mr Collins started, but the lady shushed him and glared at Elizabeth.

"I am Elizabeth Bennet, Lady Catherine. And this is my mother."

"You are Elizabeth Bennet? Well, you are not as I expected. You are very far from being a stunning beauty. Now please take me to my nephew," she demanded severely, admitting no contradiction.

"Lady Catherine, I cannot possibly do that, but I will immediately inform Dr. Cooper, as I mentioned."

"I shall come with you to see him myself. Why did nobody inform me earlier that he was being kept here? Are you keeping him prisoner?"

Elizabeth was torn between anger and amusement, and she barely kept her temper. She also noticed her mother frowning, so she knew that danger was close.

"I understand your ladyship is worried, but I am sure you were informed that Mr Darcy suffered a serious injury. He has been gravely ill but is finally recovering. Nobody kept him against his will."

"Aunt Catherine?" Georgiana's shy voice from the doorway sounded frightened. The lady turned towards her with a glare.

"Georgiana? What are you doing here?"

"I came to be with William...I am staying with him..."

"And did you not have enough consideration to inform me too? I had to learn from the letter Mr Collins received from Sir William about my nephew's condition!"

"We intended to inform you..." The girl whispered.

"Who is 'we'"? You are his only sister. Who else had to decide? I have no expectations of you, anyway, as you can barely decide anything for yourself. I want to see Darcy! Which one is his room?"

Georgiana turned pale and lowered her tearful eyes as Lady Catherine swept past her. Elizabeth's anxiety increased but in the hall Dr. Cooper appeared, cutting off Lady Catherine's path.

"Your ladyship," he slightly bowed his head.

"Dr. Cooper! Where is Darcy?"

"Resting!"

"Take me to him immediately."

"Dr. Cooper, please let my aunt enter," Darcy's voice interjected weakly.

The lady pushed Dr. Cooper away and barged into Darcy's room. She pushed the door angrily behind her but the hasty move failed to close it entirely and left enough of an opening for their voices to be heard from the hall. The others all gathered closer, listening. Mr Collins tried to follow his patroness, but he paused in the doorway, not daring to enter.

Inside, Darcy breathed deeply as he faced his aunt. He had known this moment would come, and only hoped he had the strength and the patience to handle it properly.

"Aunt Catherine, you should not have undertaken such a long journey in this weather. I am well, I assure you. It was only a trifling cold and several bruised ribs that kept me in bed. If it was something grave, you would have been informed."

"I am glad you are well. I shall take you to London straight away. Dr. Cooper can follow us and take care of you there."

"Aunt, I could not do that, even if I wanted to. And I certainly do not wish to travel to London. I will stay in Hertfordshire until after Christmas," Darcy replied, forcing himself to remain calm.

"After Christmas? Here? In this house?"

"I will move to Netherfield as soon as Dr. Cooper allows it. I have bothered the Bennets enough and I do not wish to disturb their lives more than is necessary."

"So you have no other particular reason to remain here longer than is necessary? I have heard the most alarming report that has disturbed my life and Anne's! I hope you are worried about that too!"

"What report? Aunt, please believe me that I am not well yet and I need to rest. I cannot handle absurd conversations."

"Absurd? Absurd? I heard that you show special attention

to a certain young lady that Mr Collins did not find suited to be his wife! What do you have to say about that? I hope you have not lost your good sense completely."

"As I said, I cannot handle an absurd conversation. It is not your concern who I show special attention to. This discussion is over."

"Not my concern? But you are engaged to Anne!"

"Aunt Catherine, please be reasonable. I am not engaged to Anne, and I do not wish to discuss in public what we have already argued over several times privately."

"So it is true! My authority was too good to be wrong. Then you have decided to ruin your name and to disobey your mother's dearest wish, all for a country girl? With what arts and allurements did she charm you?"

"Aunt Catherine!"

"Have you forgotten your duty and your honour? Have you lost your mind? Do you want to expose yourself to ridicule by marrying someone so below your situation in life?"

"Lady Catherine, I shall only repeat once more that who I marry is my concern only. And I shall not take this conversation any further."

"Tell me once and for all: are you engaged to her?"

"I am not."

"So you know who I am talking about! You do not even deny it!"

"I have no wish to deny it, nor to conceal my admiration for Miss Bennet. She is the most remarkable lady I have ever met and I would be honoured to gain her affection."

"You have lost your reason because she saved your life!"

"Not at all, I assure you. My admiration began long before the accident, but her courage and devotion only proved her worthiness one more time."

Lady Catherine was breathless with furry. "What about Anne? Will you abandon her?"

"I care deeply for Anne, and I will always take care of her. But I never intended to marry her, and never will."

"But...but..."

"Dr. Cooper! Stevens!" Darcy shouted and both men entered in a hurry. Just then, both Darcy and Lady Catherine saw the entire family staring at them in complete shock.

Embarrassed, distressed, ashamed, Darcy looked at Elizabeth for a moment, then at her father who was looking back at him quizzically. Next to her, Mrs Bennet was red-faced, and kept gulping and blinking, dumbfounded.

Lady Catherine glared at them, frowning in disdainful anger. "I shall never forgive this! No one will ever forgive Darcy, and he will be a stranger to his family! Everybody will laugh at him! You will all be the laughingstock of London," she spat bitterly. Then she left in a great hurry, griping and cursing, with Mr Collins following her dejectedly.

Through the open door, Darcy, Georgiana and the Bennets stared at each other in awkward silence. Bingley entered, his expression showing his complete puzzlement.

The girls looked at each other, then Mrs Bennet finally burst out.

"Lizzy? Is Lady Catherine speaking of Lizzy? Lizzy and Mr Darcy? Lizzy? And Mr Darcy? Oh dear Lord! Bless me, I will lose my mind. Lizzy?"

Elizabeth could not bear it any more; she ran to her room and threw herself on the bed sobbing from shame and anger. The beauty of her relationship with Darcy seemed polluted, and guilt penetrated her heart. Lady Catherine's spiteful words sounded real enough and the consequences of a union between her and Darcy looked devastating for him. Was she truly ruining his life? Could she bear that? And if she was selfish enough to do so, how long would pass until he came to realise his mistake and to hate her? Should she end such a prospect, before they could hurt anyone?

Downstairs, the family slowly retired, leaving Darcy with his valet and with the doctor. Once in the drawing room, Mrs Bennet kept repeating "Lizzy and Mr Darcy," in disbelief, until she finally fell onto the sofa, asking for her smelling salts.

Mr Bennet was the last to leave. With a final glance, he turned to Darcy and said mockingly, "Sir, I can hardly believe that not long ago you condemned Mrs Bennet's improper manners and lack of decorum."

Darcy smiled bitterly and replied, "I cannot believe it either, Mr Bennet."

"Well, well, this was a surprise even for me, although I had some suspicions. We shall talk more of it...tomorrow. You certainly need a good rest now, and so do we."

He closed the door behind him, leaving Darcy lonely, distressed and fearful, wondering and worrying about Elizabeth.

Chapter 19

*L*ady Catherine's departure threw Longbourn back into a state of utter distress. In their respective rooms, Elizabeth, Darcy and Georgiana each suffered from shame for themselves and worry for the others.

Dr. Cooper retired to his chamber with a glass of brandy, distraught over the embarrassing confrontation.

The Bennets and Mr Bingley, gathered in the drawing room, discussed the extraordinary news. Even if some had noticed the growing friendship between Darcy and Elizabeth, nobody suspected such a turn of events. After a brief deliberation, it was agreed that everybody was delighted for them.

Surprisingly, Mrs Bennet was the one who spoke less than usual and less than everyone else. She appeared unable to recover and took little part in the conversation. The notion of a marriage between her second daughter–whose unguarded behaviour and outspoken, stubborn character seemed an obstacle to any marriage at all–and the haughty, reserved Mr Darcy, who had refused to dance with her, was impossible to comprehend. Mrs Bennet feared to allow herself to believe such an extraordinary outcome since she was still uncertain of it.

A while later, in the middle of the heated discussion, Stevens appeared and conveyed his master's kind request for a private interview with Mr and Mrs Bennet.

Their meeting, so shortly after the scandal and the startling revelation, put together three equally abashed, utterly different people, who had barely started to know each other, having Elizabeth as their only common interest.

Darcy was the first one to speak with carefully chosen words and a hesitant voice.

"There is little that can be said in such moments, except that I am begging for your forgiveness. I have abused your generosity so utterly that I cannot imagine how I will ever compensate you for it. Until now, your care and kindness have been repaid only with offence and abuse. I have been unfair to all of you since the beginning of our acquaintance and you rewarded my rudeness by adjusting your daily life to accommodate my illness. Nobody else would have done that. I cannot apologise nor thank you sincerely enough."

"Mr Darcy, rest assured that you have no reason for concern on this subject," Mr Bennet answered.

"I am at a loss as to how to proceed further, since I am confined to my bed and I have no indication of when I shall leave it," Darcy continued. "But the matter that was so abruptly brought up by my aunt cannot be delayed since it already affects your family and I suspect rumours have already reached Meryton."

"Well, in this respect we do have reasons to worry," Mr Bennet agreed.

"So...do you have an agreement with Lizzy?" Mrs Bennet finally spoke.

"I do not. If I had, I would have certainly asked for your blessing. Miss Bennet and I have not approached this subject beyond acknowledging that our relationship has improved significantly over the last few weeks and that we both are willing to take it further," Darcy confessed hesitantly.

He paused a moment, gathering his composure, then spoke further. "I have been a private man all my life, and I rarely share my thoughts or intentions even with my closest relatives. But now I am in your house, still wounded, trying to mend a situation for which I feel guilty but over which I have no control. Everything happened so fast that I was overwhelmed, and I can barely imagine how all this seems to you. And even more so to Miss Bennet, who was put in such distressing circumstances because of me."

"Mr Darcy, what can we do now? What do you want us to do now?" Mr Bennet asked bluntly.

Darcy looked directly at them both, speaking with honesty.

"I have admired Miss Elizabeth for a long while, but only recently have I allowed myself to imagine bonding my future and my felicity to hers. For some time, I tried to observe if her wishes were in any way similar to mine. Now I have great confidence that such desires may be fulfilled and I am asking for your approval to try to pursue it as well as I can, in my present situation."

"So...you and Lizzy?" Mrs Bennet asked, dumbfounded.

"Yes. If Miss Elizabeth will do me the honour of having me," Darcy replied in earnest.

Mrs Bennet's jaw dropped in disbelief.

"Do you want me to ask her?" the lady offered.

Darcy smiled. "No, I would rather speak to her privately, if you approve of it."

"Then go to it. Or rather do not go anywhere, I will send her here," Mr Bennet mocked him. "I am glad we have cleared up this confusing matter. I only hope that the decision you make will not be unfair to your cousin Anne. Neither you nor Lizzy would be happy knowing of another's unhappiness."

"Mr Bennet, my engagement to Anne is something that only exists in my aunt's mind. Since I was very young, I have heard from Aunt Catherine about my mother's desire for such a marriage. While my duty and my affection will always induce me to take care of all my relatives, I never intended to marry Anne, and I had declared that repeatedly, long before I even met Miss Elizabeth."

"Well then, this is a relief. Gather your strength, and I will send Lizzy to talk to you."

"Thank you, Mr Bennet...Mrs Bennet."

Darcy bowed as ceremoniously as he could from his

sitting position, rubbing his hands in anxious anticipation. Part of his distress was gone; he did not expect any true opposition from Elizabeth's parents, but he feared they might feel upset and offended. Lady Catherine's accusations were equally ridiculous and harmful, and any less generous people would respond with equal harshness.

He was aware that for the Bennets, the prospect of their daughter marrying someone so far above their circle and expectations was a blessing. But he also knew that Mr Bennet and Elizabeth would never hesitate to reject a marriage proposal from someone–be he as rich as could be–who was unworthy of their admiration.

A shy knock at the door startled him and the excitement gave him chills as if he were a young boy. She was here.

"Please come in," he said, surprised by the tremble in his own voice. Elizabeth stepped in and stood by the fireplace. Darcy could see her troubled face and the shadow in her eyes.

"Miss Bennet, please...Please sit down. I hope you do not mind my boldness in asking to talk to you."

"No...of course not. I wish to tell you that Miss Darcy is waiting to speak to you too. She looks very ill. Should I fetch her?"

"No...Not yet. Please...I only beg for a few moments of your time." Elizabeth finally sat on a chair, to the right of the bed, at a safe distance from him.

"I am struggling for the best way of starting this important and difficult conversation."

"Mr Darcy," she interjected decidedly. "You are still unwell, still very weak, you still suffer from a serious wound and Dr. Cooper says you are still fighting the cold that might have affected your lungs. Let us postpone any conversation that might affect your life and your future in ways that you cannot anticipate clearly enough. I know you are affected by the last days' events and perhaps feel gratitude to my family and to me. We should not–and I will not–take advantage of your weakness and bewilderment to make decisions that you might regret later on. I do not intend to take any step that would harm you or Miss Darcy, or would destroy your connection with your family."

Elizabeth's interruption disconcerted and disappointed Darcy, as it threatened him with a refusal to the question he had not even asked yet. Then, as she spoke further, his heart swelled with pride and joy at the integrity and morals of the young woman who seemed to value his well-being more than her own. She seemed worried that his affection for her was not sound and that marrying her would harm his family.

At that, Darcy smiled with his entire being, as he well knew she could not have been more wrong. And suddenly, the words came easily and eloquently, from the depths of his heart, enhanced both by his reason and by his feelings.

"I cannot tell you the precise moment when I fell in love with you, because I was in the middle of it before I knew it. But it must have been very early in our acquaintance because for a long while, I have struggled in vain to keep my love hidden in a corner of my soul. As foolishly as my aunt, I believed that, despite all your excellent qualities, it was my duty to choose a wife with a better situation in life, with better connections, with a more powerful name perhaps, to fulfil the position of Mrs Darcy. I had been a fool for some time, but my love only grew along with my struggle. The more I knew you, the more I realised that it was not about you being worthy of becoming my wife, but about me being able to please a woman that deserved to be pleased."

Elizabeth listened to him incredulously, mesmerised, wondering how much was real and how much was in her imagination. She did not reply, so he stretched out his hand to her. She slowly rose from the chair and hesitantly stepped towards the bed. She sat on the edge, as she had so many times before, his hands captured hers, and his gaze deepened into her eyes as he continued his confession.

"When we were in the cottage, my opposition was almost gone. At the ball, my thoughts were filled with you only. I decided to travel to London, to talk to Georgiana about you, then to return. For you. While I was lying unconscious, in those few moments of clarity, it was only you. You were my light, my strength, my reason to stay alert. Every time I felt you near me, my mind struggled to recover, so I could speak to you and tell you how much I love and admire you."

Tears rolled freely down her cheeks, and his thumbs wiped them gently. His dark gaze and his hoarse voice showed so much tenderness that her senses melted in it. He was sitting, with his back against the pillows. But she was free to move, so she slowly leaned towards him, and her hands cupped his handsome face. He turned his head to place a lingering, warm kiss on each of her palms, then his fingers caressed her face. They were now only inches away, and he still had more to say.

"After your letter dissipated my doubts, I wished to propose to you right away, but I was reluctant to offer you an engagement while still ill. I believed you deserved more. So I planned to wait a little longer, and I would have done so if not for my aunt's irresponsible intervention."

"I must be grateful to Lady Catherine then, for my present felicity," she responded, then hesitantly, fighting her shyness, she closed her eyes and her lips touched his.

A chill shook them both while they gently tasted the first sip of love; but once discovered, their thirst only increased and for some long moments it defeated prudence and propriety.

When Elizabeth withdrew a little, only enough to breathe, their hands were still caressing each other's faces.

"I still need to ask you, will you do me the honour of becoming my wife, my dearest, loveliest Elizabeth?"

"I believed my answer was already clear enough, my dear Mr Darcy. But if not, let me try again," she teased him with a sweet smile that soon disappeared within another kiss.

∞∞∞

There was no happier mother than Mrs Bennet, nor a more content father than her husband and never had

Longbourn borne so much unrestrained happiness.

The turn of events, as unbelievable as it was for all of them, changed their lives entirely in only a few hours. Perhaps as happy as Mrs Bennet was Miss Darcy, whose support for her brother's marriage and affection for her future sister-in-law was immediately declared.

Mr Collins, who returned several hours after Lady Catherine's departure, was met with the biggest disappointment, as Mrs Bennet informed him there were no rooms available at Longbourn to host him.

"But my dear Mrs Bennet, I imagined that I would always have a room available to me at Longbourn, considering I am part of the family. I need accommodation for the next few days and I expected to benefit from the guest room that I have previously occupied."

"I am afraid that is not possible," Mrs Bennet stated, unmoved. "Dr. Cooper is staying in that room. And, unless you are willing to share a bed with one of my daughters or with me, we have no other to offer you."

"Mrs Bennet!" Mr Collins cried, appalled by such an outrageous statement.

"I would suggest trying at the Meryton Inn or at Lucas Lodge. I am sure your future father-in-law will be happy to host you, just as Mr Bennet is happy to host his future son-in-law–Mr Darcy, you know."

Mr Collins choked and rocked back on his heels, staring doubtfully at Mrs Bennet. She smiled widely.

"Next time you see Lady Catherine, please convey to her our deepest gratitude. If not for her visit, Mr Darcy would not have proposed to Lizzy so soon. But as it is now, we are preparing for the wedding after the new year."

Mr Collins left in a hurry, offended and hurt on his patroness's behalf and did not return to Longbourn, nor did they see him during his stay in Meryton. They only met again briefly at his wedding to Charlotte Lucas, when Mrs Bennet wished him all the felicity in marriage that he deserved. And she was being perfectly honest.

∞∞∞

Over the following weeks, Mr Darcy remained at Longbourn, gradually recovering. Dr. Cooper returned to London, leaving him under Mr Jones's supervision. The Gardiners arrived and filled the remaining chambers at Longbourn, adding to the family's enjoyment.

Mr Bingley's sisters chose to remain in London for the winter, angry and disappointed with both their brother and Darcy's marriages. To compensate for their absence, Darcy's cousin, Colonel Fitzwilliam, came as soon as he was released from his regiment and he soon became everyone's new favourite.

Wickham's fate was sealed before Darcy even had time to reveal his true character. He was caught attempting to run away with Colonel Forster's wife and with a significant sum of money. He was dismissed from the militia and sent to prison. Mrs Bennet told everyone willing to listen to her that she had guessed his real character sooner than anyone since he was unable to drive a carriage properly or to set a fire.

Despite all the deceptions and betrayals, Darcy could not abandon his childhood companion entirely. He instructed his solicitor to keep track of Wickham's fate and to search for a way to ensure a living for him abroad–perhaps a commission in India–upon his release from prison.

Christmas was a joyful time of miracles when Mr Darcy left his bed and joined his new family at the dinner table. And the second week of the new year was the moment when Mr and Mrs Bennet proudly gave their eldest daughters to the most worthy of men.

On a snowy, bright winter day, after the wedding breakfast, Mr and Mrs Bingley retired to Netherfield, while Mr and Mrs Darcy, in a large convoy of three impressive carriages, departed for their home in London together with Colonel Fitzwilliam, Miss Darcy, and the Gardiners. Furthermore, Miss Darcy generously invited Mary, Kitty and Lydia to stay with her in London for a full month, an invitation readily and cheerfully accepted.

After almost two months of continuous excitement, torment and joy, Longbourn suddenly fell into a strange peace and silence, leaving Mr and Mrs Bennet with a profound gratification and a deep sadness.

"My dear Mr Bennet, did I tell you that I confronted Mr Darcy that night at the Meryton assembly when he offended Lizzy?"

"You did not, Mrs Bennet. Was it a good confrontation?"

"Not quite; I would say rather the contrary. But I am sure it contributed, if only a little bit, to our present felicity."

"I would not dare to contradict you, Mrs Bennet. I do not always approve of your doings, but I have no objection when things turn out so well. However, you must admit that you almost forced Lizzy to marry Mr Collins."

"I did; and I will never forgive myself for such a terrible error! I thank the Lord every day that Lizzy was such a stubborn and obstinate girl. And that Mr Darcy was searching for precisely that sort of a wife."

∞∞∞

Elizabeth looked at her image in the mirror and blushed with contentment. The silky nightgown purchased by Mrs Gardiner as a wedding gift suited her nicely. The maid–her own maid, Sarah–was brushing her hair, nervous about serving the new Mrs Darcy. Almost as nervous as she was. Almost.

The house was so silent that Elizabeth could hear the fire burning. They had arrived in London late in the afternoon, and since then she had been drawn into a tumult of novelty that intimidated her more than she believed possible.

Georgiana, along with Mrs Annesley and the three Bennet girls, stopped at Miss Darcy's townhouse. The Gardiners continued their journey to Gracechurch Street, and the colonel was left at the Matlock residence.

So she had entered her new home alone with her husband, eager, anxious, nervous but very happy. Then, as if in a whirlwind, she was introduced to the housekeeper, to her maid, to the rest of the staff, and to her apartment. And it was only the beginning.

Finally, after a brief dinner and a long warm bath, there she was, in her bedchamber, arranging herself for her wedding night. For him.

"Mrs Darcy?" Sarah whispered.

"Yes?" she startled and smiled.

"Do you need anything else?"

"No, thank you. Everything is fine. Thank you."

"You may ring for me anytime."

"I am sure it will not be needed. Good night, Sarah."

"Good night Mrs Darcy."

The maid exited and Elizabeth was alone. The elegance of the room became overwhelming and she felt cold and lonely. She moved to the window and looked out at the street–lit but empty. She knew they were close to Hyde Park but she did not remember much else about their surroundings.

"You look stunning, Mrs Darcy. Truly stunning."

Elizabeth allowed a moment to enjoy her new name on his lips and only then did she turn. Her husband was slowly moving towards her, his eyes exploring her figure, his lips twisted in a mysterious smile.

She put her hands around his neck and his arms encircled her waist. She lifted her eyes to him, their bodies brushing against each other.

"I am glad you approve of my appearance, Mr Darcy. I was worried that you might not find me handsome enough to tempt you," she teased him, her eyes laughing at him.

"Mrs Darcy, I assure you that only my illness and the presence of your family prevented me from using our engagement time to show you how much you tempt me."

"And now that we are alone? Do you feel healthy enough to show me, sir?"

"Surely you do not doubt my admiration for you," he asked with a mocking concern.

"I most certainly do not. But I would be pleased to receive more proof of it nevertheless," she jested.

With his eyes holding hers and his arms embracing her tightly, Darcy led his wife to the bed and they lay together against the pillows.

"I would by no means suspend any pleasure of yours, my beloved wife," he whispered.

Their lips met in a tender kiss that slowly became eager, keen, passionate, ardent. No more words were needed.

Epilogue

Pemberley, October 1813

*E*lizabeth woke to a gentle touch on her shoulder. She opened *her eyes and met the laughing faces of her husband and her son of only one year old. She stretched out her arms and they both lay down next to her, trapping her in a warm embrace.*

"How are you, my love?" she asked lovingly.

"Which one?" Darcy whispered, placing a soft kiss on her earlobe.

"Both," she laughed while the boy giggled happily in his parents' arms.

"We are ready, all dressed up and prepared to receive our guests," Darcy declared. "We would not have awakened you if it was not late already."

She smiled and placed a quick kiss on both father and son's cheeks.

"Have Jane and Charles arrived?"

"Yes. They are downstairs with Georgiana, who is busy spoiling little Rose."

"She is a beautiful baby indeed. Very much like Jane. And she has the same sweet disposition. It is impossible not to love her," Elizabeth replied.

"I agree. But nobody is more handsome than young master Robert Bennet Darcy. He is even more handsome than I was. Mrs Reynolds herself may testify to that."

"There is no need for testimony, as this is a truth universally acknowledged. Even the Matlocks agreed on that,"

Elizabeth laughed.

"I am glad Bingley decided to let go of Netherfield and purchase an estate in Derbyshire. It was an excellent decision," Darcy declared, holding his son, while Elizabeth rose from the bed.

"Yes, it was. Having my dear Jane only thirty miles away is pure joy."

"And fortunate for the children's future too. Having little Rose around, Georgiana will not be able to spoil only Robert. My sister is a danger to the boy's discipline. And my cousin Richard, as his godfather, is even worse!" Darcy jested.

"Just wait until my parents and sisters arrive. Then you may well forget about discipline," Elizabeth laughed again. "They will only stay for the winter, but the damage might be long-lasting."

"I will take that risk," Darcy replied. "I confess I am eager to receive your parents. Your sisters and the Gardiners were here last summer, but Mr and Mrs Bennet are visiting for the first time, and I want everything to be perfect."

Elizabeth kissed his lips briefly. "I miss them dearly, as I have not seen them for almost a year and a half. But you must not be so nervous. They are family now; they do not need more than to be welcomed and to meet their grandson. The first boy in the Bennet family, can you imagine?"

"I confess I am nervous. I cannot forget that your mother offered me her own room and your father left his house and stayed at Netherfield for me. I want to be sure they feel at home at Pemberley."

"I am sure they will, my love. I believe they have arrived," Elizabeth said, looking outside at the two carriages that could be spotted entering the park. Darcy hastily took his son and left the room, while Elizabeth followed them with tearful, adoring glances.

A year and a half since they were married, she still wondered how her heart could bear so much happiness and was sure she would never have known the true meaning of felicity without him.

Elizabeth Bennet Darcy received her parents and sisters at the main entrance of Pemberley, on the arm of her husband, holding their beloved son.

Mr and Mrs Bennet exited the carriage, and for a few moments, they remained stunned and silent in front of the beauty that surrounded them.

Then they embraced each other, tearful, thrilled, joyful. And for the first time, Mrs Bennet truly kissed her son-in-law, twice, on both cheeks.

And Mr Darcy did not find it improper at all. Quite the contrary. Minutes after the Bennets arrived at Pemberley, Elizabeth had no doubts left that they already felt at home.

The End

Printed in Great Britain
by Amazon

19022487R00159